Dark Forces

'2

Dark Forces

Dark Forces

Simon Davies

Matador
5 Weir Road
Kibworth Beauchamp
Leicester LE8 0LQ, UK
Tel: (+44) 116 279 2299
Fax: (+44) 116 279 2277
Email: books@troubador.co.uk
Web: www.troubador.co.uk/matador

ISBN 978 1848767 720

British Library Cataloguing in Publication Data.
A catalogue record for this book is available from the British Library.

Typeset in 10.5pt Aldine401 BT Roman by Troubador Publishing Ltd, Leicester, UK

Matador is an imprint of Troubador Publishing Ltd

MIX
Paper from
responsible sources
FSC® C013056

Printed and bound in the UK by TJ International, Padstow, Cornwall

To Edward and Jessica.

The problem is that the gaps between the three areas of the criminal justice system, the police, the C.P.S and the courts are just too wide.

a victim

INTRODUCTION

"The District Judge is ready for you now," the black-robed usher announced, his head craning round the door.

Anthony didn't look up. Instead, in his slow and meticulous way, he gathered up his papers and tied them together with a length of pink silk.

I swallowed the last of my coffee and helped gather the empty sandwich cartons; the only bin in the room was already full to overflowing.

Finally, when Anthony was ready, he stood up and extended his hand for me to shake.

It occurred to me that this might be the last time we'd meet and I was hit by an unexpected pang of sadness, like when you part with a relative at the airport gates.

I had known Anthony for over a year and during that time we had grown fond of each other and we shared a great deal of mutual respect. I can remember the warmness I felt as we walked across the court foyer together. He placed his arm on my shoulder like he was my best man.

"Well, Simon old boy, I've explained the difference between advice and advocacy and I think we've given it our best shot. I don't think we could have done any better; it's all down now to that one man on the bench.

"Whatever happens now, I want to wish you the best of luck in whatever you do, and I just want to say what a pleasure it's been getting to know you over these past few months."

I shook his hand warmly, and together we pushed our way through the double doors and entered the warm, rather stuffy atmosphere of Court Three.

★ ★ ★

Sometimes, when faced with a life-changing incident, time can almost stand still: the world around you starts to revolve in slow motion; just a few seconds can seem like hours. There, in that court room, as the old judge coughed into his fist and began to address his court, my eyes focused on the knot of silk ribbon laid out across the desk. Although I was about to hear a decision that would affect my life, I allowed my mind to drift away from the events in front of me, taking me back in time about one year, back to Anthony's chambers and the day we first met.

As the sounds and sights of the court room melted away, my memory came into focus and I could clearly see the station.

Now, it has to be said that the London Underground, or Tube, as it's locally known, is not a pleasant place to be in the middle of summer. The intense heat can make travelling very uncomfortable down in that network of tunnels, deep below the capital's pavements, and I happened to be there on a particularly hot day.

It was the middle of a heat wave, when temperatures down below ground rose to a sweltering 46 degrees. I stood on the platform, waiting for my train; a bead of sweat went trickling down my back. Next to me, with a bucket of paste and a brush, one hundred and fifty feet below Baker Street, a worker was putting up posters advising people to drink water.

I watched as he moved his ladder ten feet down the platform and took out another poster. Just beyond him, paramedics in green jumpsuits attended a commuter who lay unconscious.

"It's the brakes on these old trains!" One passenger told another as he nodded to the man.

"When they brake, all that friction causes heat. They can't have air conditioning because there's no room, the tunnels are too narrow, just wide enough for a carriage, but this station was built in 1850."

He chuckled to himself while the passenger continued to read and the paramedics helped the casualty onto a seat.

"They've tried giant ice cubes, yeah, that's right, giant ice cubes on the trains to cool the air down, can you believe it?" The passenger studied his crossword and turned his back to the retired train driver.

A low rumble came from the deep black hole.

People stepped forward, nearing the edge, and were struck by a sudden blast of heat. Air swept along in front of the speeding train, its brakes already screeching to a halt.

Full to overflowing, the carriages took on another hundred or so humans and seconds later it was racing down the opposite hole. I held onto a strap that swung me with the motion of the train as I considered my next two hours.

For no particular reason Covent Garden sprung to mind, so I referred to my map. At that moment I was travelling along the brown line; I needed to be on the dark blue line. I could change at Piccadilly Circus, then two stops further to Covent Garden and time for a sandwich before the meeting.

I found a café on the edge of the old, arcaded square that faced the church and ordered a baguette and some coffee. An outside awning offered some shade from the boiling sun as I sat, watching people hurry about with their daily lives. In the cobbled square in front of the great portico two mime artists, both dressed in tight black-and-white clothing, attempted to find the exit to their imaginary glass box. Towards the end of the cobbles was a man juggling with fire, children tossing coins into a bowler at his feet.

The famous fruit and vegetable market had long since relocated and now the building housed an array of antique shops amongst the Victorian-style wine bars and restaurants: a magnet for tourists, shoppers and out of work actors.

As the church clock struck two I downed my coffee and checked my watch. It was time to go. Giving the fire-eater a wide birth I headed out of Covent Garden and started to make my way towards Gray's Inn.

I found the address at the corner of High Holborn and Gray's Inn Road. The place itself was quite beautiful: bathed in sunshine, the old buildings and their neatly manicured lawns had more than a passing resemberlance to an Oxford College.

I had to remind myself that this was the centre of the capital and I was about to attend, what was perhaps the most important meeting of my life.

Checking my watch for a second time, I straightened my tie and entered through the wrought iron gates, making my way over to the far corner of the square. There, engraved in brass on a board at the foot of a staircase, was the name of the person I had come to see. Anthony Hudson, Barrister at Law.

"You found it okay, then?"

Janet Ross, my solicitor, was there to meet me, and after shaking hands it was she who rang the bell. We were shown up to Anthony's room by his clerk. The room was exactly as I'd expected: it had a large, ornate fireplace, high corniced ceiling and red velvet drapes that dressed the window. The whole of one wall was bespoke teak cabinets, lined with books; behind a rosewood writing desk, a view right across the gardens.

As his clerk left the room I circled the plush office and took a glance out of the window. Two barristers walked side by side beneath me, deep in discussion, gowns flowing in the breeze.

Just as I sat down, Anthony made his abrupt and dramatic entrance and the real business of the meeting began.

He made a good first impression, beautifully tailored suit, razor-sharp mind and impeccable manners.

Now, things were so different; as Anthony stood up to address the Judge, I focused on the royal Coat of Arms in front of me.

★ ★ ★

Over my twenty years' service as a police officer I had found myself in many law courts, and for a variety of reasons, but never had I stood as the accused. Like a gamekeeper caught poaching, I was now seeing life from the other side.

Sitting in that hot court room, listening to Anthony, I had the time to reflect on the long and winding road that had brought me here: the journey that took me from my career as a police officer to a mental health patient

As Anthony presented my defence and the Judge drummed his fingers on the desk, I began to scribble notes on the characters I'd met along the way - the very people who had shaped my career.

As I wrote, I brought to mind the victims, the perpetrators, the liars, the cheats, the rights, the wrongs and all the discrimination. I reflected back on the veritable minefield of incidents, where the paths seemed to fork off in every conceivable direction with no clear guidance. Sitting back in my chair I felt an overwhelming sense of helplessness.

It was there, at that very moment, with pen in hand, that I began to scribble down the outline of a story, a loud voice interrupted my thoughts.

I looked up at the man who would be responsible for writing the final chapter.

There was a silent pause as he surveyed the Court.

"I am required to read out a statement of facts," he said, his monotone indicating that this was not the first time he'd done this.

In fact, over the course of this hearing, Jeffery Nash had shown himself to be an efficient, no nonsense sort, and he now carried on in much the same vein.

When he had felt the need to show frustration he would shake his head and interrupt. His face would then show satisfaction that some order had been brought back into his Court and everything was proceeding as he wanted.

Presiding over trials was more of a vocation than a career for Judge Nash. It was his duty to hear the case and make his judgement, and that was precisely what he intended to do.

The warmth of the room seemed to make my mind drift, visions of the characters I would be writing about sprung into my mind and, although it was difficult for me, I did my best to listen to my case.

It was precisely three o'clock when Nash cleared his throat and began to speak.

"Today, being 18th August, I have heard evidence from the following: PC Hartland and PC Cook, Sharon Brown, who was with the police for a short time on a work experience placement, Dr Strictly and Dr Stale. I have also seen and read statements of evidence from the scenes of crime officer, Balvinder Siddhu, and the hospital registrar, Dr Patel.

"I find the following facts not in dispute: that the defendant attended police headquarters on the day in question; that he had a meeting with Dr Strictly that didn't go well and an altercation took place. At that time, there was only the defendant and Dr Strictly in the consultation room.

"I have heard the evidence from the police officers who gave somewhat differing accounts of the whereabouts of the anatomical model of the human spine which was alleged to have been used in the attack. I note, that said spine was recovered but never examined.

"I've heard from Dr Stale, the forensic consultant psychiatrist, who testifies that he queried the condition of Post-Traumatic Stress Disorder during an earlier examination of the defendant.

"From the evidence, it is clear that the defendant was suffering from a mental condition at the time of the attack. It is also clear that he had been signed off from work with the condition of work-related stress.

"However, on listening to the evidence this morning, and considering the written witness statements in front of me, I have to say that I have not a shadow of doubt that you committed the offence and therefore I find you guilty."

★ ★ ★

CHAPTER ONE

Genesis

There was light rain in the air as I drove my new Mini Cooper along the dual carriageway in the direction of the town centre. It was the second time that month I'd made that journey.

I'd visited the police station once before: a familiarisation day. But this morning, it was the real thing.

I was well aware of the role I'd been trained to do. Whatever the emergency, whoever rang, however low the depths of human depravity would get, I would be called out to deal with the situation as a fully-fledged professional police officer.

If a prisoner became violent, I would restrain them. If a victim was distraught, I would comfort them. If a member of the public needed advice, I would be there to advise them. After three months of intensive training and at the very peak of physical fitness, I would be there to police the streets and make the community feel safer.

Like any other nineteen year old, I didn't have any real life experience, but who needs that when you have all the answers right there with you? As far as I was concerned, there was a right way and a wrong way and the law was there to deal with anyone who was foolish enough to choose the wrong way.

As the needle on my speedometer touched sixty, I began to wonder whether the speed limit actually applied to me and my driving.

I now had some authority: I was in charge of the road, with a uniform and badge to prove it. Surely, if pulled over, the warrant card would do the trick, along with the words, "Yeah mate, I'm one of you, on my way to the early shift."

I peered at the grey sky through my windscreen. The long road stretched out into the distance. I was driving along what was known as the 'collector road', a modern idea for town planning: designed to plug a gap in the new motorway network, this road had also formed the ideal corridor for the planners to run the sewerage and mains systems for the new housing estate.

But what struck me most of all, as I looked out of my window, was the great contrast between the different landscapes on either side of the main road: quite literally, scenes from different worlds.

To my left, across the farmer's fields, lay the market town of Coleshill, a small Warwickshire village that was once an important staging post on the coaching road from London to Chester. From my passenger window I could see the steeple of the old parish church gently piecing the grey sky above, and beyond that the historic market square, still complete with its ancient pillory and whipping post.

On the opposite side of the road lay the modern development of Chelmsley Wood, a 1960's new town, built by Birmingham City Council as an overspill estate to house its growing number of workers. The town had sprawled out across the farmland, stretching its tentacles ever further, exchanging acres and acres of the ancient Forest of Arden for tower blocks, bridged walkways and tunnels of poured concrete.

It's true to say that, in its time, it was heralded as a fine example of town planning and an effective way to solve Birmingham's overcrowding problem. But the bulldozers showed little care or respect for the ancient fabric of the landscape that would be permanently erased.

Park Hall, for example – a timber-frame manor house, complete with moat, dating back to 1265 – demolished to pave the way for the new motorway.

Castle Bromwich Mill which lay on the River Tame, grinding corn as late as 1895, was also ripped down, its foundations buried somewhere under the tonnes of tarmac. Farm buildings were replaced by row upon row of identical houses with high-rise blocks scattered amongst them, fifteen storeys high and standing firm like prehistoric stones staring out to the horizon

This man-made labyrinth was to be like a home for me for the next few months. The start of a new career, a new life … I looked out for the next road sign which soon appeared before me. Turning right at one of the many intersections, I followed the signs towards the town centre.

Twice I crossed low bridges that spanned the River Cole, their undersides daubed with graffiti and slick with urine. Either side of me, grass verges swept away, the left side leading to a rubbish-strewn footpath beside the flow of water. Yet another intersection approached and the Chelmsley Wood shopping centre loomed up ahead.

A square brick building dominated the skyline in front of me with the words BINGO and SHOPPERS CAR PARK propped up by rusty scaffolding, like a football fan holding his team's scarf but somehow tired and weary, facing relegation.

"Two people have jumped off there," I remember someone telling me on my first visit.

"It was amazing, a crowd even gathered to egg them on, shouting and swearing. At first they wouldn't do it, so the crowd shouted and threw bottles at them. The man and woman then kissed each other before they held hands and jumped off. The man hit the pavement first, what a mess. It was only ten in the morning. Scumbags."

Those were amongst the first words I had heard on that familiarisation day and they were to make a powerful impression on me. I believed that story, and various other grizzly tales told in such a callous way, could only build barriers between us and the people we were there to serve. But those barriers were deeply ingrained in the community and it would take a lot more than friendly policing to change that. I kept quiet and continued a tour of the station, learning about all the modern facilities we had at our disposal.

In the days before the development of Chelmsley Wood, policing that area of the Forest of Arden would have been more or less a one-horse affair. But now, things were very different: for the new estate, a large state-of-the-art police station was required.

Using a plot of over an acre central to the town, the new building was designed to contain every facility that modern policing would need. The grey concrete façade was four storeys high and lined with regular windows, giving it a perfect symmetry. Dull and drab, like a government building in downtown Warsaw: not big on personality, but functional and efficient. To each side of the building, double-storey wings in the same colour concrete enveloped and protected the car park.

Out there, an assortment of police vehicles would have designated parking spaces on the far side and private vehicles could be left at the near. The Inspector and Sergeants had priority.

In the far corner of the car park stood the old, dependable riot van, protective wings attached and a rusting mesh of a grill over the windscreen to protect it from flying missiles. Next to that was the old-fashioned petrol pump, specifically housed 'on site' to keep the fleet of cars self-sufficient in fuel. Behind it, the far wing of the station contained the twelve concrete cells known simply as 'the block'.

On the first floor of the opposite wing was the police social club and beneath it, a large sports hall which boasted a stage, still framed in huge red velvet curtains and braided pelmet, but dusty and neglected.

Behind those heavy curtains stood an upright piano and an assortment of chairs, abandoned in untidy stacks, dirty and grimy, some leaning one way, some the other. I suppose it was similar to most backstage areas: the walls and ceiling were painted black with rows of spotlights suspended over head.

The walls of the hall itself were covered in climbing frames and the floor was laid out as a badminton court; poles and net were lying in a corner. Outside the hall ran a corridor, one side lined with lockers topped with discarded uniform, boxes and neglected paperwork, and at the far end were two team changing rooms complete with showers.

The top two floors of the main block consisted of small dormitories known as 'single quarters'. Sixteen rooms, each fitted out identically, perhaps the size of a touring caravan, with matching overhead cupboards and a wardrobe unit with wash-basin built in. The décor looked sad and dated, with avocado green colours and ornate door trims and handles.

Across the hall from the bedrooms was a kitchen containing a washing machine, ironing board, fridge and electric cooker. A variety of pots and pans littered the worktops on units with ill fitting, broken drawers, abandoned and unused. In the fridge, a collection of margarine tubs, yoghurt pots and milk cartons lay about, waiting for the next clearout.

The freezer box door was missing and in its place stood a solid ice block with a frozen lasagne entombed (no doubt one day its owner would take an ice pick to it and exchange its frozen block for the oven, the result being the sole content of their evening meal).

They had tried to make the kitchen look homely, with splash-back tiles three high around the room, a sort of orange colour with dark brown edges. Intermittent tiles would reveal English country garden images. Primula, snowdrop, marsh marigold, sage and wild garlic, all equally-spaced around the walls, meant to make it look homely, but the signs of neglect were everywhere. The wall behind the oven had a patch of sticky grease smeared across the snowdrop: residue left over from a previous chip pan fire.

Next to the oven, screwed to the wall, was a fire blanket, fox gloves peeping out from behind it: instructions for use, spotted with gravy.

Below that, a scribbled note telling residents to wash up their plates. It has to be pointed out that residents weren't expected to do all their own cleaning: there was, of course, Mary.

The house keeper originated from County Cork and displayed the tell tale flaming red hair and caring blue eyes. Having originally come over to England to marry a coal miner, she had been looking after the single men there for the past ten years. Her early life in Ireland, surrounded by six brothers, had placed her in good stead to handle the sixteen young men all living away from home.

She took in good humour the occasional sight of a naked man padding out of the shower room. Without the faintest sign of a blush, she'd just tell him to cover up and put his little thing away. Some men saw the corridor as their territory and anyone that happened to be there should just get used to it; however, any young male who had ideas of getting a little too frisky would be firmly put in their place. No one ever did get very far that way with Mary, but it was not for the want of trying.

She had the most voluptuous figure, wore tight t-shirts and had an open mind to go with it. But when she entered a man's room, it was to take the sheets away and not to roll around in them. As soon as any attempt at horseplay was dismissed, the lads would open up their hearts and minds and rely on her for her advice for all their problems. Very often she would serve as a shoulder to cry on for any young man who was unlucky in love. Her role would thereby move swiftly from mother figure to big sister; it would all depend on the circumstances.

Underneath the single quarters, two floors below, was the parade room where officers would meet fifteen minutes before the start of duty. It was into this room that I walked at five forty-five on that morning, my first day as a fully-fledged officer.

The room was set out with a collection of assorted tables that were pushed together and around which lay a similar collection of assorted chairs. Wooden shelving was fixed to the wall, like a giant honeycomb that contained just about every conceivable piece of paperwork one could need. Next to that was a series of filing cabinets, in which each officer would have a pull-out sleeve file to keep all their work in.

I learnt very quickly that this, however, was the official storage place. Anything out of date, or slightly risky, would be filed in one of several places, including the gap behind the radiator or down the back of the changing lockers. If the whereabouts of something was queried, it was always assumed that it had previously been submitted and had got lost in the bureaucratic system; no one really queried missing paperwork.

I took a seat. One by one my new shift shuffled in, each eyeing me suspiciously, as if I was an impostor sent to spy on them and report back. Someone placed an ashtray in the middle of the table and cigarettes were handed round. I was not offered a smoke.

As officers inhaled their early morning smoke, the conversation would start and the noise level could reach fever-pitch. The noise would be broken by a surly, grey haired giant of a sergeant, who bellowed, "On parade"

In his wake came a calmer-looking Inspector, a look of mild irritation on his face at the Sergeant's noise level. This routine would signal the start of the dailey briefing where officers would be told of their duties for the shift ahead; as for the new boy, well, my first job was to make the tea.

My partner took me to a tiny room at the end of the corridor opposite the barred door to the cell block.

In there was just enough room for a sink, a kettle and a table covered with a dozen chipped mugs, most of which contained the residue of the last drink, not having seen washing up liquid for a number of days. In the corner, opposite the sink, were four square lockers, stacked one on top of the other and marked with a letter from A to D. We were 'A' unit and our locker was the one on top.

After struggling with the combination padlock for five minutes or so, I examined the contents. There was a catering tin of Nescafe, a catering bag of sugar, a bag of one thousand teabags and an assortment of spoons, most of which looked like they had been thrown out by Yuri Gellar. On the inside of the metal door was a list of people's requirements: who took sugar, who took milk, who preferred tea.

As it was my first day, I gave all the cups a wash and waited for the kettle to boil. I placed the clean cups on the tray and added the tea bags, sugar and coffee as per the list. With the whole task completed, I carefully carried the full tray back along the corridor and knocked on the door to the controller's office.

The atmosphere in that little dark room was like that on a submarine: about the size of a single bedroom. The controller sat in the middle, surrounded by panels on three sides. In front of him was the Command and Control system, looking like an old television set. The officer typed on the key pad and a flashing green square would lead the words across the screen. A series of clip boards hung all around with a series of charts plotting crimes, times and locations.

The swivel chair was well-cushioned and could swing round 360 degrees to face any corner of the room. It needed to be comfortable because, throughout every hour of every day, and every day of every year, an officer would be sitting in that chair. When the shift finished, the outgoing sergeant would vacate it and the incoming one would sit down. The room never slept. At any time, day or night, if an emergency flashed up on the screen someone would be there to receive it and despatch the necessary officers.

To assist the officer in reading the steady flow of information which passed through the office, an angle poise lamp was clamped to the ridge above the computer. It shone its light around the room like an interrogation lamp, giving an immediate pool of light but creating shadows that stretched into the corners.

When the parade was over, it was customary that members of the shift would file into this room and take their positions around the sergeant, leaning over the unit. They would listen to the seasoned officer as he recounted tales of policing in the old days.

More cigarettes would be lit up, only their tips visible as they darted around the darkness, like suspended glow worms, while people joked. A layer of smoke would gather and hang in the air, filling the dark room with an atmosphere all of its own.

All eyes would be on the sergeant and the controller's chair; only the older officers would join in with the sergeant's conversation or seek to offer any opinion without being asked first.

The younger ones would speak only when spoken to, with every sentence ending in the word, 'Sgt'. There was absolute discipline. No one would think of doing or saying anything without either having or seeking the sergeant's approval first.

Anyone trying to behave like a maverick would be ostracised until they repented and somehow found a way back into the sergeant's favour. And then, finally, freedom to enter, at will, the living, breathing heart of the station: the 'Controller's Office'.

The Inspector may have out ranked the sergeant in terms of official status, but the sergeant was the one who ran the station. The sooner you got that clear in your head, the easier your life would be.

There was also a very clear pecking order when it came to serving out the tea: the sergeant was given his first and, when he nodded his approval, the Inspector got his. This could feel slightly awkward, but nothing compared to the awkwardness of a grumpy sergeant. Once each member of the unit had their drink you could take your place in the circle. The quieter and more submissive you were the more chance you had of being accepted and the days would become a hell of a lot easier.

★ ★ ★

CHAPTER TWO

Trauma Support Network

When it seems you have all the time in the world to sit with your thoughts it's funny, the little things you remember.

"Human beings are the only animals that know they are going to die. That was one of her comments that always stuck with me. Because humans are the only animals that understand death is inevitable, we live our lives to a large degree preparing for it."

Through the rapid movements of my windscreen wipers a road sign flashed past in the rain. Six miles to Warwick. Good, almost there. I can relax and return to my train of thought.

"We go to school to get educated, to get a better job so we can save for retirement, to get a good pension plan, and then in our retirement we make plans for our funerals. Which incidentally, we actually started planning years ago, choosing our favourite pop songs and readings."

"Yes, but there's still a lot of life to enjoy, as well as all this planning!" I remember putting to her.

"Most people go for exactly the same things, choosing songs by stars like Robbie Williams or Celine Dion, which they probably have had earmarked ever since their wedding day. They've probably made it very clear to their relatives what they want playing on the little cassette player as their coffin disappears for the whole of eternity."

"I think I'd go for 'Come on Baby Light My Fire'," I offered, trying to lighten the mood.

She continued, pretending not to hear me. "My point is that animals don't spend their time worrying about pensions, savings or studying the stock market. They simply go about their daily lives eating, sleeping and making babies, blissfully unaware that their body clocks are ticking and the end is closing in."

She always did have a unique way of looking at things, which was unusual in our job. At moments like this something would remind me of her and trigger one of those memories, I've never really been sure why.

I could be driving somewhere, thinking about the past, when I'd see something that reminded me of her and a seed of a memory would germinate deep in the back of my mind. At first maybe a little grainy but becoming clearer, swimming in and out of focus until finally bursting inside my head.

If the memory was bad, I'd try and shut it down and attempt to bring up a better one. If the memory was pleasant, I'd sit back and let myself sink into it, reclining back into the warm waters of her grip. One of the best was that walk through the cherry blossom field , the sun in the sky and the colours of her dress running like a watercolour in the rain.

A screech of tyres from the car in front braking suddenly brings my focus back to the road; I peer through the windscreen looking for further road signs.

This morning, when I started out, the sky was just misty and grey but now the rain swept the windscreen in sheets. I flick the speed of the wipers up a notch. The sign announcing 'Warwick Town Centre' flashes past.

'Warwick twinned with Saumur and Verdun. Is it raining like this in the Loire,' I think out loud.

The sat-nav instructs me to turn right.

Outside my warm air-bubble the town's people are scurrying about their business, dodging the puddles and avoiding the spray from vehicles. One lady stands in a doorway smoking a cigarette, another takes shelter under a canopy as she thumbs away on her mobile phone, balancing an umbrella on her shoulder, her dress clinging to her, all soaking wet.

"In a hundred meters take the next left."

"Oh thank you very much indeed," I reply, addressing myself to the screen directly. I turn as instructed, driving under the barrier into the Castle Street car park. I've reached my destination; I must get out of the habit of talking back to the little box on the dashboard.

"Why is it, that it's always more difficult to find a parking place in bad weather?" I ask the little screen.

"More people insist on using their cars instead of trying to use their legs. I on the other hand have got no choice, I live eighteen miles away," I reply to myself.

I tend to snarl at people driving their outsized Chelsea tractors, just dropping their little brats to school when they only live a hundred yards away, bull-bars fixed in case they come across a kangaroo standing in the road.

I see that the far corner of the car park is flooded and the final three spaces are empty. I manoeuvre into the furthest one. I'm sure I can stretch my legs out to the curb to prevent my feet getting wet. I check the time.

It's not quite ten.

Leaving the engine running and blowing out huge quantities of hot air, I turn on the radio. Today there's a special broadcast on Radio 4. An African-American senator from Illinois has been elected the 44th president of the United States; the broadcaster makes constant references to a biography written about him.

"My daddy was as black as pitch, and my mommy was as white as milk," says the man born in Hawaii, who grew up to pursue his early career as a civil rights lawyer. An American commentator comes on the radio.

"Washington D.C. has descended into a spontaneous street party as people are dancing around and embracing each other like brothers and sisters. Young Americans, many of whom have distant ancestors who were slaves on the plantations, are chanting their election slogan 'Yes We Can'" and waving their election banners."

The broadcast switches back to London where the Prime Minister is in Downing Street, ready to make a statement to the world's press. A deep, dull Scottish burr comes across the airwaves and I promptly switch the radio off. A good time to make a move.

Stretching my leg out to the curb I heave myself across avoiding a dip in the freezing cold water.

The place I'm looking for, Northgate Lodge, is about five minutes away, so there's no time now for a quick coffee. I turn my coat collar up against the rain and head on up against the wind.

The house announces itself with a name engraved on a polished brass plaque by the front door. I press the intercom and almost immediately hear the sustained buzzing sound which signals the unlocking of the door.

I push my way inside, out of the rain, shaking the water out of my hair and wiping my feet, making sure that the door is firmly shut before I proceed further down the hall.

The place was clearly once a substantial town house for some wealthy family, but clearly its new occupants were happier painting all the period features and wood panelling a creamy pastel shade. A thick blue carpet leads through the hall to the rear of the house; next to the hat stand, another sign directs me up the stairs to the first floor and the area marked 'waiting room'.

The waiting room seems remarkably modern compared with the rest of the house: blue carpet tiles, light beech wood furniture, various pot plants dotted around. In front of me is a large office-style water-cooler. I take a cone-shaped plastic cup from the dispenser and, as I'm taking in the feel of the place, I'm greeted by a young woman with long blonde hair who seems to appear from nowhere.

"Hi, I'm Susan; I think I've spoken to you on the phone. Welcome to the Trauma Support Network."

"Thank you. I'm Simon. Yes, I think we have spoken: I've got an appointment with Beth Goodchild."

"Yes, that's fine; she's running a little late this morning. I don't know if you heard about it but there was a dreadful fire yesterday in one of the nearby villages. It's been on the news this morning. People are still unaccounted for. She's talking to the Chief Fire Officer on the phone. Can I get you a coffee while you wait?"

"No, water will be fine, thanks." I take a plastic cup and fill it to the top; the cooler gives a gurgle from its belly and lets off a series of bubbles.

"Okay, Simon, just have a seat and she'll call you when she's ready."

Susan disappears into the next room, a room with a security code on the door. I shun the offer of a seat and instead take a good look round. There's a column of postcards tacked up the side of the window frame. I move closer to take a look. The top one, which could only be a Greek island, catches my attention. I peer closer at the photograph. It pictures a whitewashed chapel with a sky-blue dome, high on the hillside overlooking the turquoise sea, framed with brilliant gardenias. I look out of the window down to the rain-soaked street; two umbrellas dash across the road. The turquoise sea looks inviting. The postcard below it looks like it's Edison's lighthouse; between the two there's a huge contrast in colours as the sky is grey beyond the red and white of the tower.

I quickly move away when Susan comes back to sit at her desk. I don't want to appear overbearing. I top up my half-empty cup from the water-cooler and glance at the notice board.

Childlike writing from a red crayon covers a piece of card with a spray of carnations in the bottom corner.

'A grief without pang, void, dark and drear, a drowsy, stifled, unimpassioned grief, which finds no natural outlet or relief in word, sigh or tear.' This seems to have formed part of a poem but only the bottom half remains, as though the paper has been ripped in two. The name S.T.Coleridge is barely readable under the flowers.

'Domestic Violence Kills', announces the larger poster underneath. I move in closer to study it more carefully.

The poster is by far the biggest item pinned to the board. It portrays a woman curled up on bare floor boards in the corner of a room. She's wearing an oversized dressing gown that gathers at her feet; her hands cover her face, her nails look like they're digging into her skin. Her face is all blotchy as though she's crying. Beneath her dressing gown is a telephone number: a helpline, a local number belonging to a local charity.

'Domestic Violence affects all people, regardless of race, religion, ethnicity, age or sex'. The charity's logo looks like a dove in profile carrying an olive twig in its beak, like the story of Noah and the Ark.

I move away from the notice board and glance over at Susan who's busy tapping away on her keyboard. Her eyes dart from side to side, reading something off the screen. In the opposite corner stands a large bookcase containing a variety of books. I take a closer look.

Starting at the top I read the names down the spines: 'How to cope with Stress', 'Stress in the Work Place', 'Anxiety and You'. I notice that some of books have the letters P.T.S.D in their tittles.

I'm tempted to look at one but I'm not sure if I'm supposed to: after all, this is a waiting room, not a library. Thinking about it, I doubt I could read a lot in the time I've got to wait. I may read the introduction and the subject grab my interest, I might want to find out more, and then what would I do? Perhaps I could try and slip the book into my coat and take it home to read it. That way I could bone up on the subject of mental health before I come for my next session; it might help me understand my condition better and then I could explain it to Beth.

She's bound to be nobody's fool. She'd catch on quickly and realise I'd been reading and rehearsing my lines; that would be very underhand, almost like cheating, and I don't see the point in cheating when they're trying to help you get better. Besides, things could turn out worse: Beth could recognise the style and the text and then realise that a book has gone missing and someone has stolen it. She'd be bound to kick me out or even worse, call the police, have me prosecuted for theft, and then where would I be? I step back from the book stand and glance at Susan whose eyes flick back to her screen; see, she's been watching me, probably making notes, notes for the file.

The thought of sitting in the cells at Warwick police station waiting to be charged with theft of a text book brings me back to my senses. I think I'll stick to something a little less risky than trying to steal books. I look back at Susan. I think she's reading my mind. I sit down and mouth an apology: luckily, she's not looking.

So, perhaps a little lighter reading, less challenging. I cast my eye about to see what's available.

There's a pile of well-thumbed 'Country Life' magazines on the coffee table. With nothing better to read, I select the top one. Its cover is dominated by a substantial stately home; two chocolate Labradors stretch out in the sun across the driveway, a blue Volvo Estate parked by the topiary. I open the glossy magazine and read the cover story, it tells the perspective buyer all they need to know:

'Harvington Hall, Gloucestershire, price in the region of £7 million, contact our London office for details.' A London number, but without that kind of money lying around I won't be contacting 'Evans and Sons.' There must be something a bit more suitable, something within my price range.

I flick through the impressive property section before I come to the heading 'Royal Leamington Spa'. That's more like it: just down the road. I read on. 'Number ten Cumberland Terrace is an elegant Regency Gentleman's residence. The terrace boasts a white painted stucco façade. Entry to the hallway is via a period black front door framed by two columns. Elegant wrought iron balconies afford views over Jephson Gardens. The gardens are a feature in the photographs, rectangle flower beds brimming with bright marigolds bordered with gold and red.'

That's more like it. I search for the price. 'Offers in the region of £750,000.'

Still too expensive. I feel disheartened: its pointless going any further, it will only lead to unnecessary disappointment and a feeling of inadequacy. I return to the matter in hand and remind myself what I am doing here.

I'm sitting here, in this waiting room, because today will be the first of twenty sessions with Beth, the manager of the Trauma Support Network. This is the beginning of a course that could last through to the end of the year. I'm not sure I want to dwell on it – after all it seems such a long time. I flick back to Number ten Cumberland Terrace to take my mind off things.

The inner door opens; Beth Goodchild appears in the space holding a file and sporting long brown hair and an African style kaftan.

"Hi, Simon, sorry to keep you, would you like to come through? You can bring your water."

★ ★ ★

CHAPTER THREE

The Jackie Situation

The name Kingshurst comes from the fact that the area had once been a Royal Manor; hence the first part, 'King', the word 'Hurst' meaning wood.

Early records of Kingshurst referred to it as part of the Manor of Coleshill; it was here that Simon de Montfort built a moated manor house to sit amongst the beautiful rolling landscape.

Unfortunately for the area, the First World War came along and most of the trees were chopped down to help with the war effort; however, this newly-cleared piece of land near Birmingham presented the Boy Scouts Association with a place where they could set up a permanent camp. This opened in 1923 and consisted of a training centre, wash-houses and latrines, a lido and a series of dormitory huts.

The ancient brook flowed through the base, bringing with it a supply of fresh spring water, and Cock Sparrow Farm was nearby to provide them with ample fresh milk. The entrance to the camp was famously flanked with two giant griffins carved out of stone and donated by a local business.

Today, if you were to visit Kingshust, you would find no trace of the Hall, the Scout huts or even the griffins: they've long disappeared, and in their place lies a drab, post-war housing estate.

The estate we see today was built in the 1950s as an overspill for Birmingham, ten years before the development of the much larger Chelmsley Wood. As for the Hall itself, well, the last proprietor could no longer afford to retain it and moved out. The Hall was demolished in 1962. The camp closed in 1972 and new housing crept across the remaining fields to take its place.

Kingshurst Estate was then engulfed by Chelmsley Wood: an overspill estate, surrounded by a bigger, even more monotonous overspill estate. The telltale signs of social decay emerged slightly earlier on the Kingshurst and its rot gradually spread.

When housing estates such as Kingshurst were built it was common practice to name roads after particular subjects or various groups: for example, the roads could be named after well-known rivers, birds or plants.

Ash Crescent was situated in the part of the estate where the roads were named after trees, so it stood in its section together with Laburnum, Poplar and Beech. The crescent itself was lined with cherry trees, in blossom at the time of my visit, giving the road a splash of pink, but not enough to change the mood – just as if your prison guard had hung pink curtains across your bars.

The Ash Crescent call was to be the first job I ever attended. I remember checking my appearance in the wing mirror as my partner, Jill, brought the police car to a halt.

The car only came to a final stop when she pulled on the handbrake causing a slight skid. She reached for her newly-designed 'bowler' style police hat and I reached for my helmet.

The more popular 'flat cap' could only be acquired once you had completed a driving course and for me, that was to be at least a year away. The flat cap was deeply coveted as the policeman's helmet was clumsier: it had originally been designed to protect your head from falling debris. But the awkwardness could be a handicap. Before long, I witnessed a scene of disorder on the estate; a colleague's helmet had been knocked off and had rolled under the wheels of a passing car.

There were two ways an officer could secure his helmet to his head, the first way being a webbing harness that fixed together with the use of press studs under the chin. This, at the time, would conjure up images of Margaret Thatcher's recent miner's strike: the row upon row of blue-suited 'Bobbies' holding back the coach loads of flying pickets as they guarded the roads to the collieries.

The second method was to use a patent leather strap worn below the lips, right on the point of the chin. This could also appear rather aggressive, similar to the practice of wearing black leather gloves with a short-sleeved shirt. We had to remember that the image of the friendly police officer had to be preserved – after all, we were there to protect the public, not intimidate them. But on balance, it had to be considered that, without this strap, the helmet could slip back to the rear of the head, giving the look of a Victorian music hall character.

I placed both straps inside the helmet and got out of the car.

Leading the way to the front door was a path of broken flag stones lying unevenly across a field of mud, punctuated with an occasional patch of brown grass. An old bicycle lay to the one side, sinking into the mud next to an assortment of brightly-coloured toys and a savaged bin liner spilling out dirty nappies.

On the doorstep sat a male, pale white complexion and extremely skinny, smoking what seemed to be an impossibly small handmade cigarette. At first he appeared not to pay any attention to us but one could see his eyes dart from side to side as if looking for a possible escape route. As I approached, he stood up, a little over five feet tall; he had a shaven head which made him look even shorter. Apart from his tight white T-shirt and baggy grey jogger bottoms, I remember the tattoo on his forearm: a Nazi swastika in the centre of a pointed dagger.

On leaving our vehicle, Jill had instructed that I would speak to the male and keep him outside while she entered the house and talked to the female caller. So, as the man stood up to face me, and Jill pushed open the door to the premises and went inside, I approached him as he took his last drag from his cigarette. I tried to break the ice.

"Hello mate, do you live here?"

The man flicked his fag end over to a patch of dead grass.

"Why, what's happened?" His eyes remained fixed on the roadway in front of him. I moved into his field of vision.

"We've had a report of an incident at this address; do you know anything about a call to the police?"

"No, but her in there's always ringing you lot over something or other. I wouldn't waste my time if I were you – you'd be better off doing something useful like catching burglars."

"Well, as soon as we know what's happened, I'm sure we can let you get on with your day. Can I take your details?" I took a piece of paper out of my back pocket and made a sideways turn to look for a pen in the holder on my pullover sleeve.

"So then mate, what's your name?" I looked at him, ready to record his reply.

"You've already got it down at the station. I'm not giving it you again."

I decided to change my stance before asking again. I placed my weight on the other foot.

The sound of shattering glass broke the impasse. As I looked up,

18

the front door swung open with such force that its hinges bent back and hit the house wall, smashing its glass all over the step.

From the open void, the terrifying vision of a distraught female looked out, barely human, face streaked with mascara, rouge, and blood. At first glance, I thought she was wearing war-paint, all brutal and savage, finger nails clawed into the wooden frame.

As her nails dug into the rotten wood, the red satin dressing gown fell open revealing more bruising to her chest: a purple hue that spread across the upper torso. All eyes fixed on her in a moment of stillness; then she released her grip. The half-naked woman lunged at the male, making a noise like a wailing banshee. Jill grabbed her by the arms and managed to force her back through the doorway just as her gown came off her bony shoulders and fell to the floor.

I was momentarily dumbstruck. The man with the Nazi tattoo reacted like a cat, springing to his feet and lunging back at the woman. I clambered in between them and managed to tackle him, forcing him away and knocking him down. His head hit the ground within an inch of the bicycle's handle bars, spraying flecks of mud across my neck and face. I used my weight to keep him there on the ground, securely restrained around the neck; looking up to the sky, I remember thanking God that my first struggle happened to be with a man who weighed no more than ten stone.

The front door slammed shut, a gapping whole where the glass used to be. Jill secured it as best she could, locking the banshee inside. She knelt down to help as I put the handcuffs on the man who was wriggling in the mud like a floundering fish.

"Right, let's get this twat back to the station. We can come back and take the details later." With one co-ordinated heave, she helped me get him to his feet.

Her plan sounded like a good idea, so I bundled him into the back of the car, forcing his small body down into the foot well to stop him getting the seats dirty. I for one did not what to be cleaning the bloody car seats; I had my first prisoner to think about.

It was now time for me to take my prize to the cell block and present it to the custody desk like a cat bringing home a bird. I'd been to my first real incident and come out of it relatively unscathed. I'd proven that I possessed the required abilities and now I had something to talk about with my shift, the story of taking down a violent man.

However, by the time he was placed before the custody officer he was longer a violent lunatic. He looked and sounded more like a lost child as he calmed down and gave his details at the first opportunity. Perhaps it's a case that an old villain knows only too well, there's no point giving attitude to a world-weary, dry-as-dust custody officer. They've seen it all before.

At the end of the day, it's they who get to make your stay in custody as easy or as difficult as they like. If you simply calm down and co-operate you'll make your life a lot easier and go a long way to speeding the lengthy process up.

As for me now, well, my job was to relay the facts of the arrest to the custody officer in order that he could authorise detention and formally welcome Mr Nazi to the block. I took a deep breath, not wanting to appear new.

"This man has been arrested to prevent a breach of the peace." I paused for effect before continuing, the sergeant impatiently looked at his watch.

"We received a call to Ash Crescent, following the report of a domestic dispute. While we were there, a disturbance broke out in which the prisoner became violent and tried to assault a lady at the address. He was arrested to prevent any further violence and brought here; we will need to return to the address and establish what, if any, further offences have taken place. However, I can point out at this stage that the caller does have an injury to her face."

The sergeant wrote down my words verbatim on the custody sheet. He then read Mr Nazi his rights before allocating him a cell. When the door had been slammed shut, Jill and I dusted ourselves down, straightened our ties and went to get a coffee. Having recovered from all the excitement, we sat down in the office to complete our official pocket notebooks.

Jill had been the one to speak to the caller, so she was the first to explain the job as she had heard it. She explained that the assault victim, Jackie, lived at these premises with her fifteen-year old daughter, Kelly. The prisoner, Billy, was Jackie's boyfriend.

The story was that Billy had been staying there for three months. Jackie had met him in the pub where he worked in Birmingham, and soon after they met he moved in. 'The Moon under Water', as it used to be called, closed down a month later following a drugs raid, its license having been subsequently revoked, leaving Billy without a job and an income. He'd since been living off Jackie and spending the family allowance on gambling and whiskey.

The incident today was sparked when Kelly needed money for her bus fare.

While Jackie ate her breakfast, Kelly stormed around noisily, searching the cupboards and drawers for any loose change she could find. Billy just sat there, getting angrier by the second. He began to blame Jackie for spending the last of the money on cigarettes.

It was then that Jackie made the mistake she would regret for a very long time: she answered him back.

Silence fell across the kitchen table. Even Kelly froze like a statue, her hand still in the cutlery drawer, eyes watching Billy. With lightning speed, he gave Jackie a back-handed slap across the face with such force that it knocked the cornflakes out of her mouth, spraying the residue over the wall cupboard.

Jill had made a note of the debris smeared around the kitchen, recording that it 'had a consistency like milky-white blood'. She had also recorded in her notebook that Jackie sustained a broken tooth in the assault; it was now loose in her mouth and bleeding.

Jill underlined her notes and looked towards me. She had told me about the facts in her possession and now it was my turn to explain the little that I knew about the offender. I took a sip of coffee and cleared my throat just as the radio crackled to life with a voice that sounded a little too serious for comfort.

"Zulu 45?"

"Yes, go ahead, control." I put my mug down and answered into my receiver.

"Zulu 45, you'd better get back to Ash Crescent immediately, there's been a development."

★ ★ ★

I'm not sure why the details of Ash Crescent have always remained so vivid in my memory. The details were shocking beyond belief – that's true – but then again, many other incidents are similarly horrific.

In fact, almost every day in the newspapers and on the television we are bombarded with horrendous examples of perverse human behaviour and the most terrible things that one can imagine are happening time and again. When we hear about them on the news or read about them in the papers, we tend to think we can't be shocked by anything ever again. Then something occurs that, quite frankly, defies all belief.

The most horrific stories, when they break, are often given wall-to-wall media coverage and we can become immune from the effects of knowing all the grisly facts. I remember when I first heard about the town of Amstetten in Austria, when the Joseph Fritzl case emerged in April 2008. The facts came to light after a forty-two-year old woman, Elizabeth Fritzl, told police that she had been kept against her will for twenty-four years in the cellar below the family home. The details of the crimes went back to 29th August 1984, when her father lured her into the basement. She went with him, happily believing that he needed help carrying a door. He then drugged her and bundled her into the small underground chamber.

Over the course of the next twenty-four years, Fritzl would visit the cellar once every three days or so, taking food and essential supplies. He would force her to write letters to family, friends and relatives, stating that she had gone away for good, that she was happy and content, and that she didn't want anybody to try and contact her.

During her enforced imprisonment in that underground chamber, he systematically beat and raped her and, over the course time, she gave birth to seven of his children.

Anybody who has worked in the emergency services for their whole career would have a certain sympathy for the Austrian police officers, young and old, male and female, who had to deal with such a harrowing case. There were the traumatised children to deal with, and the daughter herself, all of them the helpless victims of that monster. The images from those crimes – the sights, the sounds, the smells – would remain very real and vivid in the minds of those officers.

The fact is there's a very real problem with the way that human beings are able to process the memories of such horrific incidents. You see, in the normal course of everyday life, the details of what we see and hear first get filed in the short term memory of the brain; they remain there for a short time before they are transferred into the long term memories store. However, when witnessing extreme or shocking events, the details can get stuck in the short term memory bank and the mechanism of transferring them lets us down. In short, our memories refuse to erode or degrade.

They lie, unprocessed, and can reappear as 'flashbacks' – highly detailed, vivid snapshots of the moment in which a highly significant event occurred. Flashback memories are principally determined by events involving a high level of surprise or emotional arousal. They are extremely resistant to the process of forgetting.

Veterans who have experienced combat in war zones are susceptible to such phenomena and can go on to develop symptoms of numbness and isolation. Over the years, a great deal of research has been done into patients who have suffered as a result of witnessing such trauma, and a name has been given to the condition that can develop in people who have experienced these events.

It is simply known as 'Post-Traumatic Stress Disorder, P.T.S.D'.

★ ★ ★

I've always felt an overwhelming sense of guilt in relation to the Ash Crescent case.

However, this was to be just the first of many experiences where I would sense that society had got it wrong and failed to protect its most weak and vulnerable. It isn't as though we haven't got a plentiful supply of laws, rules, regulations and procedures to protect us. It's not as though we haven't got some good, honest, hard-working people in our services. It's just somehow, somewhere in amongst all the bureaucracy, we have collectively failed Jackie and many other vulnerable people like her.

So, how can this be? Our criminal justice system is filled with highly-educated professionals, giving advice at every turn to keep the wheels of justice well-oiled and moving. It's not as though they don't receive hansom remuneration for their work; in fact, there are a number of people who have become very rich indeed out of serving the general public.

So why is it that so many people are let down and abandoned by a system that is supposed to be one of the finest legal systems in the world? Is it that, over the years, everything has been made so complicated that real justice is somehow out of reach of the average person?

Maybe the common people have always been lambs to the slaughter when put in the hands of the people who govern us and create the rules by which we live. Have we always been exploited by the people who make the law and earn their living by interpreting the complex system of procedures that they themselves put into place?

"The first thing we do, let's kill all the lawyers," Shakespeare wrote in 'Henry the Sixth'.

It was said that the Bard often expressed the opinion that all lawyers do is shuffle parchments back and forth to each other in a systematic attempt to ruin the common people. Maybe over the centuries nothing has changed: the common people remain at the mercy of the legal system. And, as far as Jackie was concerned, after her experience – well, she never bothered with the criminal justice system ever again.

★ ★ ★

We left our coffee to go cold and within five minutes were back at the door in Ash Crescent. The atmosphere had changed, a feeling of despair hung over the house.

On this occasion, the rather sad-looking, smashed-up front door was opened by Kelly. She was angry, indignant, appearing to seep frustration from every pore on her body. She stood in the doorway like a mother about to chastise her child for coming home late without calling.

"Well, can we come in?" Jill asked, well used to dealing with teenagers.

"I suppose so." Kelly gave us a sideways glance and led us through to the kitchen, milky-white blood smeared across the cupboard door like Jill had said.

"Okay then Kelly, in your own words, tell us what's happened." Jill took her notebook from her handbag and sat poised at the table.

Kelly looked at us, one to the other, trying to work out who was in charge.

"It was just after you'd gone. I found her in her bedroom, sitting in the corner, weeping. I know I shouldn't say this to you but I had warned her, time after time, but she would never listen. I think she's a stupid cow for getting involved with him in the first place; we were

24

doing alright, just the two of us here, before she decided to bring that lunatic back to our house. I knew that this would happen one day, I just knew it. I'll never forgive the silly cow for this, never!

"I know she's up there crying right now, all beaten up and everything, but she must have been able to see this coming. What's more, she could have ended up putting me in danger with that psycho lunatic of hers.

"I've told her, I'm leaving here today, going down to London with Darren, another of my bloody friends she doesn't approve of, and then to cap it all, the silly bitch goes and brings home that animal."

"Where's your mother now, Kelly?" Jill had an impatient tone; she'd heard enough of Kelly's whining voice.

"She's up on her bed. She didn't want me to call you back. In fact, she begged me not to but I'm not putting up with this any more, and now I'm leaving it's her problem. If that animal isn't sorted out soon by you lot, then mum or somebody like her is going to end up dead!"

Jill closed her notebook and stood up.

"Right, I'm going up to see Jackie. Kelly, I want you to stay here with my colleague, Simon, who is going to take a statement off you. Before you go anywhere at all, we'll need all your details together with any address in London where you're going so that we can contact you."

"Yeah, whatever." Kelly forced a sarcastic grin and reached for one of her mum's cigarettes. She lit it, eyeing me all the time from across the kitchen table. She took a long, deep draw on the cigarette before exhaling up to the ceiling. After a short pause, she began.

"I've warned her you know! Warned her about what a dirty, rotten pig he is, he even made me feel uneasy, the way he looked at me, so God knows how mum must have felt. That bastard always wanted to push the boundaries, there was no satisfying him.

"Once, he left one of his filthy, dirty magazines in the living room on the sofa, as if mum would have accepted that, he just gave me the creeps.

"Then, there was the occasion when he deliberately walked in on me when I was having a shower. He tried to pretend that he thought the bathroom was empty, but he would have been able to hear the shower from the landing, even with the closed door. I was there, standing up washing my hair, and all of a sudden, the door was wide open, the shower curtain had blown up against me and was clinging onto my skin. I washed the soap out of my eyes and looked up. The pig was standing there, staring at me.

"I remember he was smirking. I panicked and tried to pull the curtain around me, but the thing was just so wet and clingy that I couldn't move it properly; the shower was blasting water all over the floor. He pretended to reach for his shaving foam, saying he was in a hurry. I screamed at him to get out and give me my privacy, but he just laughed.

"'What's the problem?'" he said. "'I've seen your mum in the shower, what's so different about you?'"

"I was about to burst into tears, I couldn't keep myself covered and turn off the shower at the same time; I was trapped by that animal. After a moment or two, he made a big show of holding up his razor and walked out of the bathroom. I spent the next hour scrubbing the hell out of my skin as I felt filthy."

"Did you ever tell your mum about this?" I looked up at her from my notebook.

"No, I didn't, but I did tell her that he was a dirty little creep and she should boot him out. She promised me that she was going to tell him this weekend, but when this weekend? That's what I want to know!

"Anyway it's too late now, look what's happened to her, the bloody silly cow. I've just been having a go at her; just before you two came back, asking her if she gets some pleasure being slapped around. It's not as though he brings any money into the house or provides food or anything, he just takes and takes from her. I've told her that he's a waster, she's stupid just putting up with him and now I don't want to see either of them, ever again." She paused while she stubbed out her cigarette, grinding the filter hard into the ashtray.

Momentarily, she took her eyes off me and I stared at her pouting, childlike face, as she ground away with the cigarette end. It struck me just how much she resembled her mum. Although I'd only seen her mother for a brief second or two, they had a similar look: there was of course the physical resemblance, the body shape and hair colour. But then there was also a particular demeanour, as though the weary desperation of life was wearing away at them, eroding their personalities.

Kelly was just a child at the time of my visit, but she was talking like an adult, somebody who had experienced things in her short life that people should never experience. And now she was about to embark on a new life in London with Darren. Maybe her mother, Jackie, was the same twenty years ago, sitting in her mother's kitchen, smoking her mother's fags, planning on leaving home to start a new life with some young man. Perhaps she has watched her life unfold over the years and decided that she wanted something better for Kelly, a better life with a loving partner, not a violent monster.

Maybe Jackie is making up for the fear of failure by accepting a good beating every now and then? Telling herself that life and all its miserable events are beyond her control – she's a victim, whether she likes it or not. Like acting out a recurring part in a play, she hopes and prays that Kelly will see for herself and decide that she doesn't want to go down the same road, living in some squalid flat with a violent man and no money.

She takes another cigarette from her mum's packet, flicks the lighter and pauses, her eyes following Jill as she returned to the kitchen.

"Right, I'm going to be staying upstairs with Jackie. I want you, Simon, to stay here with Kelly. In the meantime, get onto control right away, tell them to get S.O.C.O with their cameras down here, and get a message to the duty Inspector. "Jackie's been raped."

★ ★ ★

You could be forgiven for thinking it, but the old building situated in the unlit car park at the rear of the hospital was not named after Florence Nightingale, the founder of nursing: no, not at all.

The name came from that small passerine songbird belonging to the thrush family, and the block bearing its name stood alongside the mortuary and the other buildings which bore the names Chaffinch, Kingfisher and Peregrine.

Most of these buildings used to house new student nurses who would come to do their training at the hospital. But as the years passed, and more and more targets and league tables were introduced, the buildings were taken over by accountants, statisticians and managers, all brought in to manage 'change' in the modern-day service.

As soon as the first group of nurses had been moved out, it paved the way for all of the available nurse's quarters to be re-allocated to serve a more cost-effective purpose. Hence, with the help of social services and a variety of other agencies, the Nightingale Suite came about, situated in a ground floor flat which would previously have accommodated three students.

Like all the other flats in the Nightingale block, it consisted of three bedrooms, a bathroom and a kitchen diner. Specialist equipment, like cameras and an examination couch, were moved in, along with comfy armchairs, a television set and some second-hand toys that were donated in an old cardboard box.

As you entered the suite, the first door on the right led to the reception room. This was where people would wait for interviews, examinations and the like. The tired-looking box sat in the corner full of kid's toys, the kind you see in waiting rooms up and down the land.

Next on the right was the recording room. Microphones and television monitors were built into the wall above writing desks and filing cabinets containing all the necessary video and audio tapes and the obligatory forms.

Last door on the right was the interview room. Two large armchairs and low lighting set the scene where victims would have their accounts taken in a safe and secure environment. Four cameras, secured high in each corner, saw everything and captured it on the tapes which revolved above the heads of officers in the recording room.

The last room on the left was the smallest: the examination room. It was in here that victims would be required to be naked. There was a mat for them to stand on, a bed for them to lie on and a desk for the doctor.

And so, everything was up and running, ready for the first victim.

★ ★ ★

While Jill and I escorted Jackie to the Nightingale Suite, specialist child protection officers were interviewing Kelly at the police station. Jill was now in the hands of the criminal justice system and would not be able to contact Kelly until initial enquiries had been completed.

On entering the hospital grounds, the barriers automatically lifted allowing our police vehicle to the service area around the rear. Jill tapped the alarm code into the key pad and we entered the darkened suite and searched for the light switch. We found the reception room and made ourselves comfortable. There would be a two hour wait for the arrival of the doctor.

Jill had instructed Jackie not to drink, eat, smoke or use the toilet in the intervening hours; her body was full of forensic evidence and procedures had to be followed. So, without the chance of so much as a cup of coffee, we all settled down to watch the early evening talk show. A story had broken that day about a Hollywood film star who had assaulted his wife and left her in a coma; one of her friends was being interviewed. I turned it off, leaving an awkward silence over the room.

For a minute or two we just sat there. Jackie rocked backwards and forwards in her chair, mumbling something that only she herself could hear. We looked from one to the other, wondering who would be first to break the uncomfortable silence; then, all of a sudden, Jackie began to tell her story.

"The stupid thing is ..." she wiped away a tear. "We were going to leave him today. I was going to pick Kelly up from school at four and we'd have been gone. I've been in touch with Maureen from Women's Support who's been advising me on what exactly to do. She's been a real angel over these past two weeks, helping me set up a new bank account and getting everything ready for the off.

"As she suggested, I rounded up our passports, medical cards, all the forms of identification that we would need; they're all in a box at the back of the wardrobe, ready and waiting. The suitcase is packed, paracetemol, prescriptions, school work, two sets of clean clothes and some coins for a laundrette, all the things I wouldn't have thought about without her.

"The plan was, I'd pick Kelly up and go straight to the refuge. Maureen would meet us there and get us booked in. The next day, she was going to contact a solicitor that helps women, he would start proceedings to get Billy out of the house and kept away for good. The council would have gone in to change the locks on doors and windows and made the place safe with a personal attack alarm that goes straight through to the police."

Jackie paused and looked directly at me.

"The bastard would have got the message."

I leant towards Jackie; her eyes were melting away.

"So Jackie, what went wrong?"

She shot me a warning look, like a cornered animal, but then drifted back to her hypnotic state. She looked drained and helpless. I'm not sure that she realised exactly where she was or what was about to happen to her. Of course, we explained to her that she was here voluntarily, that she could get up and leave at any time, but she was unable to think clearly and had no will to question us. Even if she did leave, what would she do? Wander the streets perhaps, nowhere to go, nowhere to hide, no one to turn to. No: her only option was to stay here; stay and endure her worst nightmares.

It was our job to keep her there, and we could be pretty persuasive. Her body was now a piece of evidence and would need to be forensically examined. She would have to go through the whole thing completely naked so to avoid cross-contamination, her body belonging to the system to reap and plunder the evidence. Of course, the doctor was there to help put her at ease and explain every inch of the examination: her breasts, anus, pubic hair, each being studied, swabbed, and recorded for evidence.

She would be on autopilot, vulnerable, naked and humiliated, but she wouldn't protest. She was like a dead woman walking: just the shell of a body with the humanity ripped out. She would think about the moment she could get away, far away, hide in a corner and weep alone.

"He found out about the plan," she said at length.

"He overheard a conversation, this morning, in the kitchen. I was talking to Kelly, asking her to be ready; it was the first time I'd mentioned it to her and she got angry. I never mentioned it up until now – she would have said something, given the game away and ended up putting us both in more danger. I told her I'd be picking her up from school and that she would need to be prepared, I told her we'd be off to meet Maureen and that she would look after us.

"Kelly started banging around the place, making noise. Billy hates noise. She was looking for bus fare but the money jar was empty. She started shouting. I told her the money had been put safely in the bank but she was talking too loudly. We looked round and Billy was standing there. He'd heard every word.

"He stood there, motionless, piecing the details together in his mind. Then he nodded to himself, as though he'd thought there had been a conspiracy all along.

"Kelly couldn't sense the danger but I could. I looked at Kelly, my mind pleading with her not to make a scene. She banged the last two cupboards and slammed the kitchen door; that set him off.

"I tried to act as if everything was normal, not to antagonise him or provoke him. I carried on trying to eat my cereal but I felt sick to the stomach. Then he hit me.

"His back-hand caught me straight across the mouth, splitting my lip and knocking the food from my mouth."

Jill looked up from her note book.

"Has he ever been violent to you before?"

"He's only done it once before, again, he thought we were leaving him. Kelly rang the police. They said it was my word against his and they let him back. Within three hours he was back at the table, silent and dangerous; Kelly had to go and spend the night with a friend. Later that night, he stood at the kitchen table playing with a bread knife. He told me that if I ever spoke to the police again, he would teach me a lesson that I would never forget."

"Where was it that the two of you met?"

"That's the really good part; it was on a mate's night out, celebrating her divorce. We'd gone to a karaoke night at a pub up town: there were about ten of us in our group, having a right laugh until this barman came over. Just my luck, when the other girls went up singing, he started to chat me up. He was giving me some sob story about his wife leaving him and taking everything; he said he was now sleeping on his brother's floor and all he wanted to do was rebuild his life. He said he would have asked me out, but he didn't have any money until payday, and he said that I deserve the best, and guess what; I went and fell for it.

"After only two dates he told me he had to move out of his brother's house because his wife was expecting a child. He said if he moved in with me he could pay half the bills and do the odd jobs, he seemed so helpful and harmless. I thought to myself, it can't hurt. As soon as he moved in things changed: there was always some reason why he couldn't help towards the bills. When the pub closed down he got made redundant and started to borrow money off me to tide him over before he could sign on. It was then that he started to pressure me into having sex with him whenever he felt like it. I started to worry about the way he would look at Kelly, and I told her not to walk around the house in her nightie anymore. I noticed that his tastes in that department started to change and become really weird".

"What do you mean by his tastes were weird?" Jill asked hesitantly.

Jackie had returned to her trance-like state; her eyes were wide open but she was miles away. She was delving into the darkest recesses of her mind, going through the collection of images, sweeping them up ready to unload.

She was trying to move Billy into the section marked distant past: the part of her that respected Billy had died. It died the moment he raped her; he'd taken a part of her away that could never be replaced. If she had to kill him to protect her daughter she would do it – but then, instead of sitting in this foreboding rape suite, she'd be in a police cell.

It didn't really make much difference. It was all the same to her; in fact the prison cell would be easier: no one to question you, prod you, poke you, swab every intimate part of you and probe every corner of your mind.

In prison you would not be judged, nobody would enquire into your past, you could remain anonymous. You could take your place among the failures and the rejects and become institutionalised, protected from the outside world, its reality and its cruelty. The bars and stone walls would keep you safe.

"What do you mean by tastes, Jackie?" Jill tried to bring her back from her trance.

"First it was just stockings and suspenders, a cheap set bought in the market and a pair of cheap leather boots. He would ask me to pose around the kitchen as he took photos, I tried to pull the blinds down but he'd stop me, get me to pose by the sink, washing up. He always wanted to humiliate me – he liked other people to see me humiliated. He got a kick out of treating me like dirt, his own personal property, his own Barbie doll, dressing me up and making me feel like his toy.

"He wanted to have total control over me and my body, it gave him a feeling of power. He craved total control and as time went on things went from bad to worse. He came back home one day and brought with him a dog collar, the kind you see on one of those Staffs: thick leather with studs all over it, three inches wide. I must have been so bloody stupid; I actually thought he was going to buy a dog.

"He wanted me to wear it in the bedroom; he wanted me to stand to attention by the bed and beg. I stood there for a minute feeling silly and embarrassed but he insisted I wear it. The next night, when he put it on me, he put it on too tight, I couldn't breathe; I couldn't nod my head or move it side to side. He then got on top, with his normal brutish approach. I was choking but couldn't move my jaw and couldn't scream. My vision went blurred and I felt my eyes roll up into my head. Everything went black. I felt myself slowly passing out. Just at that point, he finished with a series of violent thrusts. I clawed at the buckle, trying to loosen it; I fell to the floor, gasping for breath. I loosened it and held my throat, all the time struggling to breathe.

"I begged and begged him not to use it again; he smiled and put the collar back in the drawer."

"You said earlier that Kelly stormed out of the kitchen, slamming the door. What happened after that?" Jill turned a new page in her pocket book.

"She went upstairs to her bedroom and put her music on, a new tape that Darren had bought her: rap music or something; just boom, boom, boom. Billy hates that music, it drives him mad.

"Well, Kelly's put this rap music on, very loud, it's banging through the ceiling, boom, boom, boom, a dull, rhythmic boom. The place was shaking.

"Billy just froze.

"His face was red. I thought he was about to explode, boom, boom, boom! I kept thinking, 'For God's sake, Kelly, turn that bloody noise off.' Billy had that look in his eyes. The one when he puts that collar on me. I know I'm in danger, I know I'll be punished. Nothing left but to prepare myself for a beating.

"I sat waiting. Upstairs the music got louder, boom, boom, boom, through the ceiling. Then, something strange happened: his behaviour changed.

"He tilted his head upwards, like an animal scenting the breeze. He was looking up at the ceiling, below Kelly's room. He smiled this chilling smile. I felt sick.

"I felt this cold hand stirring in my stomach as it dawned on me. I began shaking my head, no, please no. I was mouthing the words, 'No, God no, anything but that, don't hurt Kelly.' There was no sound coming out.

"He was halfway up the stairs before I could move. I chased him up the final steps and caught up with him at Kelly's door. It was a couple of inches open, she couldn't hear us – she had the music up too loud and she was lying facing the wall.

"I looked at my daughter, young and innocent, lying there in her dressing gown. I turned and looked at Billy. Suddenly all the threats and all the bullying came together.

"I was only concerned about Kelly – I'd never have forgiven myself, I was her mother, I needed to protect her. My mind was pounding, trying to think, there was no time to call the police.

"There would have been no use in pleading with him: it would have made him worse. I had to save Kelly.

"I undid my dressing gown and let it fall. I felt stupid and bare; I must have looked like a prisoner, standing naked against a cell wall. I leaned over him and pulled Kelly's door shut. She was still unaware of our presence.

"I put my finger up to my bloody lips and went 'ssshhh'. He looked at me; a little confused by then, his wolfish smile came back.

"'Come on honey, I don't want Kelly to hear us.' I led him through to our bedroom, holding back the tears and trying to remain strong. He thought it was a trap and I saw the danger in his eyes. I held up the dog collar and smiled, tears running down my face. He nodded and slammed the door.

"He squeezed my neck and threw me onto the bed. The tears were coming faster. I tried to stop. I knew I had to go through with it to protect Kelly, keep him distracted. I felt the collar being pulled tightly around my neck. My breathing became harder, I had to keep alive. He fell beside me, the bed shook and I felt his hands all over me, hard and rough, pulling at me, this way and that; then he got on top and held the collar, forcing my head back. I started to pray.

"Suddenly the weight was lifted from my back; I felt a rush of relief that lasted only a couple of seconds, then immense pain.

"He pulled me back by the collar and threw me onto the floor. He picked me back up like a rag doll and threw me against the wall. I felt a punch to my back and then more to my side as I slid down the wall to the ground."

Jackie paused.

"Were you unconscious, Jackie?" Jill stopped writing, a tear welling up in her eye.

"Yes, for a moment; at least I think I was. I was worried about Kelly and if she was safe. I pulled myself up by the window sill and undid the collar. I looked out the window.

"Billy was sat outside, smoking a cigarette. I took the opportunity, got to the phone, rang 999."

"What happened then, Jackie?"

"As soon as I saw the police car, I grabbed my dressing gown and ran down the stairs, that's when you came in." She looked at Jill, a longing smile.

"Well, after you took Billy away, Kelly came to my room. She saw the collar, the bed and my bruises. She went for the phone. I pleaded with her not to ring. I told her he'd gone, couldn't hurt us again, we were safe, but she wouldn't listen.

"All my strength had gone, I couldn't fight anymore."

"What will you do now?" I asked.

"When I get out of here, I want to make it up with Kelly. I will never put my daughter in danger again. Can I speak to her?"

"No, not now, Jackie, she's being interviewed. They'll let us know when you can speak with her."

A shadow crept over Jackie's face.

"You're not going to take her from me, are you? Please no, you wouldn't do that, would you?"

There was a knock at the door. Dr Porlock had arrived and he was running late.

★ ★ ★

CHAPTER FOUR

Introduction to Therapy

I'd been with Beth at the Trauma Support Network for over half an hour before I noticed that the mantelpiece was covered in birthday cards. This gave me the ideal opportunity to take a break from all the psychological cross-examining and engage in a little harmless small talk.

"I didn't know it was your birthday, Beth. Is it actually today?"

"No, my birthday was yesterday, but my partner's taking me out tonight to celebrate."

"Well, that sounds good. Are you going anywhere nice?" Already I was feeling a sense of relief as we moved to a different subject.

"She's taking me to Symphony Hall to see Puccini's 'Tosca', and then I'm being treated to dinner at Le Petit Chateau."

"That sounds all very grand; I'll spare a thought for you while I'm eating my fish and chip supper." Beth laughed and I looked around the room for any other birthday clues. As I did, it suddenly occurred to me that my seat was placed with its back to the window, facing towards the fireplace, whereas her seat faced the window, looking to the outside world and the view of the medieval castle wall. Things like this were done to focus my attention in the room without being distracted by anything outside: to concentrate my thoughts on the session, without diversion. That's why the place was painted white; nothing to focus on but your thoughts. From the skirting up to the coving, the ceiling over to the mantelpiece, everything was painted white. A white vase holding white twigs stood on the hearth, and even the logs under the sealed-off chimney were painted white. The birthday cards had provided some relief.

Beth was making some notes; I continued to look around the room.

Just like outside, in the waiting room, the carpet tiles and the two easy chairs were a striking cobalt blue colour. Between Beth and me was a low beech-coloured table, a vanilla-scented candle and a large box of mansize tissues placed carefully on top; I wondered if these tissues were for her male clients and a more suitably feminine box was hidden away to be used for female clients. My eyes darted around the room again, looking for them.

Beth's voice cut across my train of thought.

"We've got about ten minutes left before my next client and I wanted to say a bit about the next few sessions. Are you familiar with the term 'Trauma Focused Cognitive Behavioural Therapy'?"

"Well a little. I mean, I think I've heard of it." I began to stumble, my attention focused back on Beth, the small talk over.

"Well," Beth decides to help me out. "We at the Trauma Therapy Network believe that the best results can be achieved when Trauma Focused Therapy is combined with the necessary anti-depressant medication.

"The psychotherapy programs with the most proven results include variants of exposure therapy together with what we call 'stress inoculation training'.

"I don't want to cause you any panic or blind you with science; after all this is only your first visit. I just wanted to give you an idea of the ground we'll be covering over the next few weeks.

"Before you head off home, though, I just want to say how impressed I've been by the way you've opened up and felt able to talk freely today. It's very important that you feel able to talk openly about these incidents, particularly if you're serious about confronting your condition with a view to moving on.

"In one sense, it's good that you've been able to talk about this Jackie case, because this and similar cases seem to have had such a profound affect on you. But just for the moment, I want you to leave her to one side while we concentrate on some of the other incidents that have shaped you and your career over the past couple of years. As I read into your case, I can see that you've certainly been exposed to a number of very nasty incidents, some of which have taken their toll on you, and it's important that we have a chance to examine each one, make a clean sweep of things if you like. I can help you to understand your own anger and frustration and help you understand that these emotions are perfectly normal and that we just have to learn the right way to deal with them.

"However, the Alton matter is slightly different, due to the intensity of the exposure you suffered; so, I will make it clear to you now, that when and only when you, yourself, are ready to talk about the case will we go into detail on that one.

"I don't want you to feel under pressure to tackle those issues. Only when you have the confidence in me and the therapy will we be able to tackle the real causes of these flashbacks and nightmares that have been causing you so much distress.

"The symptoms you're displaying are part of what we call 'persistent re-experience' and I can understand your hesitation and reluctance to tackle these so early on in the therapy.

"So, when you're ready, we will explore the Alton case and the affect that it has had on you. We will then go on to deal with the causes of stress, the things that trigger the flashbacks and the panic attacks and try and get you back on the right track – you know, get a sense of normality back to your life.

"However, as I've already said, that's for a later session and what's important right now is that you feel comfortable and confident in talking to me. For my part, I must say you appear to me to be a pleasant, genuine sort of guy, who has just failed to get the support that's been needed, and throughout this course I hope to remedy this and provide the support that has so obviously been lacking."

Beth reached for her handbag, removed a business card and began scribbling on the back.

"That's my mobile phone number. If at any time you feel the need to talk just give me a call, okay?" I took the card and looked at the number written on the back.

"Thanks Beth, I really appreciate this." I shook her hand and left the room.

★ ★ ★

I left the meeting in a more positive mood. It was still raining heavily, but for some strange reason I've always found it easier to think when the weather is bad. Maybe it's because, like the therapy room, there are fewer distractions. People dart around under their umbrellas, taking less notice of things around them.

On the corner of Castle Lane I saw a familiar sign and walked into the café out of the rain. The warm air, heavy with the smell of coffee, washed over me with a welcoming breeze. I closed the door leaving the bad weather outside.

I always take my coffee in exactly the same way, but when asked by the assistant what I wanted I couldn't help perusing the menu board.

"A large cappuccino with an extra shot and a cinnamon Danish, please," I say at length.

"Yes, sir, coming right up."

There is always a couple of minutes to wait while the coffee is being prepared, the beans are ground from the supply at the top of the machine and the various gauges, levers and spouts do their thing. A strong black liquid is produced and poured into a waiting cup; the milk is then frothed and poured over the coffee producing a creamy peak higher than the cup rim.

"Do you want chocolate on your cappuccino?"

I nodded a 'yes' and the server held a template over the cup and sprinkled chocolate powder onto the froth. I thanked him and took the coffee over to a sofa by the window, where I could watch the people dart around in the rain.

I felt a sense of satisfaction with the world now that I'd had my first session and met Beth.

I'd had some bad experiences with counsellors before. I'd sat there, facing some stranger who sat in a comfy chair, wearing open-toed sandals and white socks. I'd bared my soul and told my innermost secrets to some do-gooder who really didn't give a shit whether I lived or died; someone who no doubt started their career with the best intentions, but had spent the past few years being ground down.

They probably started off with the right ideas, wanting to help people to get better and all that. But, all too often, it's the other professionals that have not shown the same dedication.

They had tried to get used to doing the best they could with such a lack of resources and they too were fed up with passing people around the mental health system. They no longer felt that they could really make any difference. Yes, they were happy to listen, happy to pass the hour with you nodding and agreeing, but that still didn't stop you leaving with the same sense of emptiness with which you arrived.

It didn't help you understand what was going on in your mind or help you find a way out of the darkness. For some professionals, their work is nothing more than an endless conveyer belt of sad, pathetic people and, after each client leaves, they just file the notes away with the hundreds of others and the next weary soul shuffles in to take the seat.

As for me and the Andrew Alton case – well, I wondered if any therapist could sort that one out. How could something be tackled when everybody else did their best to avoid responsibility? The whole thing just festered like a giant sore, spreading its poison around until it destroyed yet another life.

But I have decided that I'm going to give this a chance. I've got nothing to lose; the first session went all right.

Now, I suppose all I need do is sit back, enjoy my coffee and consider what I will say at our next meeting.

★ ★ ★

CHAPTER FIVE

A New Station

"I just wanted to grab five minutes with you, to have a quick chat, but also to say welcome on board and I hope you'll be very happy on 'A' unit here at Solihull."

He introduced himself with a hand on my shoulder and a firm grip in his handshake.

"I'm very happy to be coming over this side, particularly on 'A' unit. I know Tracey and Paul from my days over at the Wood, and from all the things they've been telling me it sounds like there's a great team spirit here," I replied.

"Yes, indeed, I think it's the best of the four. But then I would say that, wouldn't I? It's true to say that we've had the best prisoner figures for the last year, but what's just as important for the team, as well as a good work rate, is that the shift has a good social set-up with most people taking part. I don't know if you've met Claire yet – she's our social fund organiser.

"The last event being a tour of the Black Country on the official Tour Bus with their famous 'faggots and peas' evening; I don't think they'll be inviting us back anytime soon, but that's another story!

"I trust you'll be joining us at the Coach House for our normal end-of-tour drink this Thursday; you know, get a chance to say hello properly."

Inspector Andy Stewart was the old-fashioned kind of police officer. After serving fifteen years with the Metropolitan Police at West End Central, he'd spent his last ten in the West Midlands here at Solihull. Throughout his policing career he had achieved sporting success in both forces, representing the police at cricket in the summer and rugby union in the winter. If there was any time left over, he would be found coaching the polo team in the swimming baths.

According to the word around the station, he was always the first to arrive and the last to leave most of the social events, and if any one thought they could drink him under the table – well, they would normally end up being carried out.

He sat at the Inspector's desk, flicking through my file.

"I understand that you've completed Part One of the sergeants' exam." He stood up and lent forward to adjust the blinds; the sun shinning through the large south facing windows was making the room uncomfortably hot.

"That's right, sir." I looked across to his sideboard where a stainless steel desk fan stood idle, electric cord gathered beside it, almost mocking us. He sat back down.

"And the second part?" He made a steeple with his fingers and rested his chin.

"I had my first attempt at the second part last year. Unfortunately, I failed it, but I'll be giving it another go this October."

"You know, when I was your age I had to do the old-style exam. We had none of this multiple choice, put a tick in the box stuff. It was all long-hand answers, with a text book the size of a telephone directory." He leant back in his high-backed leather chair. A satisfied smile crept across his face.

"I just found Part Two a little bit tricky, so I'm doing a course with the training department. With any luck that will help me next time."

"Any idea what your weak areas were?" he asked, swivelling from side to side in his executive chair.

"I've had some feedback on my performance but it was quite limited in what it told me." One attempt to swivel my chair and I found it stuck on four rigid legs.

"Did they indicate which of the scenarios it was that you struggled with?" This time he leant right back, touching the wall with the back of his chair, knees up to the desk, fingers back under his chin.

"The first scenario that I felt I didn't perform particularly well in was the one with the old boy who had just come out of headquarters. He'd been posted at a busy town centre police station after twenty years in licensing, or some other dead-end job like that. You know the sort of thing: he'd got eighteen months to do before collecting his pension and heading off into the sunset in his camper van; then, all of a sudden, he finds himself back on the streets of Sandford, wearing a top hat and not having a clue about new procedures. He's de-motivated and quite frankly doesn't want to be there, dealing with all the crap on the streets. To cap it all, the dinosaur has been put on patrol with a young female probationer, and, well, let's just say he's a bit rough around the edges. So, to all intents and purposes, it's a grievance procedure and a claim just sat there, waiting to happen."

"So then, you'd got a clear picture on the issue and the factors to be considered – how did you approach the problem?" He reached over, took the cord again and made another adjustment to the window blinds.

"First of all, I took him through the various training courses that I thought he'd benefit from, and I also pointed out the recent changes in the law that he needed to be aware of: you know, stop and search, arrest details and so on.

"However, looking back at the scenario, I think if anything I was a little harsh on him, maybe a bit impatient. I should have looked further into his welfare needs and the support he needed, before simply suggesting a training course."

The Inspector slowly nodded his head as though considering what I'd said, before returning to swivelling in his chair.

"Did they give you any details of any other scenarios?"

"The other one where I seem to have been marked down was the one where you have to approach and deal with an officer whose work rate is poor. This officer was failing to arrest the required amount of prisoners and his paperwork was always late and below standard. I sat him down and went into detail on subjects like 'performance indicators' and our league tables, but what I failed to do was to probe deeply enough into the underlying reasons for the downturn in his work.

"Apparently, the story was that his wife had just left him and he was having problems with alcohol. The first thing I should have considered was making a referral to occupational health, so he could speak to someone about his stress issues."

He nodded his head again, obviously satisfied with my account, before finally plugging in the fan and switching it on. A cool wave of air swept across my face.

"And what do you think they would have done?"

"Well, they would probably have told him to go and see his GP, who would probably have asked what occupational health was doing about the problem. After a couple of months of going back and forth he would probably have given up the ghost and killed himself; at least then the problem would have gone away!"

He smiled a knowing smile and leant back.

The phone on his desk gave a high-pitched trill and he grabbed it with a grip like his handshake.

"Duty Officer," he growled.

He began listening carefully to what was a good five minutes of speech from the other end, his pen poised, scribbling the occasional note on his desk pad. I pulled open a little gap in the blinds and craned my neck slightly to look out into the street and towards the town.

The town centre lies south of the borough and is in the centre of a very affluent area where the people with money live. Its wealthy and highly-skilled population makes Solihull one of the most prosperous boroughs in the Midlands. People who live in the south are known as 'Silhillians'.

Having lived in Solihull for most of my life, I can tell you that the name dates back to medieval times, when travellers would refer to the clearing in the forest as a muddy or 'soily hill'. Later, the area progressed to be a mail coach stop and, as it became more populated, a thriving market town.

Unlike Birmingham, its big brother neighbour, the industrial revolution largely passed Solihull by, so to this day the town retains many of its original features: its timber-framed, Tudor-style houses and pubs.

Throughout World War II, the German Luftwaffe really couldn't be bothered with Solihull; they didn't think it was worth their while. So it wasn't until the 1960's that anyone was able to inflict any real damage on the town's ancient fabric.

It was in the 60's that the then Town Clerk, Mr Maurice Mell, ordered the demolition of the old market square to make way for a new shopping centre – the thoroughly modern and modestly named 'Mell Square.'

This open-air shopping complex, complete with marble façades and water fountains, was indeed a sixties showcase. People were now able to bring their motor cars into the town and park right outside their new department store; then, with their goods on board, they could drive around the little ring-road that encircled the fountain pool. However, with a modern shopping centre came new devices known as 'parking meters', and double yellow lines appeared with penalties for those who ignored them.

Solihull ended up with a significant 'north-south divide'. The two opposing sides of the borough came with profoundly different policing needs.

As a general rule of thumb, Silhillians in the south paid more money in taxes, but would tend to have lifestyles that relied less on the modern range of public services. However, it has to be said that if the richer people did ever have cause to use the services of the public sector, they would require, and normally demand, the highest standards and almost impossibly high levels of service.

Some would think nothing of pointing out to a busy nurse rushing around the chaotic hospital ward, that they played golf with the chairman of the board and they expected to be treated all the better because of it.

In the north, however, people generally paid less money in taxation; but in contrast to the south, their day-to-day lives would be closely interwoven with state services. Some families would even have their own network of social workers, health visitors and education welfare officers, and were well-used to the constant intrusions. For some, it was just a necessary part of everyday life.

They would not always be so insistent on such a high standard of service, but would be more likely to resort to violence if they thought it would help their cause.

As far as reporting crime was concerned there was also a difference. In the north it was more likely that a victim of domestic violence would call the police and report an assault; they would be more used to the police being an intrusive part of their lives. It would be more likely that disputes would be held in public, perhaps outside in the street, the offender often carried kicking and screaming to the riot van.

As would quite often happen when the dust settled, the victim would then consider their position and a call would be made to the station because they wanted to retract the complaint and get their partner back. The cycle of behaviour involving complaint and retraction would come to be a constant source of frustration for the local police. The incident would no doubt rear its ugly head again and the police would be called out for a repeat performance. Some addresses could log up a huge list of calls for help, with never an end to the problems.

On the other, southern half of the borough, it was a totally different story. Before the authorities were called into somebody's private life, there were more important things to consider.

There were mortgages, savings, pensions, careers and reputations at stake. An arrest for assaulting one's wife could lead to loss of career, loss of income and a lower standard of living for the family, let alone the public shame of being named in the local newspaper.

Instead, a call to an expensive lawyer the following morning might be a bit better in the long run – better than having Plod charge in with his size ten boots all over your Berber carpets. Of course, the family lawyer came at a price but would be more than happy to give advice on matrimonial rights and entitlements. It is a sobering thought, if your children attend public school, that you can't live off maintenance payments if your partner's in prison with no income.

The family solicitor, although a very expensive crutch to lean on, would indeed be glad to offer whatever support they could – at a price of, let's say, £200 per hour, upfront on account, naturally!

The telephone receiver was slammed back down.

In the office, the Inspector's voice brought my attention back to the room and I give him my full concentration.

"That was the control room," he said, standing up and reaching for his briefcase. "There's a suspected child suicide out near Berkswell station. I'm off there now to take a look."

I took my cue and followed him into the corridor. He spoke as he walked.

"I'm teaming you up with PC Collins." His pace quickened and I hurried to keep up. "I believe you've already met her." He was now well ahead of me, exiting out of the rear door.

"Yes, err, I have. Bye, sir."

I watched as he got into his police vehicle, turned on my heels, and walked off in the opposite direction. I took the stairs to the second floor and found myself in the real heart of the station: the canteen.

My new partner to be, Tracey, was sat in the far corner playing with a cheese salad by jabbing it with her fork. A quick glance at the menu board told me that chilli con carne was today's special. I approached the counter thinking about the chilli and for the first time in my life heard myself ordering a cheese salad.

Tracey saw me, beckoned me over to join her, and I sat down while my salad was being prepared.

"Hi Simon, welcome to the funny farm!"

I gave her a smile and reached over for a knife and fork.

★ ★ ★

It's an interesting point to consider: throughout the 1980's, as the number of women joining the modern police force increased, some of the shifts, which could be up to twenty officers, became an even split in numbers of male and female constables.

During the passage of time, throughout the force, more and more officers became, let's say, romantically attached to one another, having first met in the station or even out at jobs.

On some shifts, teaming up with somebody of the opposite sex was like a police version of 'speed-dating', where it was quite possible that a deep and meaningful relationship could blossom. The reasons for this were quite natural and simple.

Working with somebody on frontline policing could often be an intense, highly dangerous and almost intimate experience. A normal, everyday shift would last at least eight hours and that's a lot of time to spend with somebody and get to know their personality. In fact, other than the act of sleeping, you would spend more time in the close company of your work partner than your husband or wife at home.

Even when at home, things wouldn't be that intense. For example, one of you might be watching T.V. while the other is having a bath; one might be taking the dog out while the other cooks the dinner, or one might be working on the computer while the other snoozes in the armchair.

When it came to work, you'd always be with your partner, sat right next to each other. You'd be eating together, fighting together, enduring periods of extreme boredom together, then tackling life-threatening emergencies together, and you learnt to rely completely on one another. You needed to know each other's strengths and weaknesses and how the other would react in any given situation.

As a partnership, you came to learn that even the smallest of incidents could turn out to be very important and you needed to be able to trust each other implicitly. Each day was like a jigsaw, made up of many parts, and you never knew how the pieces would come together, but you had to be prepared, ready to back each other up to your bosses or even a court of law.

You needed to know what the other would say, would they back you up, would they stand up for you and support you when things took a turn for the worse?

You had to remember that sometimes, someone's memory can get a bit hazy. It could be difficult to remember exactly what happened. Would that person go along with your version? Would they automatically agree with you as a matter of course, without query or doubt? In the world of policing, having your story straight could be the difference between success and failure.

Two police officers testifying with the same account to the same incident would be the difference between a conviction and the criminal walking free. For the sake of the vulnerable victim, you had to make the case watertight: one of the officers not being sure of the course of events could put enough doubt in the minds of the jury for the case to collapse. Could the shift then trust that officer in the future, or would they be seen as weak?

If you gel together, it's like the two have made a commitment to each other, forming a bond on the basis of mutual trust. After that, well, anything could happen – especially when you consider that protecting somebody in danger can prove quite an attraction.

There are plenty of examples of people who face trauma together and go on to form deep and lasting relationships. It seems that, sometimes, the more traumatic the incident, the deeper the devotion.

In the aftermath of the September 11th attacks on the World Trade Centre, up to a dozen New York fire-fighters left their wives after falling in love with the widows of comrades killed on that day. Amongst the abandoned wives, the phenomenon was branded the New York Fire Department's 'dirty secret'. Although it's never been officially sanctioned, the tradition of caring for the widows and families of fallen colleagues has been an unwritten rule in the New York fire service for more than a hundred years.

Families who were not actually bereaved by the terrorist attack itself would be devastated as the ripple effect reached out and touched them. What was worse, as secondary victims of the tragic event, they'd never receive any compensation for loss of their man.

Psychiatrists have explained this type of behaviour by stating that the family liaison officer moved into a new 'rescue' role, in which they went on to save the vulnerable victim by stepping into the void that the husband had left.

A great deal of work was done to try and ensure that more of the surviving officers didn't leave their families to take up the hero role with a grieving widow. We have to bear in mind, that out of the 3,000 or so people killed that day, 343 of them were fire-fighters.

However, on that summer's day when I took my seat opposite Tracey: 9th September 2001 and the New York attacks were a long way in the future. A catastrophe of such magnitude defied imagination.

★ ★ ★

"Are you having a coffee?" The sound of Tracey's voice made me look up.

"Oh, yeah, a cappuccino please." I did my best to shake myself back to life.

Tracey walked over to the serving counter and placed the cup under the drinks machine. The machine got to work and soon produced two cups of hot, milky coffee.

"I'm popping next door for a fag. You coming?"

I finished what was left of the salad and got up to follow her out of the room. I had only given up smoking six months ago but I had no problem being in the company of other smokers.

"Yeah, I might as well join you."

We carried the coffees out into the lobby area. The exit to the stairwell lay straight ahead and there was a doorway on either side of us; the door to the right was closed, with a brass plaque on it saying, 'Officers' Mess'.

This concept was a relic of bygone days, when officers of the rank of Inspector and above would take their morning coffee and afternoon tea in their own mess, away from the hoi-polloi. It gave the place a military feel, more suited to the days of the authoritarian Police Force, and it did little but emphasise the boundaries that had always existed in the service. The senior staff would dine in the mess and be served through their own private door at the rear of the kitchen: that way their food could be wheeled straight to them on a trolley.

I couldn't resist opening the door just a little and peering in.

On the wall beneath the dining table was a portrait of a young Queen Elizabeth II, seated and smiling down on her subjects; white dress, elbow gloves, blue sash and diamond tiara.

The walls of the mess were decorated with a rich, gold paper with vertical stripes; a mahogany sideboard containing china gave the place the feel of a gentleman's living room. The place was clearly out of bounds.

I followed Tracey through the other door into the smoking room.

This room, supposedly there to service the needs of all the nicotine addicts in the station, was less than half the size of the mess. The ceiling was stained a dirty yellow colour that seemed to creep down the walls.

The 'broom cupboard' as it was known, looked old and tired, suffering from the effects of years of smoke. This was the only place left inside the police station for smokers to meet and, at peak times, it could get quite crowded: in fact, sometimes it would be quite unnecessary to light up – just breathe in the atmosphere and you could get your daily dose of cigarette smoke.

For the smokers' comfort, four low, black, faux leather chairs just about fitted into the room, together with a fruit machine in the corner by the window. It, too, bore the effects of smoking: tiny burn marks were visible where cigarettes had been balanced while the smokers played the machine, concentrating on nudge buttons and the lure of the big cash payout.

The damn machine's lights flashed continually in its carefully programmed sequence; left to right, up and down, the lights followed each other round and round, hypnotising the player. The theme of this particular fruit machine was 'Popeye the Sailor Man'.

It had the nasty habit of suddenly bursting into chorus, like a bird singing its lungs out to attract a mate. After the chorus, Popeye's unique way of speaking would sound off and his picture would light up, beefy forearms displaying anchor tattoos, corncob pipe tooting like a steamship's whistle, reminding people that money needed to be fed into the slot.

A range of pictures lit up around the cash prizes. The old sea-hag 'Bluto' chased the stick-like 'Olive' around a ship's deck. Popeye squeezed a can of spinach to open the top. As a player nudged up their points, they lit up a tower of spinach cans until they hit the jackpot and the machine burped out dozens of ten pence pieces.

Deliberately ignoring the brutish Bluto, I leaned behind the machine and pulled open the window to allow some fresh air into the room. Tracey took a cigarette from her red and white box. Behind me, a metallic sounding 'clunk' and a whiff of lighter fuel signalled her Zippo had lit up her smoke and she was up and running.

She seemed to gain satisfaction from holding the smoke down for longer than normal, closing her eyes with a look of sheer pleasure. Then, she'd purse her lips and exhale her smoke up towards the yellow ceiling.

She re-opened her eyes just as I was staring at her, watching her lips move, trying to make out the shade of lipstick. I looked away and caught Popeye just as he gave a final 'toot' on his pipe.

Slightly embarrassed, I felt in my pocket for some change. The whirling lights had begun to reel me in, but a couple of five pence pieces and a petrol receipt wouldn't go a long way in the world of gambling. I returned my attention to Tracey.

"What's the plan then?" I asked, as she deliberately exhaled closer to my face, a warning shot.

"I've got about an hour of paperwork left to sort before we go out. After that, well, I don't know if you fancy a trip out to Henley? I know a little tea spot I think you'd like."

"Sounds good to me. I've got to take a little trip to admin to sort out some new uniform, so once I'm done I'll come and find you in the parade room."

She exhaled again, this time back towards the ceiling. I found myself staring – this time it was at her neck, how white it looked against her black hair, combed back and scraped mercilessly into a tight bun on the back of her head.

"Sounds like a plan," she said with the cheeky raise of an eyebrow, conscious of the fact I'd been caught staring at her: was it a challenge?

I left the room and headed upstairs.

* * *

The administration area of the police station was on the top floor, just along from the offices of the senior members of staff. Accordingly, and in contrast to the rest of the station, it was tastefully decorated and carpeted, with rubber plants growing in the corners. I strolled along the corridor and found the door marked 'Admin'. I entered the room with a spring in my step and approached Sandra.

"Hi Simon, how are you finding it here on the sunny side?" she said, biting the tip of her biro and flicking back her hair.

"Well, the admin assistants are much better for a start!" I perched on the end of her desk and she leant away just a little. "Over there they're rubbish, no use at all, won't help you with anything. Over here it's totally different; people can't speak highly enough of you, they say the staff are really friendly and are always willing to help".

"Okay then, buster, that's enough. What is it that you want?"

"Who me? Nothing. I just came here to say hi and to see how you all were. I don't think enough people tell you what a wonderful job you do and in the most difficult of circumstances, too. But now you come to mention it, while I'm here I need two new pairs of trousers. Oh yeah, and I could do with some more of those cleaning tokens." I leant forward across her desk, giving her a grin. She backed her chair away.

"And there was me thinking you'd just popped in to give us a compliment."

"No, that's precisely how it was, but it's when you jogged my memory, I just thought, you know, while I was here …"

"Well, we wouldn't want you to leave the office without your trousers, would we?" She pushed herself back from the desk.

Stooping down to the lower drawer of a metal filing cabinet, she pulled out a requisition form. Like in most police stations, the filing cabinet was huge and must have had thirty individual trays, all with an index card on the front displaying the form name and number. You can't do anything without a form in the police force: there must be a whole office of people employed to come up with new reasons for forms.

"I positively refuse to leave this office without my trousers." I raised my eyebrows but she wasn't looking. She was concentrating on filling in the form with her chewed biro.

"Will you stop flirting with our younger members of staff? She's at rather an impressionable age is Sandra."

A voice came from the corner, somebody behind a computer screen.

"Yes, I mean you; don't leave us out just because we're older!" It was Jenny. Perhaps the longest serving member of staff, she stood up to water a series of potted plants which were sitting on her window ledge, soaking up the sun.

"Let me make it absolutely clear that, as far as flirting, as you put it, is concerned, I don't discriminate on the grounds of age, race or religious belief."

"Many a good tune played on an old fiddle, or so they say." She gave a cheeky wink, put the jug down and returned to her keyboard. This time it was me feeling slightly awkward, best thing to do was to come out with a joke.

"You know they say that women of different ages are like the continents of the world."

"Oh no, I can feel something totally inappropriate coming on here." Sandra shook her head as she scribbled away, face buried in the form.

"No, it's actually true: women of different ages are like the continents of the earth. Let me explain. Right, under the age of twenty, a woman is like Asia. Dark, mysterious and only partly explored. Then, from the ages of twenty to thirty, she's like Africa...."

Sandra coughed a warning sound and inclined her head towards the door.

"Afternoon, ladies." The voice indicated another male's presence in the room.

"Ah, good afternoon, Sir!" It was Chief Superintendent Wallis, a man I'd known for some years.

"Yes, good afternoon." He turned his attention to Jenny.

"Could you let me have these figures in time for this afternoon's tasking meeting?"

Jenny accepted the file from the boss and flicked through the pages.

I took the opportunity to quietly slip out, not wanting to be hanging around the office while the boss was on the prowl.

"I'll get back to you with the results as soon as I can." Sandra nodded at me, understanding the code.

I felt like a naughty boy, scuttling off after being caught lingering around the office, telling jokes to the female members of staff. I thought I'd nip back up later and pick up the form when the coast was clear.

Down two flights of stairs, I found Tracey in the parade room. She'd finished what she was doing and was now packing her paperwork into her briefcase. Her cigarettes and lighter were on the table next to a diary with a picture of Pooh Bear holding a blue balloon on the cover. She continued getting ready for patrol. I watched as she fastened her utility belt round her waist, with its hand cuffs, CS gas and expandable baton all attached. Then, she placed the Pooh Bear diary in her case; on top of all the paperwork, the simple, childish cartoon on the cover seeming very much at odds with the brutality of the police utility belt and its array of weaponry – an 'oxymoron' if ever there was one. The Pooh Bear diary and the utility belt: two opposites, part of the enigma that was Tracey.

My good reflexes allowed me to catch a set of keys that came flying through the air.

"You can drive, honey!" An instruction, but teasing all the same.

"Right you are, boss!" I extended my arm, signalling that I'd follow her.

We left the parade room and exited the building onto the flight deck – the mezzanine car park for all police vehicles. A new Peugeot was there waiting for us. Tracey placed her gear on the rear seat while I got inside and started to complete the vehicle's mandatory log book. When all the necessary checks were completed, I eased the police patrol car out of the yard and we began our rounds.

★ ★ ★

Every area of greenery in the town centre was covered with office workers enjoying their lunches in the sunshine.

Convertibles with their hoods down screeched past blasting out music, the young drivers, wearing the obligatory sunshades, checking out the ladies walking by. Yes, this was summer all right, with all its beauty. I considered suggesting an ice cream when the radio crackled into life.

"Lima X-ray to Mike 4?"

Tracey pressed the talk button on the radio attached to her breast pocket.

"Mike 4, go ahead."

The receiver pulled on the shirt, opening a small gap between her buttons. She caught my glance for the third time that day. I turned my attention back to the road, biting my lip.

A convertible flashed past with a bass beat pounding in its slipstream.

"Bloody hooligans!" I shouted backwards, realising that Tracey was transmitting a message. The reply came back and I listened in.

"Mike 4, message from Inspector Stewart. Could you liaise with him at White Gables, Manor Farm Lane?"

"Yes, that's received."

"Further to that, Mike 4, make sure you have the camera on board."

★ ★ ★

CHAPTER SIX

White Gables

The house known as 'White Gables' sat halfway down the lane, on the left-hand side if you were heading down towards Manor Farm. The name came about because of the three acutely-peaked gables to the front.

Although the gables were painted pitch-black, the undersides were white, hence 'White Gables'. Two very large, leaded-glass front windows and a double-width front door made up the impressive frontage.

Whenever I saw places like this, I couldn't help but feel a little envious of its owners. What must it be like to live in a house like this? I'd always dreamt of one day owning such a house, the sort of place you could retire to, enjoying the beautifully landscaped gardens in the summer and taking an afternoon snooze by the large open fire in the winter.

The full extent of its gardens came into view as we entered the driveway between the two stone pillars which held the automatic wrought iron gates. It was the highly polished brass plaque on the left-hand side that confirmed that we had indeed found 'White Gables'.

There were a total of six different cars parked outside on the gravel. I brought the police car to a halt at the far end of the line. Tracey grabbed the camera, placing it out of sight in her briefcase, not wanting to cause alarm. Together, we got out of the vehicle and began to crunch our way across the Cotswold Stone path to the front door.

They must have been expecting more people to arrive because the front door had been left slightly ajar. I eased it open and quietly entered the cavernous hallway. I wasn't disappointed.

Wood panelling ran chest high around the hallway, with a gap for the carved staircase that led to the gallery landing. In front of us was an impressive stone chimney breast, with green leather club chairs either side. A grand piano sat proudly between the fireplace and the underside of the staircase, its top wide open, revealing rows of strings, hammers and buffers; sheet music open on the stand. Above the fireplace hung an old English oil painting depicting rolling countryside, hounds and horses galloping over hedges in pursuit of a fox.

A total of four separate doors led off the hallway. We crept quietly onwards, listening out for the sound of voices.

The sound of a woman sobbing came from the doorway to the right of the chimney breast. I took the lead, carefully pushing the door open and entering the room.

In front of me, on a large sofa, were three people, sat around a fireplace which must have shared the chimney in the hall. They all sat together, two men on either side both comforting a woman.

Her face was worn and weary: the same painful expression I'd seen on Jackie; twisted and contorted as if fighting a migraine, eyes tightly closed as if the agony was forcing its way out through the very sockets. A mixture of mascara and salty tears collected on her lashes before finding its channels and following them down her face.

I didn't need to ask any questions. To me it was very clear: she was the mother and one of her babies was dead.

It was harder to guess who the two males were; they didn't display emotions as overtly as the woman. Men will always try and remain strong to support their wives in times of crises. They won't release their pain till later, maybe much later, and it'll be quieter, less obvious, when they're on their own.

"Your Inspector's waiting upstairs with the doctor," one of the males offered softly. His words were answered with a low, agonising groan from the woman.

"Thank you, sir. We've been sent to liaise with him. I'm sorry to cause any further intrusion."

He turned and kissed the brow of the woman's pain-ridden face; so he's the husband, I made a mental note.

Quietly and respectfully, we backed our way out of the room. It must have been a mixture of the silence and the sense of grief hanging over the place that made us feel we had to tip toe up the stairway. Perhaps it was out of respect for the dead; not wanting to distract from the mournful stillness, we crept on, speaking in whispers and the occasional hand signal.

On the wall up the staircase were a set of school photographs, three in total: two boys and one girl. They must have been taken at the same school judging by the uniforms. The girl in a blue gingham frock and straw boater, the boys in blazers with school badges; I studied each photograph, looking for the clues.

Which of these children was it then, who displayed the tell tale signs of weakness, vulnerability, whose photo portrayed that sense of loneliness? It proved impossible to tell, but I knew that soon it would all become abundantly clear. We were about to meet one of these people, and they sure as hell wouldn't be speaking to us.

One of the people in the photographs had left White Gables for the last time and would never be coming back. We were about to find out which one.

I reached the top of the stairs and saw another four doors leading off the gallery landing. I was still a little in awe of the impressive hallway of the house. I looked back over the banister, down into the entrance hall. I imagined the scene: the lady of the house elegantly gliding down the stairway for the Christmas cocktail party; fire roaring in the hearth, the piano playing popular carols, a huge Christmas tree lighting up the hall, sparkling with colour.

But life had been sucked out of the very fabric of the place. It felt like an empty shell; there would be nothing this Christmas. Festivities would not be the same ever again. Death had come to visit and from now on its presence would remain, hiding in the shadows, haunting those parents for the rest of their days.

Up on the landing there was still total silence. We stopped moving and listened hard, waiting for a clue.

I envisaged the horrifying scene of opening a bedroom door and being greeted by a pair of legs in front of my eyes. A shiver ran down my spine as I slowly pushed open the first door.

Peeping round it, I saw that this room was not lived in. A bed with hospital corners, a guest towel, a musty, non-lived-in smell. No, it's not this room: no one's been in there for a while. I quietly closed the door behind me. Again, like hunting animals, we stood still and tuned our ears in.

Voices came from down the landing, so we followed the sounds till we got to the foot of a drop-down ladder leading up to the attic trap door.

The voices became clearer. There was a conversation taking place between two people, one of them the Inspector. Tracey and I had our last squabble, playfully whispering "You go first," in a Scooby Doo type way. Then, giving in to professionalism, I decided to take the lead.

Step by step, up the metal ladder until my head poked up above the floorboards. I was greeted by the sight of two people and a body suspended from a joist.

"Hello again, Sir."

"Simon, this is Dr Boardman, and we have here a confirmed sudden death. If Tracey's behind you, can you both come up here and take over responsibility for the scene?"

The doctor continued to relay his findings to the Inspector as we joined them in the large dusty void, that dark attic beneath the slates.

"You see, Inspector, among children in particular, hanging is a common method for committing suicide. The materials needed are easily available. It remains a simple yet highly effective method as it's difficult to go wrong, to succeed in killing yourself. Not even full suspension is required.

"People prefer this method because it's not as messy as what we call blunt force trauma, for example jumping off a tall building or stepping out into the path of a train. Hanging is commonplace amongst juvenile suicidal prisoners. Death is often achieved by self-strangulation using a ligature on the neck. As I said, only partial suspension of the body is required.

"Now, when I take a look at this child – Ben, you say he is? The first thing I tend to look for is evidence of severing to the spinal cord, which in basic terms is a functional decapitation. This itself doesn't bring about instant death; the person could remain conscious for some minutes, hanging there, very much alive."

The doctor continued, very much in his stride.

"In the absence of fracture and dislocation, occlusion of the blood vessels becomes the major cause of death, rather than asphyxiation. Looking at this child, I can see that his face has become engorged: look, you can see that he has turned blue due to lack of oxygen."

He was now in full flow, taking the Inspector through every detail with the enthusiasm of a car dealer shifting a car.

"Here we see little blood marks on the face and in the eyes, caused by the bursting of blood capillaries – a classic sign of strangulation."

Wearing a rubber glove and gripping the chin, he turned the young face towards the Inspector while shining a pen torch into one lifeless eye. The face caught the light, giving a grotesque stare: a stare that looks out but sees nothing.

"Here, here and here. Do you see?"

"Yes, I can. What are you recording as the time of death?"

"I pronounce life extinct at 15:50hrs."

"Thank you, Doctor."

"I don't suppose you have any idea as to what would cause this young gentleman to hang himself from the rafters?" the medic asks, still absorbed in his work and peering at the face over half-moon spectacles, pen torch shining on the dead skin.

"We found a note, which we've already sealed up safe and secure, but I can't start to draw any conclusion until we've interviewed the parents. And, as you can see from the state they're in, that could take some time."

The doctor switched off the torch and addressed the officer as if he were a student.

"With child suicides, never rule out the possibility of the copy-cat." He switched the torch back on and pointed to the rope marks. "Copy-cat suicides account for about six per cent of all suicides. They can trigger off what we call a 'suicide cluster.' One child will do it and then others follow, usually taking up exactly the same method as was used by the first. A terrible sequence of events, very hard to explain."

"Yes, I'd imagine so, but are these people – the ones that copy the first death and take part in these cluster suicides – mentally ill?"

"Opinion has always been divided on the subject, but my approach is quite simple, that is to say: all people who attempt suicide are mentally ill. Why, you may ask. Because it's clear that only people who are suffering from a mental condition would indeed attempt to take their own lives."

He gave a nod to the Inspector, signalling that he was satisfied with his final examination.

"I'll be off now, and will be sending my report to the coroner this afternoon. Good day, Inspector."

The doctor picked up his case and, stepping backwards, carefully descended the ladder to the landing, leaving three of us staring at the body.

"When do we take him down then?" I asked.

"The body remains in situ until S.O.C.O. have examined the loft.

They're held up at a murder for the next two hours, so you two have won the job of babysitting young Ben here. I want pictures taken of both Ben and the loft so that we have an accurate record of the golden hour as things were when we found them. S.O.C.O. will do their own when they eventually get here. Well, that's it for me – good luck team, and don't think you'll be off by four. I'm leaving you the running log. Just make an entry for anybody, and I mean anybody, who comes up here. I've left it over there, together with the note which I've sealed up. Once the body's been removed, bring it all back to the station and book it in. If you need me again, or have any problems or queries, get onto me via the control room."

The Inspector descended the ladder in the wake of the doctor.

"And then there were three," mumbled Tracey as we stood on either side of a suspended child. We both surveyed the lifeless figure, like a sculpture in a museum.

"I don't think you can count Ben. I think there's just the two of us."

Tracey raised an eyebrow.

"Well then, you're right. There's just you, me, and that camera. What are you waiting for?" She gave me a shy smile and cocked her head.

For a second or two I was frozen to the spot. Was she actually flirting with me? Here, next to a body? Or was she just teasing, trying to break the sombre silence, putting on a brave face amongst the gloom?

To my relief she sat down on an old tea chest, studying the running log; I started to line up a shot of the body with the camera.

The attic was split into two halves by the giant chimney breast which rose up from the hall. We were high up in the left-hand gable, underneath solid oak rafters. The hatch was the only entry or exit and only the thinnest shard of daylight shone through a couple of gaps in the slates above our heads.

A single bulb hung from a cord, eighteen inches from Ben's face and lit him up with a ghostly yellow glow.

To carry out his plan, Ben had secured a length of rope over the central rafter and stood on a stool to tie the noose; he had then kicked away the stool, which was now lying on its side at his feet.

I took the first picture of his body from the front, making sure I captured the bruising to the neck. The second one gave a clear picture of the rope around the rafter. I took a few others from around the attic.

"What do you think?"

Tracey was reclined across the tea chests, posing like a model.

"Go on, one for the scrapbook." She placed her hands behind her head, and lifted one leg up to rest on the chest.

"Yes, I'll take a few photos of you and then I'll hand my notice in to Inspector Stewart before I get sacked, oh yes, and you'll be joining me too."

"Are we really going to have to wait up here for two hours?"

"Yes, so just get used to it. Stop messing about trying to wind me up and find something to read."

I sorted through a box of old books.

"Look, here you go: 'Alice through the Looking Glass'. Why don't you read that to keep yourself out of trouble?"

The well-thumbed book had been on top of the pile, above a set of geography text books. I picked it up and tossed it over to her.

"Good lord, I haven't seen this book since I was in junior school. Do you think Ben was reading this before he – well, you know?" She mimed her own hanging.

"I don't know. It stands a good chance. Flick through it, see if he's left any cryptic codes in the margins."

Tracey flicked through the old book, finding nothing of note, so she tossed it back onto the floor next to an old chessboard.

"Perhaps he wasn't reading this book, perhaps he was playing chess with himself. Look: no white pieces. Maybe he was just a total loner, just himself and his red set; you don't need both if there's just one of you."

She took hold of the clipboard containing the running log.

"Maybe this will shed some light on the matter!" Her eyes lit up with excitement. "You know, explain what he was doing up here all alone with a piece of rope."

She started to fumble with the cellophane wrapping around the suicide note, holding it up to the light in front of Ben's face.

"Are you supposed to be messing with that?"

She rolled her eyes. "Here you go, listen to this: 'These are the last words of Benjamin Hamilton, aged 15.'"

She posed like an actress about to deliver a comedy news sketch on stage. She coughed for effect and read the note out loud:-

My dearest Becky,

Since you made your decision, I have found it increasingly harder to keep myself going.

You were the only ray of sunlight in what was a dark and dull existence. You understood me in a way that no one else could. We shared our life, our love and our thoughts.

Life to me is nothing but someone else's idea of a joke and I simply don't get it. I feel that everyone's at a party and I'm not invited.

Without you, life is dull, people are dull; food tastes dull.

I have no wish to carry on

I want you to have your half of the chess set, so I have left the red ones for you to do with as you please. Someone will get them to you.

I have no use for the white pieces so I have destroyed them, if you want to, you can do the same with the red.

Yours,

Ben x

"Oh for heaven's sake, put the bloody thing down! It's private, the last words of a suicidal mind. Can't you find anything else to occupy yourself with? And before you say anything, don't even think about lighting a fag up here, this place would go up like a tinder box. I don't know about you, but I want to make it home tonight."

Tracey went back to studying Ben's distorted face.

"He must have loved this Becky very deeply, if he was to hang himself because of her. Do you think she'd just dumped him or something?"

"I've no idea, but it's not easy being a young lad with raging hormones and girlfriends dumping you all the time."

Tracey left the body and stooped down to the board. She picked up and started to examine the exquisitely-carved red King.

"If you were going to do it, how would you go about it? Suicide, I mean."

"I haven't really thought about it, and I have no intention of thinking about it. I certainly wouldn't hang myself in my own dusty attic."

"It's interesting, though, isn't it? I mean, why humans can decide to just end their lives; animals don't think that way. Did you know that human beings are the only animals who know they are going to die? Because we understand that death is inevitable we live our lives to a greater degree preparing for it."

I sat back down on the box and listened to Tracey. Still examining the chess pieces one by one, she talked as she held them up to the light bulb. I looked at my watch and tried to get comfortable as the time dragged by in that hot, dusty attic.

She was examining the underneath of the red knight when she stopped and looked directly at me.

"Do you know where the most popular suicide spot in England is?"

"It's not in here, is it?" I tried not to appear bored.

"No, you great ape, it's not here." She gave a sarcastic smile. "I saw it on the news last week. Beachy Head, down in Sussex; some old git had driven his car off the edge. Apparently, people are always doing it down there, five or six every month, the same place, the same bloody cliff.

"If the Martians were to land at Beachy Head after a long journey through outer space, they'd see all these human beings, sad, lonely creatures, throwing themselves to the rocks below. They'd probably report back to their mother planet, saying 'don't bother coming to this bloody place, it's crap: full of selfish people messing each other about. Even the human's don't like it.'

"They all look happy, but inside their hearts they're not. They're all a bunch of selfish morons, only interested in making more and more of this human paper which they call 'money'. They put this 'money' into these things called 'banks'. The 'banks' piss around with it for a few years until the person dies and it's all left to their offspring.

"The humans all live a crazy, senseless cycle of work, work, work, and no one really cares about anybody else. So for God's sake, don't bother coming here. Go back to Mars, where there aren't any bloody humans at all!'"

"My, my, we do need a fag, don't we?"

"Well yes, I suppose I do. But nevertheless, I find it really weird that so many people could all flock to the same place, just to kill themselves. Why Beachy Head? Why not just jump off a tall building, the kind you find in every city? All you need to do is go in, get the lift to the top floor, find the fire escape, stand on the edge, count to ten and 'Tally Ho!' You're a gonner."

I'd never really thought about it. Still, conversation seemed like a good way of relieving the monotony and passing the time.

"Perhaps it's something to do with the avoidance of other people. You know – the bloody interfering do-gooders. You stand on a window ledge, right, about to jump, and you're in the centre of the city – well, of course some bloody do-gooder is going to see you and ring the Old Bill. Then you'll have some sad old copper trying to win some medal by talking you down and saving your sad little life. You know: telling you how wonderful life is, and how people love you, and you'll feel better tomorrow – all that kind of usual crap. But here's the point – the person who is seriously contemplating suicide has been through all that bullshit before with a load of other do-gooders. Most will have been through the health system, had their counselling, been seen by the local mental team and been let down time and time again.

"They've heard it all before, they've heard all the Good Samaritan crap, and they've realised that, after their allotted hour of therapy, nobody cares. They've all seen how the system is failing and how far the resources are stretched, and they don't want to keep getting let down all the time.

"So, what do they do? They go somewhere far away, somewhere tried and tested by others who have been in the same predicament, like a high cliff top with jagged rocks two hundred feet below. It's only in a place like that they can get their last few minutes on this planet in peace and solitude: no more heroes, no more counsellors, no more professionals; they've all had their chance and failed miserably.

"It's just peace and quiet, with two hundred feet of cliff standing between them and freedom from all the crap.

"When they're good and ready, they take that final step into the abyss and it's all over. The lights go out and finally, once and for all, the pain stops."

Tracey sat upright on her tea chest, bringing her face out of the shadows. She waved an unlit cigarette as she spoke.

"Yeah, but now they've got all sorts of tossers patrolling those cliffs every night. You've got the Samaritans and the God squad and any one else who wants an award. Then you've got every other interfering nutter that lives or works in the area – they can spot a suicide case a mile off. The local pub, the taxi company, they're all used to seeing people who look out of the ordinary: the ones moping around like zombies, looking like they're carrying the weight of the world on their shoulders.

"So they ring up the bloody patrols on the cliffs, describe the nut job, and then everybody's on the hunt for the jumper, trying to intercept them and talk them out of it.

"There was one story of a lady who came from out-of-town, a smart cookie, took a ride to the cliff top. Didn't want anybody trying to talk her out of it. She just got out of her taxi, paid the fare, ran towards the cliff and jumped off. No one got a chance to get near her.

"So, in the long run, either the jumpers are going to get wise and do running jumps, dodging the Samaritans, or they'll find a new beauty spot to become the latest location. It wouldn't be difficult to find a new place, it could be literally anywhere. On the same programme they went on to say that the chosen place for people in America is the Golden Gate Bridge in San Francisco. Yeah, people have been jumping off that since it was built.

"And the Japanese, well, they've got some forest somewhere where people go to kill themselves. Yeah, it's as simple as that: a forest. You know, the funniest thing about watching that programme was this guy who was going to jump off the Golden Gate Bridge. As he stood there trying to make his peace with God, some tourist came up to him with a camera and started lining up the shot. Another person asked him when he going to jump?

"The guy was so amazed at this pitiful side of human nature that he decided not to jump after all, but to go off to Las Vegas, write a book on suicide, become a priest and conduct celebrity-style weddings at the Chapel of Love."

"So it worked out for him, then." I tried to be discreet as I checked the time on my watch.

"Yeah, he ended up with his own evangelical show on cable – the kind where you ring up and donate your money, the number passing on the tickertape at the bottom of the screen."

I sat back and looked at Ben.

★ ★ ★

It was going to be another hour we would be sitting there, like actors in some macabre stage play. Talking to each other, it seemed that no subject was out of bounds as we shared this horrible scene: the old tea chests, Ben hanging there, lit up like a Christmas tree.

Tracey sensed that two hours was almost up. She leant back on her makeshift bed of boxes and flicked the flint on her lighter. The flame appeared for a second, then died, throwing a shadow back across her face. Again the flame appeared, illuminating her features and those red, pouting lips. Once again, she disappeared into shadow. She knew that I was looking at her, mesmerised, and she repeated it again and again, the lighter acting like some magnetic force pulling the two of us together.

The sound of tyres coming to a halt on the gravel driveway brought us out of the lighter game. Tracey seizes the opportunity.

"I'll go down and show them up. We can't have them wondering around in paper suits scarring mum and dad, can we?"

She backed her way down the ladder, her face disappearing below the hatch, and left me alone with Ben. I quickly became restless, craving human company. A lifeless body makes an unsettling roommate. Before long, the first of two paper-hooded crime experts lifted their head above the parapet, signalling my release from that dreadful, dusty hole.

I joined Tracey in the hallway and we nodded our agreement that we should say our farewells to the parents. The three adults were standing by the fireplace, the lady of the house holding a cigarette but with an uneasy posture, as though not used to holding one. One of the males spoke.

"Officers, we've left some refreshments out in the garden if you'd like to help yourselves. I'm sure you could do with a nice, cool drink."

"Thank you, sir, that's very kind of you," I said, preferring the idea of a quick exit but grateful for a cold drink.

Laid out on the lawn was a table with a white cloth draped over it. A jug of homemade lemonade sat next to an ice box and two glasses. This was obviously a house where they were used to entertaining; in their own way, the show would go on.

I poured Tracey a glass and used tongs for the ice. She headed straight over to the arbour with its love-seat, which lay out-of-sight of the living room and its occupants. As I joined her, she was taking pleasure in the first drag of her cigarette, eyes closed in deep satisfaction, before exhaling to the roses above her head.

I sat back and took in the beautifully-tended gardens, the strategically-placed box topiary, the stone pillars and curved borders, eager to escape the horrors of the house, to wander around the rose beds, explore the arches cut into the hedge, but Tracey was sat in her own world, lost in the pleasure of her cigarette.

So I just sat next to her, enjoying the balmy afternoon – the kind that distant summers were made of.

The peace and quiet only tainted by the thought of that young body hanging there, high up in that attic.

★ ★ ★

CHAPTER SEVEN

The Chandler Situation

Today the room looks bare. The walls are bare, the mantelpiece is bare.

I'd been rabbiting on for half an hour, a constant niggling in the back of my mind. It took a while but then the penny dropped. I paused briefly, Beth looked up.

"Birthday cards!"

"I'm sorry?" she replied, a little taken aback.

"It's your birthday cards, they're no longer on the fireplace. You've taken them down."

Beth looked behind her at the empty mantelpiece.

"Yes, they only came down yesterday. They kept reminding me I was getting older."

"Well, I hope you had a good one. Did you go to see 'Madame Butterfly'?" I asked, scanning the room to check that they'd all gone.

"Not quite, but you're close – it was 'Tosca'."

I decided a brief spell of small talk would come as a relief. I continued, eating up time.

"Oh, I thought it was one or the other." I was trying to recall the details.

"'Tosca' remains my favourite; 'Madame Butterfly' is a little modern for me."

I nodded in agreement; I wasn't familiar with either. "How was the meal? You were going to err.....?" Beginning to struggle a little bit.

"'Le Petit Chateau'. It was amazing, have you ever been there?"

I gave the appearance of trying to recollect, jogging my memory.

"No, I don't think I've actually been to that one."

"I treated myself to the Filet Mignon; it's just to die for. I haven't tasted beef like that anywhere. However, if you do decide to go, make sure you book up well in advance – it's very popular."

Alas, feeling that I'd exhausted the birthday conversation, my eyes flitted around the room looking for another subject; there wasn't one. Maybe that's why everything was painted white; maybe that's why I was the one with my chair facing away from the window.

I sensed that Beth had cottoned on, she steered me back to the matter in hand.

"Simon, as I've pointed out to you before, I note that the referral mentions flashbacks and nightmares – what we know in the trade as 'persistent re-experience'. Are these still occurring at the same frequency?"

"Yes they are, but I've learnt to deal with them by avoiding some of the things that trigger them off. For example, if I'm driving about the place, I try to avoid the areas and the roads that I associate with the case. I've found that's the best way to prevent nasty flashbacks, but the nightmares – they still remain."

"Do your nightmares always involve the same characters? I'm thinking of this Alton chap."

"Yes, they tend to involve him in one way or another. There may be variations in time and place and the surrounding circumstances, but generally he'll be there, somewhere in the background. Recently, though, they've tended to include bits and pieces from Ben and the White Gables. They're like that: they can take any direction with any cocktail of images. But the answer is, yes, he always seems to be there, hanging around in the background, like a ghost."

"And Jackie?"

"Well, yes, Jackie can be there sometimes. I think she's there because of the impact of the case. After I heard what happened to her, I got quite depressed. I felt that somehow, like the others, we had failed to help her and somehow we were responsible.

"The same with Ben, the same with all those people who needed our help and didn't seem to get it. All those people who found themselves let down by all the crap. They wanted our help, they needed our help, they sought help, but … somehow, they slipped through the net or got lost amongst the incompetence and the bureaucracy. And then, the same bloody words, time and time on the television: 'We're sorry, we're learning the lessons from our mistakes, we're holding a review, we're doing an enquiry into who cocked up.'

"Then someone inevitably gets moved, to another department, where they can make another balls-up. Everything settles down again, new people are brought in, the public are happy, until it happens again.

"Like with every mistake they make, everything gets lost in a bloody inquiry. The bloody people involved move on before the results are out, then the new manager comes in and wants to stamp their authority. The review gets forgotten about – until the next cock-up. The cycle never ends.

"You know, in the days of constant inquiries into failures, the amount of money involved is totally obscene. I suppose if you're the lucky one asked to set up an inquiry into somebody else's cock-up, you're given a license to print money.

"I don't suppose you heard that article on the ten o'clock news? It was about the 'Bloody Sunday' inquiry. Something had come out following a Freedom of Information request. The reply was to the effect that the inquiry is running up costs of £500,000 a month. That includes the times when the flaming inquiry isn't actually sitting. The total so far, the amount the inquiry has cost you and me, the tax payer, is something in the region of £400 million. Most of that is legal fees. The whole thing is just a feeding frenzy for the establishment, while the real victims stand by and just watch.

"There's never any time limit, there's no limits at all. The only question for the legal people is how much money can they possibly claim? Everybody's happy; the lawyers are happy, the experts are happy, the politicians are happy; they can say that they've done everything they can. It becomes a political football to kick around when it suits them. I've no doubt, most of the politicians involved in these inquiries have connections with the legal profession – they ate their meals in the same dining rooms at the same Inns of Court. Then, when they finally get elected to power and feel the need for an inquiry, they go on to appoint their old chums as the officials.

"When it comes to events on their own watch, well, that's a different story: no, enquiries have to be avoided at all costs – like 7th July.

"On July 7th, terrorists managed to bring the whole of London to a standstill after three bombs were set off in the underground system. The country wants to know how a group of terrorists could cause such carnage in the capital and bring the whole city to a halt. Well, too many of those politicians are still about so, in answer to that one, an inquiry is deemed to be 'too expensive'!

"Anything that happened before the same people took power, well, no amount of effort or money is too much in the painstaking search for the truth.

"It always boils down to the same thing: extortionate amounts of money for the law-makers and absolutely sod all for the ordinary, everyday people on the ground!"

I realised I'd gone on a bit and sat back, my pulse racing. I took deep breaths to calm myself down. Beth waited a moment or two before she spoke.

"You don't sound very keen on lawyers."

"No, I dare say I'm not. As far as my experience goes, they seem to cause friction where there isn't any, they muddy clear waters, they expect you to run around doing all their leg work for them then they provide you with a gigantic bill for your efforts. Either that or the buggers want payment in advance – that way, if they're useless at their job, well too late, you've paid! Then, if it goes to court, you have to pay again, for a barrister to speak for you: likewise, you pay upfront. When you've finally got no money left and you're bled dry, they stop returning your calls."

"Did you have any involvement with lawyers during the Alton case?" Beth asked.

"You could say that. I've had them circling over my head like vultures for the past three years. Their costs ran into tens of thousands of pounds but I could see very little benefit in having them; any success came from me and my relentless search for justice. If it had been left purely to my solicitors, I'd have come away with nothing."

Beth referred to her paperwork.

"I've read from your file a little about the uphill battle you've faced, the way in which you've had to fight each step of the way . The whole thing has caused you a great deal of anger and frustration, and in turn, that intense feeling of neglect has worsened your already fragile condition.

"Episodes of what we call 'explosive anger' are symptoms of post-traumatic stress disorder and organisations like the police who, more often than not, ignore the conditions, can tend to enflame the situation; you've been stuck in a vicious circle.

"Just one look at your file indicates the size of the mountain you've had to climb. You've had to cope on your own with very little support from your senior officers. What we aim to do in this program is to put a stop to all that, try and break the cycle, get you the support you so desperately need."

Beth flicked over the page and scribbled a note.

"I must say that just the first couple of sessions have really helped me, I can see things a lot clearer, just being able to talk has helped."

"Well, that's what we're here for; as long as you keep talking, we'll keep listening; we're here to get you back on your feet."

★ ★ ★

Kate was very distressed, to the point of delirium, when she stumbled into the front office that April afternoon. She approached the counter and used it for support; taking deep breaths, she tried to compose herself. The front office assistant stood behind the desk, pen poised, waiting for her to say something.

She did try but she just couldn't get the words out. Then, as if to release all the pent-up emotion, she let out one almighty scream, stumbled backwards, fell into a chair and wept.

Down the corridor, the four of us were sitting around the table eating fish and chips, brought in by Tracey: a present from our local chip shop.

The sound of the scream echoed down the hall and reached the parade room. Everybody stopped eating for a moment and froze.

"Keep it down, will ya!" Ted shouted as he shovelled a piece of cod into his mouth. A ripple of laughter went round the room and everyone resumed chomping. The tomato sauce was passed across the table.

Shirley had been a fully-functional police station for the last twelve months. Prior to that it had been partly used as offices for the force's photographic department but following the implementation of 'sector policing' this and other buildings had become fully functioning sub-stations. Tracey and I had been working at Shirley for the past three months.

Sectorisation was the brain child of a previous, somewhat bureaucratic Chief Constable, the idea being that each area would combine its community and response policing and tailor its service to the area's particular needs.

There was only one problem, it was a disaster.

It proved to be dysfunctional and provided a fragmented, insular approach to problems. Before long, a more centralised, joined-up approach began to creep in by stealth. The architects of the system were pensioned off one by one, heading off to the Palace to collect their knighthoods.

So, in January of the New Year, Tracey and I found ourselves assigned to the Shirley policing sector. Little could I have known it, but that one decision was to put me on a path that would change the course of my life – for ever.

★ ★ ★

The reason that Kate had come into the police station that day was that she feared for her life, and she had every reason to be scared.

Over the past five days, she had been followed by an unknown male. At first she was unsure if she was just imagining things, but it soon became apparent that this man was following her every movement. She was terrified.

It was after work that day, while driving down Shirley High Street, that she noticed the same man behind her in his car. She was at her wits' end and felt like driving her car into a brick wall. Suddenly, almost as a spur of the moment thing, she swerved into the slip road at the police station, abandoned her vehicle and ran in through the front doors, into the safety of the office.

Down in the parade room, as Tracey cleared away the chip papers, I was just a little concerned. I was well aware that if there had been a problem, Janice would have called down to us; however, I still felt uneasy that she was up there on her own, and the sound of that scream had focused my attention.

As someone volunteered to make another cup of coffee I took a stroll up the corridor and put my head round the door. Janice was leaning over the desk, taking notes; the lady had now composed herself and was giving her details.

Satisfied that everything seemed in order, I was just turning back when Janice called out, "Oh, Simon, can I just get a bit of advice from you about this one?" I went through the door and joined Janice at the counter. The lady opposite seemed to fill up with a sense of relief at the sight of a police officer's uniform.

"This is Mrs Chandler. As you can see, she's very distressed. She says that over the last five days she's been followed around by a man. Events have gone from bad to worse and things came to a head last night about ten o'clock. She was at home, alone as normal, and had just taken her bath.

"She walked through to her bedroom to prepare herself for bed. As she walked over to the windows she looked out into the street to check her car. She noticed at the end of her path was this very same man: this time he had a camcorder which he was pointing in her direction.

"She says she got into a right state, just didn't know what to do, hardly slept a wink! When she looked out in the morning this man's car was still there, parked at the end of her path; it was all steamed up, like someone had slept in it.

"She got herself ready for work and as she walked past the car she saw the back window had been cleared of condensation from the inside. She peered in, and amongst some sleeping bags she saw this man's face looking out at her. She says it was the same man who had been following her all week.

"On leaving work today, his car was parked in the car park. He began to follow her again; she almost lost control of her car twice as she tried to lose him. She then saw the police station and ran in here. She's extremely distressed."

I looked at the woman and saw the tired expression of someone who hasn't slept. The woman, no doubt beautiful in her own way, now had a face that was drawn and ghostly, her eyes pleading like those of a prisoner in some far-flung jail, her spirit broken.

Janice continued with the details. "She took down the registration number of his car."

She handed me a tissue, the car number written in red lipstick, like a child's playful scrawl.

"She reckons it's a blue Ford Focus or similar. I was just about to run the number through the box."

I took the piece of tissue: the child, the mother's make-up, all ran through my mind, but this was desperate, a note full of fear, screaming for help. I couldn't just ignore such a desperate act.

"Yes, Janice, if you'd do that. I'll take this lady into an interview room and get some details. Just let me know what comes up on the vehicle."

I showed her into a room and was joined by Tracey, who cornered me outside.

"What you got?" she whispered to avoid the lady hearing.

I pulled the door and spoke quietly to my partner.

"This lady says she's being followed by this guy who films her or something. He was outside her house last night and was still there when she woke in the morning. She was the one who screamed down the corridor. I'm just trying to get some details and find out what's going on – would you get her a cup of tea while I have a quick word?"

"Yeah, no problem. I'll then come and join you. Just make sure that it's not going to turn out one of those long drawn-out things."

I returned to the interview room and took a seat opposite her. She gave her name as Kate Chandler. I made a note.

"Now, Kate, I can see you're very upset; just take your time and start at the beginning. Tell me what's happened."

Slowly but surely, wiping away the occasional tear, she told me the story of the last few days. I tried not to interrupt as she recalled the details. She then got to the events of the previous evening.

"I walked over to close the curtains; I was just in my dressing gown."

She dabbed the corner of her eye, still fighting back the tears.

"I just started to close them when I happened to look out into the street. We have a street light just up from us, it lights up the pavement in front of my house. Standing in the shadows at the end of the path was a man. At first I thought it must be a dog walker, you know with the time and all, but as I looked closer I felt sick to my stomach.

"As he moved in and out of the shadows, I saw it was the same man who had been following me. He was now stood right outside my house looking up at my bedroom window. He was doing this awful, grinning thing, showing his teeth.

"I yanked the curtains together and looked for somewhere to hide. I slid under my bed. I mean how bloody stupid is that, hiding under your own bed, as if it could protect you from some mad man?"

I handed her a clean tissue.

"Right, Kate, thanks for that. I know it hasn't been easy for you but we'll deal with it from now."

She gave me a smile and I noticed the colour starting to come back to her cheeks. I stood up to leave.

"There is one thing I don't understand, though: why didn't you call the police last night?"

Kate's face changed again, anger returning to her eyes, but she spoke quietly.

"I did."

For a moment I was speechless, my silence broken by a knock at the door.

"Excuse me." I slipped out of the room. Janice was holding the ownership details of the offending vehicle. I took the paper from her and read it.

"Okay, so the owner is one Andrew Alton, last known address 5 Maybrook Road, Solihull. Thanks Janice, you can leave it with me." Tracey caught up with me outside the door, holding two cups of tea.

"Well, go on then, what's the score?" Again she was whispering.

"Apparently, this fruitcake spent the night outside her address, then he followed her after work today. She says she rang the police last night but it doesn't appear they did anything about it – see if you can find a log for last night and work out what happened. I've got a bad feeling about this one; I'm going to have a word with the sergeant."

I took the tea into Kate and told her I was just going to check on a few details. I left her alone while I went to track down my immediate supervisor, Sgt Moore.

After a few minutes of phoning around I located him at the main station; before long, I was listening to his familiar tone coming down the telephone line.

"Do we know anything about this man?" he asked as he considered the story.

"We're not even sure that it was the registered keeper who was driving the vehicle. At the moment we can't confirm who was in it; all we know for certain is that we have the car registration number and that it is registered to a local address.

"The problem is though, Sarge, I feel that there is a degree of urgency here. This man has been persistent in the way he's followed her, he's been quite blatant about it. She's seen his face and he knows that she's at the police station. There's every reason to suggest that all this will continue, and that could be as soon as she leaves the station. I think that we have to assume that she's in some degree of danger and needs protection."

"Okay then, once you've got all the details, make sure she gets home safely and then pay a visit to the registered keeper. See if you can find out why this character is so intent on causing so much grief, give him some kind of warning and update the log accordingly. Hopefully we won't hear anymore from this, what's his name again?"

I jumped in, "Alton, Sarge; a Mr Andrew Alton."

"Yes. Hopefully we won't hear from this Alton guy again."

I returned to Kate's interview room. Tracey caught up with me, just outside the door.

"I had a look at last night's log for Mycroft Avenue. I've got a copy here."

Tracey started to read it out loud, "'Distressed female on line, states that a man's been following her, he's outside now, been following her for some days, please can you come?'"

"What's the response?"

"Mike II asked to pay passing attention during night. She was advised about ringing 999 if urgent. One hour later, Mike II became committed, dealing with a drive-off from a petrol station; the log was then closed: 'no further action'."

"It's nice to know they take these things seriously. It's a good job she wasn't murdered in her sleep by the axe-wielding maniac. While she's still in one piece we're going to follow her home to make sure she gets in safe and sound, then we're going to pay a visit to Mr Alton to see what he's got to say on the matter."

"Right you are, boss, I'll grab my gear."

★ ★ ★

Within the hour we were in our police car, heading towards the Blythe Way estate, one of the most prosperous areas in the whole of Solihull.

It was a favourite residential location for senior police officers, lawyers, and even the occasional premiership footballer. Other residents were the people lucky enough to have bought their property at the right time and who were now set up for life. The ones who decided to put their moving plans on hold for a year found themselves having to kiss goodbye to any chance of living on the Blythe Way estate; they had missed the new millennium property boom.

Maybrook Road proved easy enough to find. The planners had made it simple: the roads on the estate always followed the same pattern. From the main arterial road, smaller roads came off, left and right. From those came smaller roads, then finally tiny cul-de-sacs sprouted off the ends. Just like the blood supply in human organs, the arteries feed into arterioles, then finally into the little capillaries, ending in tight little clusters.

Number 5, Maybrook Road, was at the end of such a cluster, tucked neatly away, very quiet and very anonymous. It was the perfect hideaway for anyone who happened to suffer from paranoia or was particularly 'surveillance conscious'.

Set back, behind a patch of lawn, deep in the corner of the basin, it was shielded by neighbours on either side; likewise, its garden was completely surrounded at the rear. From the front view, an ancient oak tree stood to the right hand side, its great branches reaching out and covering the roof, protecting it from anything above. To cap it all, the curve of the road made it impossible to see it from the junction.

In short, it was not possible to take a look at the place without sitting right outside it. Anyone inside would see you first.

Whoever lived here had selected this house very carefully.

★ ★ ★

Tracey brought the car to a halt across the driveway. The Ford Focus was parked in front of the house. I double-checked the registration number with the one in my notebook.

Having some experience as a police officer, my senses were already telling me that something was wrong. This came from a combination of two things:

Firstly, the ridiculous, almost clumsy way in which Kate had been followed, so blatant and obvious. The man wanted to be seen.

Secondly, this house indicated that whoever lived there was a person of considerable means – not a thug or a loser, but someone who had made something of themselves and enjoyed a high standard of living.

If this was indeed our man, those facts alone made the case more complicated than at first glance. The notion that this job would turn out to be quick and simple was draining away, leaving a cold, stirring feeling in the pit of my stomach. Trusting my instincts, I felt a sudden impulse to protect Tracey. I had already seen one woman who had been on the receiving end of this man's work.

As we walked up the path I decided to take the lead. I knocked on the front door. We then stood there for a moment, looking at each other with anticipation. I was just about to knock again when I heard a noise; the garage door swung up above our heads and a middle-aged man appeared, looking tired and drawn.

He looked at us before silently retreating back into his garage. Pulling the cord, he left the garage door half way up. We looked at each other and nodded before ducking down and following him.

Unusually, for a residential house, a CCTV camera was on the wall above the inner door. Although this was pointing away from us, it seemed to me that this male had deliberately bought us in here. He had us where he wanted us; the cameras around the garage were all part of a plan.

I felt out of control of the situation. We were being led into something; I would need to recover, and fast.

Without preamble he spoke.

"What are you doing here?" His eyes darted to and from the corners, and my eyes followed his. Sensing a trap, I composed myself.

"We've just received a report from a lady that she is being followed by a male and that he is using a Ford Focus vehicle. She's given us the registered number that she wrote down on a piece of paper. The registration number is the same as the one on that vehicle parked on your drive. I just need to ask you, is that your vehicle out there and do you know anything about such an allegation?"

The man in front of me paid no attention to Tracey: as far he was concerned she was invisible. He put his hand to his mouth and let out a sound, as if contemplating a speech. A brief shadow of satisfaction passed over his face, like an inquisitor who had finally unmasked the traitor. The hand came away and made a claw. He jabbed a stubby finger in my direction.

"What's it got to do with you? What has anything I do have to do with you? If I want to follow someone then I can follow them!" The finger was pointing just short of my nose. I could feel Tracey trying to move position, maybe to butt in, in an attempt to defuse him. Without even turning his head he held a hand up to silence her. He nodded at me, expecting a reply. I tried not to show any emotion.

"Well, if what she says is true there may well be an offence of harassment. What we're trying to do is to find out what the problem is, to see if we can resolve the issues. I just need to know if you have been using that car and following this lady."

He took a couple more seconds to contemplate me before he went red in the face. His whole body seemed to tense up with rage.

"Get out!" He gave a low growl. "You've got no right coming here, asking your stupid questions. It's none of your business what I do. I've done nothing wrong. If I want to film someone and follow them about, I can.

"Go on, bugger off. If you come round here lecturing me again, then I can assure you, your arse won't touch the ground." His open palm pushed my chest, shoving me backwards. I turned and ducked my head, avoiding the garage door, and found myself back on the lawn.

He was now pulling down the garage door by its cord. I shouted underneath.

"I must warn you that if you continue any behaviour that constitutes harassment, you will be arrested."

The garage door slammed shut. A cloud of dust blew around the ground.

Somewhat shocked, we got back into the car.

We decided to drive off, away from the house, before resolving what to do next. I had a bad feeling about the place; it made me feel claustrophobic, as if the road were closing in around us. The giant oak tree made the place look darker, the entrance to the little cul-de-sac appearing narrower, as the light faded.

Meeting this man after Kate's report, had been a disturbing experience. We both felt uneasy. There was obviously a lot more to this man than met the eye. As far I as could see, nothing was adding up or making the slightest sense.

I tried to think.

"I want to nip into Solihull and have a word with the sergeant about this one. There's something wrong, I don't like the feel of the thing, it gives me the creeps. You know, in all my years, no one has ever pushed me like that without being arrested."

"Why didn't you lock him up?"

"I thought about it, but it's always a different story when you're in someone's house and they want you to leave. You're on a sticky wicket. I'm sure that's why he got us in there: you know, didn't want to talk on the front lawn.

"If I'd gone and locked him up, he'd have said that he'd asked us to leave his house and we didn't; he'd have tried to cause the maximum amount of trouble; it would have got very messy. Besides, I'm sure that's what he wanted.

"He would have made up some story and caused as much grief as he could. We'd be the ones defending ourselves to P.S.D. for the next twelve months – believe me, I can't be doing with that crap. I'm not in the habit of letting somebody else dictate the agenda, no matter how mad they are. No, this whole thing runs a lot deeper than I thought.

"This man Alton, whoever he is, is just challenging us. He wants us to do something, so he can prove a point; believe me, he wants to cause a whole, stinking heap of crap. I just don't know why. One thing's for sure: the fruitcake has got a screw loose, that's what makes him all the more dangerous. I can smell it. I think it's time I had a chat with Sarge."

Tracey stopped at the junction, watching the line of traffic. She looked at me from the corner of her eye.

"Well, one things for sure: he's a creepy son of a bitch."

I didn't hear her because I wasn't listening. I sat back in my seat, wandering what this Alton guy had in mind for us.

★ ★ ★

Outside the rear door was the designated smoking area. That's where we found Sergeant Moore finishing his fag. That gave the ideal opportunity for Tracey to light one up; she opened a new packet, flicked her lighter and took the first, deep, satisfying drag.

As always in these situations, a non-smoker can feel a little left out. The two of them puffed away in their own little group. Part of me wished that I was still a smoker; I could join their club and escape for five minutes in a cloud of smoke, numbing my senses with a lethal concoction of drugs. Moore spoke first.

"How did you get on?" he asked, stubbing his cigarette out on the dustbin.

"Not good, I'm afraid." I thought I'd be honest. "It didn't feel right at all. At the very least, I think he'll complain about something or other. I've never come across someone as uptight as him. He doesn't seem right in the head.

"One thing's for sure. There's something missing. I don't think we've heard the last of this man."

"So what are you going to do now?" He took out another cigarette.

"Well, we'll update the log, and I'll give this woman a bell and tell her that we've been to see him. I'll record the fact that we've spoken to this character and if he continues, then I suppose he gets locked up. Maybe, if that does happen and he does get himself locked up, then everything will become clearer."

The sergeant took a deep drag. I was succumbing to temptation.

"Make sure you give this lady the log number and make sure you've fully updated it. Also, make a note to brief the other shifts, just in case there are any more incidents tonight."

"Yeah, we'll see to that. Oh, and by the way, do you remember Tracey and I mentioned knocking off an hour early to go to that leaving do? Perhaps knock off around nine? Otherwise we'll find ourselves short on drinking time and we don't want to let the side down now, do we?"

"Go on then, if you must. Just make sure you update the log."

★ ★ ★

A favourite haunt for off-duty police officers was the Coach House.

Quietly tucked away from the main road, with a friendly landlord who put out the 'private party' sign for the occasional do, it had a warm, intimate feel to it.

It was there that tired and weary officers could drink, dance and party in a safe, hassle-free environment.

Most old towns like Solihull would have old coach or carriage houses dotted about here and there; the ones that hadn't been demolished in all the regeneration were refurbished as antique shops, restaurants or pubs. Some of them were fairly substantial buildings: they would have included considerable living quarters for the staff who tended to the horses.

This old coach house had been converted, providing two floors of open plan drinking space. It was on a balcony suspended over the bar area that Tracey and I sat on leather chairs, looking over the dance floor at our colleagues, dancing and cavorting in the party atmosphere.

Tracey took a swig from her bottle of lager; she was deep in thought.

"You know how you're always saying that this country is going down the pan – you know, everything is turning into a load of crap?"

"Did I say that?" I replied with my normal sarcasm. Tracey continued.

"You're always saying it. Going on about how standards are slipping and no one cares about anyone else. How people are only interested in themselves and how much money they can earn. How they screw up other people's lives by doing as little as possible for as much as possible and no one bothers anymore. Then you're always going on about the court system and how the scum of the earth seem to get away with murder all the time, but, on the other hand, if the police do anything wrong then the system comes down on us like a ton of bricks."

"Are you sure that was me?"

I examined my beer label. Tracey gave a playful nudge and turned to look at me, moving her face to within inches of mine. The warmth of her breath had an immediate intoxicating effect. I looked into her eyes and drifted even closer to her.

My senses were alive; colours and smells so vivid they blocked out everything else. I became trapped in the moment. Everything was frozen, the world stood still, like when you pause the video halfway through a film and see the still frame.

Her raven hair, no longer pulled back into a tight bun, flowed down over her shoulders, resting on her chest. Her silk dress clung to the curves of her body like paint. High heels only served to emphasise the softness of her legs.

I didn't recall seeing her like this before. I was used to seeing her as a colleague and friend, but this is something different, something more dangerous.

Gone was the utility belt around her waist, the police officer's hat and sensible shoes. Right now, she was more like a woman, with needs and vulnerabilities. I suddenly felt a connection with someone who had shared the last two years of my life, the tragedies, the sorrows and the trauma.

We just sat there, locked in each other's gaze, waiting for something to happen, waiting for each other to move. Something stopped us.

She broke off and sat back in her chair; my body relaxed. I breathed out as she spoke.

"Simon, I've had enough of all this crap. I've been thinking about this for some time and I wasn't sure, but now an opportunity's come up and I have to decide whether to take it."

I pulled myself up from a slouching position deep in the sofa cushions.

"What are you talking about? Anything in particular or are you just pissed off?"

"No I'm not just pissed off, you buffoon. I'm trying to tell you something."

"What is it then? Don't say your bottle's empty because if I remember correctly, it's your round."

The smile drained from her face.

"Well, here goes. I've applied for an Australian visa."

My smile went the same way. I held the bottle halfway to my mouth.

"An Australian visa – well, that's for people who want to work in Australia. Why would you want an Australian visa? You work here, with me!"

"Yes, I know I work here with you, but it doesn't mean I'm going to be working here in England for the rest of my life."

"Yes, but Australia, that's, well, miles away. You have had a look at the map, haven't you?"

"Will you stop pissing about? It's not something I'm considering lightly, and I haven't made my mind up. It's just something I've been considering, that's all."

"If you've already applied for a visa then that sounds to me like you've done a bit more than just consider it. I mean, when are you thinking about going, and who with? It's a bloody long way if you're not sure!"

Tracey took a long drink before looking me in the eye.

"Have you heard me talk about Michael?"

"Let me think … Michael? That's the computer nerd who sits playing his Playstation all evening. Yes, I've heard you mention his name. Loser, I think you said."

"Well, he, Michael, has been accepted for a programmer's job out there. He fits into their skills shortage program and the career path is fantastic. He's asked me to go with him. I was shocked at first, it took a while to sink in, and then I made a few initial enquiries. I approached the police in Queensland and ran it past them and, subject to the normal conditions, they've offered me a job."

"So what have they said?" I could feel myself sobering up.

"As I said, subject to all the normal entry requirements, they said they'd be pleased to welcome me to the force. I just need to apply."

Someone had pressed the play button on the video; the room is full of noise and movement. From an intimate moment, I am now shouting just to be heard.

"But Australia! I can't believe you're talking about Australia! On top of that, you're thinking of going with someone who acts like a ten year old! Have you gone completely insane?"

She looked over my shoulder, into the distance.

"I might consider staying; if things were different."

"Oh yeah, shall I change the criminal justice system for you, sort out the bent lawyers, tax those barristers – I don't think it's in my power, do you?"

"I'm not talking about them. I'm talking about you."

★ ★ ★

The evening came to a close after we had been joined by two of her friends. I made my apologies and left to get a taxi. The next morning was difficult – a chilly atmosphere hung about the office.

Tracey and I had hardly spoken to each other. Too much had happened the night before and there was a sort of agreement not to revisit it. There'd been too much information all in one go and drink can lower the defences.

Talk remained stunted as we flicked through our paperwork, updating reports with fancy words before filing them. A steady flow of coffee with a breakfast of muffins had helped the morning pass and the day was starting to pick up.

Tracey was returning from having a cigarette on the back step when the phone rang. She picked it up as she passed.

"Hello, Shirley Police Station, WPC Collins speaking."

I breathed a sigh of relief that the thing had stopped ringing and carried on with the reports. It seemed like one of those long drawn-out calls, somebody complaining. I was pleased that she had answered it.

I remember thinking that it must be a real boring bugger, as she'd held it to her ear for a lot longer than normal without any butting in. What concerned me was that her face had drained of colour; she had turned as white as a sheet. I gave a little chuckle and shook my head, but it felt like a shadow was creeping over me.

It may have been the effects of the night's alcohol that made my reactions slower. When the penny dropped, it did so in slow motion.

The look on Tracey's face was not boredom, it was horror. I got up from my seat and moved towards her mouthing, "Are you alright?" As I got to her, she slowly replaced the receiver and looked into my eyes.

"That was Andrew Alton. I think we need to speak outside."

The sense of awkwardness was now mixed with a heightened state of alert. I had the obvious questions spinning around my head but still felt the need to clear the air with Tracey before we tackled the Alton matter. Tracey lit a cigarette.

"Look, about last night ..." I said at length.

"There's nothing to say on that, let's just forget about it," she snapped and looked away, exhaling her smoke.

"Tracey, I'm flattered that you have such strong feelings for me and I have very strong feelings for you."

She half-turned away and took a long draw.

"I don't know if you'd noticed, but I'm married. Leaving my wife for you is not the right thing to do. I know we're fond of each other and we watch each other's backs, but we've also got separate lives outside the police. I'm totally flattered, but the fact is, I love my wife. The last thing I want you to do is to bugger off to Australia – that would mean I'd never see you again. I'm not totally convinced that it's what you want anyway."

She rounded on me, frustration in her eyes.

"Look, let's just leave Australia for the moment; I think you've made the situation perfectly clear. I'm now just left with a lot of thinking to do. I hope you didn't mind me asking you like that. It's just something I needed to do, I needed the answer."

"Right, well at least we know where we stand."

"Yeah, Simon, we know where we stand, so let's just leave it and move on."

She stubbed out the cigarette that was hardly smoked and paused.

"Simon, as I said, that person on the phone just then was Andrew

Alton. Simon, he used your full name, he told me where you live, he says he knows everything about you. He told me that you violated his privacy and you're going to have to pay. He says he's going to complain about you, but before he does he wants you to write him a letter."

"Write to him!" I shouted. "Why in God's name would I write to him?"

"He wants you to say sorry!"

★ ★ ★

"Simon, Simon, are you okay? Can I get you a drink of water? Come on, Simon, everything's fine, there you are, have a drink. I think we lost you there for a moment."

As I came round, I smelled the familiar vanilla aroma from the scented candle. Beth passed me the cup. Just then, her lips had been moving, but with no sound; now her voice became much clearer. She was saying something about water, asking me if I wanted a drink.

"Oh, thanks." I took the cup from her and finished the last gulp, still feeling a little fuzzy. Beth sat back and scribbled a note. She looked concerned.

"I think we've done enough for today. You look a bit drained. I know how emotionally demanding this can be." Her voice was perfectly clear again. As I said to you on the first day, intrusive thoughts can be present for any trauma survivor, but you'll begin to find it easier. I promise you, we will work through all these flashbacks and their causes and things will get better for you. Was it this Alton chap again?"

"Yes, but it isn't always just him. I seem to recall events a little too vividly. There are times, you know, following a flashback, when I can't even remember what I was doing or where I'd been. That can be worrying."

Beth gave me one of her sympathetic looks.

"This is all part of your condition: it's what we in the trade call a 'dissociate flashback.' During these sessions we will work together to deal with these intrusive thoughts in the hope of preventing the condition getting any worse. We try to expose you to your fears whilst you're in this safe environment, in order for you to learn to process them and file them away."

I looked at my empty glass. Beth continued.

"You were telling me how you met this chap, your first visit to his house, then I think we lost you for a moment. Is it just him that's causing these episodes?"

"No, no, not just him; there's the others, too."

I didn't want to talk about Alton anymore. Beth looked suspicious. I needed to say something.

"If you must know, I was thinking about Jackie and that poster out there – the one in the waiting room, the one that says 'Domestic Violence Kills.' You know: the one with that picture of that dove with the thing in his beak."

Beth thought hard.

"Yeah, I know the one; it's produced by one of our local charities – what about it?"

"It reminds me of Jackie."

As I was speaking, my mind was painting a picture; I felt like I was drifting back into that bedroom.

"I sometimes feel like I'm losing control. Sometimes, it's like a world of dreams. I feel detached and find myself living in the story, the memories come without particular order, running into each other and distorting, creating a dream. Maybe all those files in my brain got mixed up, perhaps they were never filed away in the first place – they just lay about the place, cluttering it up.

"When memories get mixed up I sometimes get images that run into each other, you know, like one of those old slide shows. The old and dusty slide projector propped up on a table, facing a plain wall.

"One by one the faces flash up as the slide moves through the light. The faces flash up, a button is pressed, another one slides through, throwing itself up. The last image was that poster, the one with the woman sat on bare floorboards, big dressing gown gathered at her feet, her hands covering her face. That bloody dove was hovering over her head, looking directly at me – olive twig in its bloody beak.

"The woman was weeping, her hands holding her face, nails digging into her skin, there's a thin trickle of blood down her cheek.

"I can hear myself telling her 'release', so I can look at her face, but she's too distressed. I take hold of her hands and try to force them. She's resisting, she doesn't want me to see, her nails dig deeper. She's trying to rip her face off; her sharp nails leave deep ridges in her skin.

I pull them away to save her injuring herself, her eyes are swollen up like wasp stings, all puffed up, she can hardly see.

"Her lips and nostrils are burnt. The skin is cracked and swollen. She can't breathe. She starts scratching like a woman possessed, pulling at her nose, trying to stop the air from burning her nostrils.

"Her breathing gets harder and harder, the back of her throat is all swollen, she's making a curious whistling sound, fighting for breath.

"Confused and in panic, I scan the room for clues; then I see it: a blue plastic bottle by her feet. I examine the label, front and back, but I can't read the writing, it's too small. I open the top and smell it. The stench shoots up my nose, like jumping into a swimming pool. It smells like chlorine, a smell from childhood.

"But I don't recognise that brand; I haven't seen it advertised, it's got some red and blue strips. That's it: it's the value brand. It's value bloody bleach.

"Jackie has drunk a bottle of cheap value bloody bleach!"

I stopped talking, sweat pouring from my forehead. Beth looked up.

"You never got as far as telling me what happened to her. I think we left it. Would it help you to talk about Jackie?"

"I'm not sure. It was all along time ago, I can't see the point in bringing it up again."

"It's not a problem for me. Although we're making progress on Alton, don't feel that you can't talk about anything else. I know we've spoken about Jackie before; there's no problem in returning to the subject. You might feel that it helps you as it gives you a break from your man. And if it helps, well, that's all right by me."

"Do you want hear what happened?"

"That's entirely up to you. This is your time and everything you say in here is between us two. I'm here to listen and if you feel that you want to, go ahead."

"Well then, how far did I get?"

Beth flicked through her file.

"You were telling me about the rape crisis centre. She was talking about her partner, Billy I think his name was."

"Yes, that's right Billy Macrow; you couldn't meet a nicer bloke. I'll tell you what happened to him, it's bloody priceless. But first, Jackie.

"We'd managed to keep her at the centre for three long hours until the doctor arrived, making sure that she didn't wash, drink or go to the toilet. The forensic examination room was laid out and Jackie was sent for. Her legs went to jelly as she tried to stand up. Jill was having difficulty supporting her so I lent a hand as far as the doctor's room. The sight of two uniformed police officers carrying her was a scene that wouldn't make it onto any publicity posters.

"A sharps container overflowing with used needles had put the doctor in a bad mood. This was clear as he ordered Jackie to remove all her clothing and stand there naked for his examination to begin. She would stand totally naked for twenty minutes, during which she was given a list of instructions that she could hardly understand.

"She stood still, weeping, looking down at a man inching a comb through her pubic hair and moving inch by inch over her lower body. She thought back to the rape, feeling helpless and ashamed, yearning to cover up and regain her dignity.

"The weeping got louder; I could hear it from the next room, the dull sound broken only by a man's voice. As a victim, she would feel totally humiliated, her body would now be examined inch by inch; then later, the lawyers and barristers would be waiting, eager to do the same. The procedure in the suite is meant to be degrading: it's meant to see if you have the bottle to go further, to see it through.

"After her body is violated, the lawyers start with her sexual history, piece by piece, recording every detail. Then they probe every second, every detail of the incident, implying that Jackie herself was the instigator, someone who actually consented to the sex and is now on a vindictive campaign, trying to ruin an innocent man's life.

"Maybe Billy will produce some of the photos taken of Jackie, just to show what kind of a woman she was – happy to pose nude around the house while her child slept upstairs. Those photographs could seriously damage the good character of a victim and put question marks in the minds of a jury.

"However, as we all know, the reporting of rapes is notoriously low, prosecutions are lower still and convictions are rare. In Jackie's case, it never got through to the prosecution stage, not after what happened."

Beth closed her file.

"I never realised how hard it would be for a victim in this day and age." Beth's voice was filled with sadness.

"It's like so many other things today: there's a gulf of difference between what people are told and the experiences they face.

"Every organisation has a PR machine, churning out sound bites and glossy brochures, showing a system working efficiently like a well-oiled machine. But when people find themselves in need, the reality of the situation kicks in. When the system fails the individual, all the authorities do is wheel out some bigwig to tell us that they've learnt from their mistakes and new procedures are now in place.

"I mean, everybody must have heard it so many times. I'm amazed that people fall for it anymore. No one seems to be able to distinguish the bullshit from the facts."

"What happened to Jackie in the end?"

"You mean after the rape suite? We took her home. She wanted to go in the house by herself. She pleaded with us to leave her alone and give her some space. So we left her outside and told her to contact us if there was anything she needed. Apparently, when she got in, a letter was there from Kelly.

"Kelly had been brought back by the police earlier and left in the care of the neighbours, but she sneaked out the back. She got into the house via a window, grabbed her belongings and left a note for her mum.

Mum,

I've gone to London with Darren. I love Darren and he loves me. He says he will always look after me and care for me. Money will be tight, but I know we will manage; he would never let me go without.

Now I've found the right man and I'm in love, I want to move away from you and Billy and all the crap. I've told you, time and time again that he is nothing but a pig, but you never listened. I will never let a man treat me like that and you need to get some self respect.

Please don't try and find me, I do not want to be found, please leave me to live my life without you.

K

"Jackie frantically searched the whole house for her daughter but saw that all her stuff had been taken. The house was empty and quiet, just the bloodstain on the cupboard door – a reminder of Billy.

"We know that she got all the old albums out, the ones with Kelly as a baby, photographed on holiday in Wales. Photographs and letters were strewn across the table.

"She then opened the cupboard under the sink and took out the bottle of bleach. She went up to her bedroom, the room where she'd been raped, and sat down on the floor. She opened the bottle and drank.

"It was the same neighbour who heard the screaming. Jackie was found writhing in agony, burns around her nose and mouth. After twenty-four hours in intensive care she was sectioned under the Mental Health Act and banned from any contact with her daughter. The rape case was dropped a week later; it was deemed not to be in the public interest.

"Jackie was sectioned and her evidence was seen as unreliable. There was no prosecution, no day in court, and no conviction.

"There can be few things worse than to keep locked up within you a terrible secret, to finally pluck up the courage to tell somebody about it, and for them to brush the matter aside.

"As for the others ... well, Hackney Social Services took care of Kelly. And as for Billy, good old Billy, well – he was last seen with his new partner in The Drum and Monkey. A single mother of two, fifteen years his junior.

★ ★ ★

CHAPTER EIGHT

Andrew Alton

"Okay Tracey, start at the beginning and tell me everything." Sergeant Moore leaned back in his chair and lifted his knees up to his desk.

"Well, like I said, I was in the parade room this morning when the phone rang. I answered it as normal. There was a man on the line; he said something along the lines of 'This is Andrew Alton, do you remember me?'

"I told him that I did remember him and I asked him what he wanted. He said he couldn't speak to Simon because he was now subject to a complaint. He said he had no problem with me, just Simon.

"He told me that he was working with a television company who were making a documentary about the Force. He said this documentary was all about the failings of the police and how badly they treated their staff.

"He said that he had been in touch with the production company who now wanted the details of yesterday's visit – all part of the documentary into how the police were harassing him

"He went on to say that our visit yesterday was captured on audio and video tape and that he was preparing to release the recordings to the producer. In the meantime, he asked that Simon write to him to apologise for violating his privacy and continuing to harass him. The thing was, he sounded quite mad: very angry and threatening. He said he'd got all Simon's personal details, his full name, his address, his car number and everything. If Simon did not make a formal apology forthwith, then he would be forced to 'take the appropriate action', whatever he means by that. I'll tell you one thing: he sounded like a guy with one hell of a screw loose."

Sergeant Moore sat upright in his chair and placed his head in his hands, deep in thought.

"Okay then, Tracey, I've heard what you've said but I don't see why he would want Simon to apologise for something that, as far as I can see, hasn't happened. The whole thing doesn't make any sense, unless there's something that you're not telling me. Are you sure there's nothing else?"

"No, of course not! I'm as in the dark as you are. Maybe the guy's just crazy. I suppose that one option is to go back, maybe take you with us this time, try and clear the air, ask him what his problem is."

Sergeant Moore started making some notes as Tracey continued.

"He did say that he'd already made some complaints about officers and that these were all part of this documentary. Is it worth you giving Professional Standards a bell, see if they can tell us anything about him?"

The sergeant finished scribbling and looked up.

"One last thing," Tracey said, trying to recall all the facts. "I know it's only a minor detail but Simon was the only one to introduce himself. He used the words PC Davies. No other details were given to him."

"So what are you saying?" Sergeant Moore looked up.

"Well, there's only one way he could have got his full name since our visit."

"And what's that?" He placed his file in his brief case.

"Someone here has told him."

A silence fell across the room as the last sentence sunk in.

"Right," the sergeant said, after a short pause. "I'll do as you suggest, give Professional Standards a bell, see if they know anything about this chap. You keep in touch with Kate and see that she's all right and nothing else has happened. We need to make sure that she comes to no harm. In the meantime, I'm telling you to stay well away from this character. We'll cross the next bridge when we come to it."

Sergeant Moore picked up the receiver and Tracey took her cue to leave.

"Tracey, one last thing."

She turned.

"Just be careful."

★ ★ ★

I remember how she was that day, her mind miles away, brow furrowed in thought.

I sat and passed her the cup of coffee, left to go cold. She took a sip, her eyes focused on the wall behind me. It was some time before she finally spoke.

"I've got a bad feeling about this. There's something somebody's not telling us. I've been thinking: if Kate Chandler rings up to report anything else, I think someone else should deal with him, you know, take the heat off you. The more I think about it, the more I think he's playing a game, trying to isolate someone in the organisation to target his grievance. That's what all the pushing was about – trying to cause an incident. I think the guy's just a low life and we shouldn't make things easy for him. If someone else picks up the case, he'll find it harder to call the shots."

Tracey stood up, gathered her things and beckoned towards the smoking room, the cigarette already in her mouth, lighter at the ready. At the door she stopped, lit the thing up and inhaled deeply.

"Well, maybe you should have a word with Sergeant Moore; let him worry about what to do. One thing's for sure, he's a god-damned scary freak."

I watched Tracey exhale her smoke and began to realise just how much I'd miss her. It could have been the events of the past thirty-six hours that made me realise how much I relied on her.

I remember thinking about the irony of the timing; just when I need her most, she was trying to escape this bloody country and make a new life.

I watched her and considered bringing the subject of Australia up, but then thought better of it. The subject was still raw and I thought it best to lighten the mood.

"What do you fancy for lunch?"

Tracey could see right through me.

"I don't mind." She examined the tip of her cigarette.

I decided to say it.

"When do you need to make the decision about going?"

"I'm going to give it one more week. I keep weighing up the pros and cons and it's driving me mad, I'm going round in circles. One thing I have decided, though."

"Oh yeah, what's that?"

She placed the tip of her finger against my lips. Her gentle touch had a dominant edge.

"You will be the first to know."

Thursday was the start of late shifts. Duty time started at two in the afternoon.

Around that time, I was in the habit of swimming before shifts, making use of the quieter periods at the baths, without the teenagers showing off.

I would push myself hard, ploughing up and down the baths, averaging sixty each time. After a good swim that morning, I took an ice-cold shower and walked to work. I got changed and entered the parade room, bang on the dot of two.

"Hello Sarge, what are you doing over here? We don't normally have the pleasure of your company."

The smile quickly drained from my face.

"Can we have a little word?" He gestured up the corridor.

"Yes, of course Sarge, lead on."

I followed him to an unoccupied office; when inside, the door shut behind me.

"Simon, I've just had a phone call from DCI Bailey. Do you remember I said I was going to call her and ask if she knew anything about this Alton character? Well I've just spoken to her and she's not very happy, she's not very happy at all."

"She's not very bloody happy, that's rich, I'm not very happy."

I could feel myself on edge, losing my composure.

"She is angry that an officer has been around to his home and upset him. I don't know why she should be so annoyed about this in particular. All I know is that she wants to know who, why, when and she wants to know by this afternoon."

I tried to cut in.

"But …"

"No buts, Simon; this afternoon. I tell you, she's got her knickers in a twist about something. I just suggest that you keep yourself out of the station and for God's sake, don't go near this bloody Alton chap until you hear from me. She instructs that on no account whatsoever should anybody make contact with him. She forbids any type of 'clear the air' meeting, so don't even think about it; just keep your head down."

"Yeah, okay, I'm sure we can find something to do. I'll speak to you when she's gone. Will you give me a shout over the air?"

"Yes, of course. As soon as I know what's going on, you'll know."

I left the office in a gloomy mood.

Tracey must have known what was coming; she was ready, waiting outside the back door.

"Is everything okay?" She stubbed out a cigarette on the bin lid.

"Come on, I'll tell you in the car." She held the keys towards me, dangling off an extended middle finger.

I took them and we drove out of the yard towards the more peaceful, rural area. We soon found ourselves driving along winding country roads between fields and farmhouses. When we were far enough away, I began to speak.

"DCI Bailey's coming down from Professional Standards to see Moore; she's really doing her nut about something. I reckon Alton must be one of these persistent moaners who make everyone's life a misery.

"He goes and makes life difficult for the pen pushers up at PSD, who in turn make life difficult for us lot at the sharp end. I take it you've noticed that everything that smells in nature rolls down hill.

"But I still can't see what the problem is. As far as I'm aware, some woman has come screaming into the station after being followed, presumably by this Alton bloke. We go and see him and all of a sudden the whole thing goes tits up.

"Neither of us has done anything wrong, it's just those time-wasters up there in their ivory tower creating a load of bullshit over nothing. I'm sure it will sort itself out."

Neither of us really believed that. There was a part of the jigsaw missing and we didn't know which part.

Sometimes these small, seemingly insignificant details can go pear-shaped, when the bigger, more important matters get resolved.

We spent the next few minutes in our own private thoughts, driving aimlessly round the chocolate-box villages of the green belt. When it was time for a break we took the advice to stay away from Shirley and headed into Solihull.

While Tracey drank her coffee, accompanied by a cigarette in the smoking room, I took a stroll up to admin to search out some friendly faces.

I entered the office and it was very much the same as I'd left it. I was pleased to see Sandra sitting at her desk, pouring over files, with her blonde hair tied up, her figure-hugging pullover showing her assets.

"Did I ever say how brilliant the staff were over here compared with those over on the Wood? No, really, they're bloody useless, not helpful at all – while over this side, there's always a friendly face."

I was forcing a smile on my own face.

Sandra looked up from her diary, faking a yawn, a manicured hand to her mouth.

"Oh, hi Simon, I was just thinking about you the other day. I remember you telling me something about women under twenty being like Asia or something. But unfortunately, before you got any further you had to go. I assume there was more to your joke?"

"Did I mention Africa?"

"I think you were just about to."

"Yes, I remember that. Oh, and by the way, I almost forgot to say thanks for that uniform, it came two days later – just another example of how much better things are over here."

Sandra rolled her eyes. "It's always nice to be appreciated for all the fantastic work we do, but do you think we are ever going to get to hear the end of this joke, or do we have to wait until your retirement do?"

"I won't be having a retirement do. As soon as my last day is completed, I'll be out of here and you won't see my heels for dust. I won't be hanging around for a disco and a sausage roll. But anyway, where was I? Oh yes, African woman, yes, that's right; I think I was talking about Africa. Here goes."

I cleared my throat for effect.

"From the age of twenty to thirty a woman is like Africa: wild, exciting and dangerous. Between the ages of thirty and forty, she's like America: bubbly and warm and welcoming. Between the ages of forty and fifty, she's like Europe…"

The phone rang on Sandra's desk. She picked it up.

"Yes, sir, he's here; he's standing right in front of me. Okay, I'll pass you over to him."

I took the receiver.

"Hello?"

Tracey's voice had a sense of urgency.

"Come down as soon as you can. Sergeant Moore wants to see us at Shirley."

"Right, down in two ticks, meet you out by the car."

I leant across the desk towards Sandra, who was already pretending to ignore me as she studied her fingernails.

"Sorry, Sandra, I promise I'll be back as soon as I can to tell you about European women, but I really do have to shoot right now."

I started retreating towards the door.

"You'll do anything to keep me in suspense."

I charged down two flights of stairs and out into the car park. Tracey was already waiting for me.

"Did the sergeant say anything else?"

"No, he just said get back here. He wants to see you. He certainly doesn't sound very happy. I think Bailey's gone and put a rocket up his arse."

"Oh crap. Tell you what: you can have a drive, and don't spare the horses."

I threw the keys to Tracey who made an expert catch. I jumped into the passenger seat. We were back at Shirley police station in five minutes. I found the sergeant in the office where I'd left him.

"Come and have a seat, Simon. Tracey, you can go and have a break if you want."

She took the hint and backed out through the door, giving me one of those 'I'll be waiting for you when you've finished' looks.

"Simon, I've just had the DCI grill me for two hours about Alton. She wants to know every detail about it, everything from the circumstances of the call, to how we handled it and why we went round to his house."

"Is she allowed to do that, Sarge? I mean, just come down and sort of interview you like this about an official complaint? Aren't there procedures and proper interviews where you can have somebody present? Surely they can't just do as they like?"

"Well in this case it appears they can do just what they like. But after our meeting, I think I can safely say I now know what the fuss is about."

"Well, come on then, Sarge, I'm all ears. Spill the beans." He now had my complete attention.

"Okay, brace yourself. Up until two years ago, Andrew Alton was a Midlands police officer – wait for it – working on the anti-terrorist unit with Special Branch."

"So what's all this drama about? I can understand that being a bitter and twisted ex-employee is one thing, but all this is going a bit far!"

"The facts are that Alton's expertise was in the area of surveillance and his knowledge on the subject was profound. He was developing some sort of surveillance equipment when there was an accident and he injured his back. It appears that the Midlands police took the opportunity to get rid of him, pension him off, probably as an excuse to get him out of the organisation. But he didn't take it too well.

"There are concerns over his mental state. He was becoming eccentric and very awkward to handle. In laymen's terms, he had a mental breakdown.

"It's more than likely that twenty-or-so years of sensitive police work had a very deep psychological effect. Alton had been involved in a large number of high-impact cases, some of which have had serious repercussions for the security of the country.

"The hierarchy found themselves with the problem of an experienced and highly valued officer losing his marbles, going mad.

"Having worked in the sensitive area of counter-terrorism for so long, he held an awful lot of information on past cases. The more they tried to adapt him to the new world, the new way of doing things, the more of a maverick he became.

"It appears that before he totally lost his mind, he went and injured his back on a surveillance job and this gave the police the golden opportunity to get rid of him. It was a chance too good to ignore, so they pensioned him off using this injury as an excuse."

"So what's his great beef? He must have been coming close to natural retirement age, when he would have been pensioned anyway; this way he just picks up his pension early – most people would be jumping at the chance."

"Maybe so. But not him. He sees it as the ultimate betrayal after all his work. He dedicated his life to the Special Branch. There is no doubt that the work had a huge impact in reducing terrorist activity. He worked on cases that brought suspects to justice in some high-profile cases.

"All that work, dedication and commitment, and then his mental breakdown – he sees his medical pension as the ultimate betrayal, and he's angry. However, instead of providing help and support, they've rather just left him to his own devices. I think they assumed that he was going to get an allotment and grow vegetables, but it didn't work out like that.

"He's loose in the community with a giant chip on his shoulder and a lot of anger; that's what makes him very dangerous."

"But surely they must have some sort of duty of care to him – they can't just let him loose. Couldn't they have carried on supporting him through occupational health?"

"Well, that sounds very nice and cosy, but in the real world there's a cost involved. As far as they're concerned up at headquarters, he's gone and that's it: it's no longer their problem. They'll keep humouring him and keep him at arms length, but I suspect one day he'll go too far and end up doing something stupid. Then he won't be their problem: he'll be someone else's."

"So what happens now?"

"Well, Alton has submitted a formal complaint to the Professional Standards Department, so everything is now investigated in the normal way. Because of the sensitive nature of Andrew Alton and his circumstances, DCI Bailey deals with him as a special case. It is her and her alone; no other person in the department has access to his file. She tells me that she is officially investigating the complaint about you but, to date, Alton won't release this audio and video that he claims he has. He claims all the evidence is in the hands of some television company, so at the moment, she is trying to arrange a copy."

"There's no bloody audio or video, that's a load of bullcrap, nothing controversial was said or done; he's just playing games."

"The DCI does concede that he has made allegations on a number of previous occasions that were not substantiated. But they have to take each individual complaint separately and on its own merits. So they carry on believing that he has evidence until such time as they are given cause to think otherwise."

"Well, I'm glad that they spend so much time and effort entertaining time-wasters. It's just a shame they haven't got the same amount of time to put into dealing with the serious villains."

I'm aware that my tone is beginning to sound a little despondent.

"Oh yeah, one last thing: last year he tried this same sort of thing with a young female officer, started following her around to her children's school. She went half mad. Just you be careful. Hopefully he'll have a heart attack or get locked up. Then we can all have some peace!"

★ ★ ★

CHAPTER NINE

Kate's Statement

It was the British Prime Minister, Harold Wilson, who once famously said, "A week is a long time in politics."

I have no doubt that's true, but it can be said about any profession. Life can change on the flip of a coin.

For the six days following DCI Bailey's meeting with Sergeant Moore, nothing happened. Days of dealing with trivial incidents all seemed to flow into one.

Then it all happened at once.

First, Tracey broke the news that she had made her decision to go to Queensland. She had just given in her notice and had one month left to do. That set the tone for the day; at six p.m. precisely, I received the message I hoped would never come.

"Lima X-ray to Mike 4?"

"Yes, go ahead Lima X-ray."

"I've just had a log flash up from a call taken yesterday. No one was sent, but a delayed action was agreed for today. You're instructed to attend the address yourself; apparently, you've had dealings with this lady. Could you attend and speak to a Miss Kate Chandler, reporting being followed by a man in a blue Ford Focus. She wishes to complain about harassment."

So he had continued to follow her. And, when she rang up the police, someone had seen my name on a previous log and decided to bat it back to me. Like playing a game of cricket, when a job comes your way that you don't like, you see if you can hit it into the long grass and let someone else deal.

No one wants a hysterical female, ranting and raving. However, I was stuck with it. I'd previously had dealings with Kate Chandler; I could see why everyone else would run a mile and leave it all with me.

The lazy buggers could have gone yesterday, sorted the matter out, put her mind at ease. But no: it was left there for me. Just what I bloody needed. I looked at Tracey.

"I don't like this. I'm going to end up lumbered with this crazy bastard for life. I think we'll go to the job, take the details and any statement that's required, and when we've done the paperwork we'll go and see Moore and tell him that someone else must pick it up.

"We need to point out that Alton has made an official complaint so we should not be dealing anyway. Let's keep our fingers crossed. If we weren't on duty, those lazy tossers would keep delaying the job until she finally gave up or was bloody murdered, that's how much they care."

"Let's just go out there, see what she's got to say and then worry about it."

I could tell that Tracey's mind was on Australia. She could now take a back seat, relax and see out the final weeks as quietly as possible.

I, on the other hand, felt myself getting sucked deeper and deeper into a battle between an ex-police officer and his former force.

The feeling of being a pawn on a chess board was real. A shadow seemed to pass over me as we drove. I felt like I was getting myself into something, the politics of which I could not understand; to them it was just a game. A game in which this mentally ill ex-officer was challenging his force, saying, 'Come and get me, go on, make a fuss, let me show you how mad I am.'

The force in response was being distant and unapproachable, keeping him at arm's length, watching the events unfold. Their objective was to avoid liability.

I was stuck in the middle of these two formidable players, a pawn on the chessboard, and they gave me no way out.

Another shadow passed over me as we parked our vehicle and walked up the path. Someone was there to open the door; they had been expecting us.

We were shown into the living room where Kate sat, curled up in a giant cane armchair, sobbing into a tissue. She looked up at me and I saw a look of hope in her eyes, as if I was the only one who'd believed her.

The middle-aged man, who she later introduced as her uncle, spoke first.

"This damn business is absolutely intolerable. Can nobody stop this crazy man before someone gets injured? It's affecting Kate's health and making her life a living hell. First it was just following her, then it was parking outside her house, then it was following her to and from work, and now this. I want to know what the hell you're doing about it, or are you just going to wait until she gets killed? Why don't you lot do something about this man?"

He paused, took deep breaths and supported himself on the back of the armchair.

"Sir, I was the officer who started the inquiry and we've already had a chat with this man. I can assure you that we are taking this matter very seriously. What I need to find out are the precise details of what has happened since I last spoke to Kate. Only then can I reassure you on what we can do about it."

I looked at Kate, who was staring back with those big, brown eyes.

"Kate, I need you to tell me what's happened up to when you called the police."

Kate reached for the box on her coffee table and pulled up a couple of pastel tissues. She dabbed the corner of each eye before turning to me and clearing her throat.

"The day after you rang me to tell me that you'd been and spoken to the owner of that car, he started following me again. I saw him in the morning, waiting at the end of the road; he followed me all the way to work. I thought that if I just ignored him for a couple of days he would just go away. He'd do whatever he wanted to do and then leave me alone. I felt a bit safer in the knowledge that you knew about him. I thought at least you'd be able to track him down if he did hurt me. But after yesterday, I don't think he cares about anything – now I'm terrified and I'm going to have to leave my house."

"Have you any idea where you're going to go?" I reached for my notebook.

"Harry, that's my uncle, has insisted that I go and stay with him until this nutter is caught. I think he's right, I can't stay here, I don't feel safe in my own home."

"Okay then, Kate, tell me what happened yesterday." My pen was poised.

"I was leaving work at about five as usual, and I was just driving through the gates out onto the main road. You have to drive very slowly because your view is restricted and there's a junior school round the corner. As I came out of the gate, I saw his vehicle parked on the road facing the gates. Normally, he'd be further up the road, almost out-of-sight, but on this occasion he was parked just there, almost blocking the driveway.

"I had to drive slowly out, edging forward, and I could see his face through the windscreen. He was staring right at me, but this time with a menacing look on his face, all screwed up and angry. I watched him as he raised his hand and made like a barrel of a gun with his two fingers. He then did some kind of shooting action before holding his fingers up to his mouth and blowing them, like he was a cowboy in the movies, blowing the smoke from the barrel."

Kate started to weep again. Tracey walked across and passed her some clean tissues.

She took them and mouthed, "Thank you."

"I know this is very hard for you, but I think he's done enough to be arrested. We will also try and give you some protection. If you're able to, just carry on with what happened."

Kate fought back the tears, dabbing her eyes. Tracey sat down on the edge of the chair and held her hand.

"I was just terrified. Although he's been around, following me for some time, he's never done anything like that – it frightened the life out of me. I just put my foot down and sped off down the road. Goodness knows how I didn't knock anybody over, I was in a panic. I got home as fast as I could and went straight in and dialled 999.

"I was distraught and screaming down the phone, asking for help; they just asked me if the man was still outside. I hadn't been thinking for the last five minutes and I had no idea if he'd carried on, so I went over to the window and looked out. There wasn't a soul about and then I realised that he must have turned off. I think he was just trying to terrify me, in the hope that I'd panic and cause an accident.

"I told the lady that the man was not outside my house and I didn't know where he was. They put me through to the local police station and I spoke to a police officer in the control room. He told me that if the man wasn't causing a threat to my safety at the time I rang then I should not ring the 999 number, as that was for emergencies. I remember just crying and crying and the man said he'd get a local officer to ring me back that afternoon."

Tracey reached for fresh tissues.

"Can I get you both a drink, a coffee perhaps?" The uncle spoke; I sensed we all needed a break.

"Yes, thank you very much: a coffee would be great, that's very kind of you."

Uncle went into the kitchen to fill the kettle and Tracey rubbed Kate's back.

"You're doing fine, Kate. In a minute we're going to take a statement from you and then we can get down to the business of sorting this matter out."

Kate's large eyes turned to Tracey, who gave a reassuring smile.

"Yes, Tracey's right, once we've taken the statement we're going to speak to our supervisor and sort out getting this guy arrested."

"But what happens when you release him?" Kate sobbed. "What if he tries to find me and does something horrible, what if he's angry and tries to hurt me? I've told you what he's like with that gun thing he did with his fingers."

"If he's charged with an offence of harassment we can give him bail conditions, which means he can't come near you or try to contact you. If he was to breach these conditions then he could get locked up again and find himself in court."

The uncle arrived with the coffees and handed them out. Tracey gave a final rub on Kate's back and moved over to her own chair. Kate cupped her hands around her warm mug and stared vacantly across the room.

After a sip of hot coffee and a pause, Kate was ready to carry on.

"I waited by the phone for four hours but all that time it didn't ring. Then a young officer rang and again told me that he had to explain the 999 procedure and that I should only ring it in an emergency.

"He was angry and made me feel so small, I almost told him not to worry as I wouldn't bother them again. He said that they were only trying to help and told me to calm down. I was just trying to tell him what had happened but I don't think he was listening.

"After it went quiet for a moment I asked him if he was still there and he said he was reading the previous logs. He asked me if I'd spoken to you and I said yes and told him that you'd come to speak to me at the station when I first reported it. He said that in that case it wasn't worth him coming out to take a statement today as you knew all about the case. He said you were working tomorrow and he would delay the log for your attention, and when you were next on duty you'd come and see me."

Tracey and I both sighed as we realised the job had just been left to us by someone who couldn't be bothered to come out.

"Okay, then, what I want to do is to take a formal statement of complaint off you and then deal with the matter as a crime of harassment. We then have the power to arrest this man and interview him. It might then go to court, but the main thing is to start some measures to protect you as soon as possible and that means getting him off the streets as soon as possible. The statement should take about an hour or so – are you going to remain here tonight?"

"No, I'll be going to my uncle's address as soon as you've finished here, so if you need to you can contact me there and I'll make sure you have my number. I won't be coming back here until it's safe to do so."

There was a long pause as Kate wiped the tears from her eyes.

"You will help me, won't you?" Her teary eyes darted from me to Tracey and back to me. I had the statement paper on my clip board and my pen at the ready.

"Of course we will. That's what we're here for. Now, let's start again from the beginning . . . What's your full name? "

★ ★ ★

CHAPTER TEN

Duty of Care

"We're now at the stage where I like to start recording the sessions," Beth says, flicking through her notes, holding a pencil to her lips.

Next to her is a tape recorder, its deck open and a tape lying next to it.

"Once the session is finished, the tape is yours; you can keep it somewhere safe, you can listen to it, or you can throw it away, the choice is yours. We will concentrate on the events that have caused you the greatest concern, the flashbacks and the images that you suffer from. So, this is the tape recorder and this is the microphone, how does that sound?"

It was certainly a new concept in the therapy and I had no problem with Beth recording the session, but almost instantly I'd decided that I would not want a copy.

As far as my treatment was concerned, everything now had its place, and that's how I wanted it. There were the places where I'd go to relax and think: the places where I felt safe. There were the more sinister places that I would avoid, the ones that would evoke the bad memories.

I had built up my own routine of where I would go, what I would say and who would I trust.

Beth's consultation room was the only place where I would allow Alton to emerge, where I would release him from the darkness and allow him to come back to life. Beth and I would sit opposite each other, probing deep into the past, inviting his presence to join us, bringing it out into the daylight.

As far as I was concerned, during the therapy sessions he could sit on a chair next to the fireplace, his image fading in and out of the wallpaper, not threatening or interfering – just there.

When it was time for our session to end, I'd get up and thank Beth, preparing to leave the room with him still sat there. Only when I'd left the house would she finish her notes and clear up, before spiriting his ghost back into the file.

Then she'd go and file him away, safely under lock and key.

Her next client would arrive and the next session would start, the room would fill with other people's ghosts. They'd be waiting on the stairs and moving in behind the curtains as the client entered the building and made their way up the staircase.

Taking that audio tape out of the sanctity of those four walls was out of the question. I'd feel somehow that he was still clinging to me, hanging on and harassing me, following me around. I'd sooner take it out, drop it onto the pavement and smash it into a thousand pieces than carry it around.

Just then, a memory came flooding back, a hazy memory of a summer holiday: a rainy day on a caravan site in Cornwall.

The caravan site lay high above the cliffs at the end of a road lined with miners' cottages. Way down below us the Atlantic rollers battered the rocks, and up above, the lanes with their tufts of grass that ran between the cottages.

Our old tomcat, Fudge, would prowl the cliffs, killing mice to bring back to the caravan. In order to frighten the other kids, I would pick up the mouse and put it in my pocket, ready to creep up behind some girl and drop it down her back. After the fun, the mouse would go back into my pocket and the lads and I would take the cliff path back to the site.

Then I would begin to feel uncomfortable with the mouse in my pocket. I wanted to get rid of it, I wanted to hurl it into the sea; I no longer wanted that little stiff body near me.

But the joke had been too funny and the lads would expect me to repeat it. Hoist by my own petard, the joke was on me: I was the one feeling awkward and uncomfortable. I dropped the little body on the ground.

An instant flood of relief would wash over me. I would lose that bloody tape in much the same way, discarding it to the bin and feeling that same sense of relief.

The noise of her unwrapping the cellophane brought my attention back. Beth looked at me one more time, as if she was seeking final approval, before she closed the deck and pressed the record button. I couldn't help myself from focusing on the tape spools, both turning slowly in unison, as Beth began to speak.

"Looking back at everything you've been through, tell me how you feel."

I took a last look at the spools and cleared my throat.

"Disappointment, neglect, anger, frustration, an overwhelming sense of being let down by the very people I trusted; a feeling of being let down by the very people who could have helped, or should have helped; a feeling of being pushed aside by people who had a duty of care but instead decided to do nothing."

"Are these feelings of frustration and anger directed towards Andrew Alton or the police?"

"The police," I said, not pausing for breath.

"Why do you feel that way about the organisation? Wasn't it Andrew Alton and his actions that affected you so badly and made you ill?"

"Yes, that's right, it was certainly his actions that caused my illness, but he had been let down himself; not one of the bloody-minded idiots helped him. He was mentally ill due to the stresses and strains of his job. After saving lives and countless crimes, they abandoned him and threw him out."

Beth adjusted herself in her chair and tucked her hair behind her ear.

"Out there, he would have worked under the most stressful conditions; the sort of ungodly hours that some people don't know exist, carrying out surveillance on people who wouldn't think twice about killing a police officer. I've no doubt that he dedicated his working life to make the Midlands a safer place.

"Then, finally, after all those dedicated years of work, when the pressure starts to take its toll and he becomes ill, they decide to throw him out with the waste. Worse, this man is now living his life like a ticking time-bomb, full of anger, frustration and bitterness.

"But instead of treating him and providing support, they just washed their hands of him, passing the responsibility to an already overstretched NHS.

"The NHS itself, although hard working and committed, it is hugely under-resourced in the area of mental health. The staff utilised at the primary care trust level are good at caring, but couldn't possibly understand the pressures of all that danger he faced.

"Some of his work touched on areas so sensitive that he wouldn't divulge it to professionals outside of the service, so instead it would remain bottled up, stockpiled in the back of his brain, and one day he'd simply explode.

"In the meantime, he sits idle, brooding, with time on his hands, plotting revenge, the type of revenge that is fuelled by bitterness, the type of bitterness that needs revenge.

"The revenge would have no clear motive to it, no particular structure and no particular goal, other than to cause as much trouble as possible and create the disruption he so desperately craves.

"The police themselves are slow to react. Their hope is that it will all just go away, burn itself out; he'll eventually get better. But the slow, arm's length approach only fuels the need for attention and from that moment on, someone, yes, someone, is going to suffer.

"It won't be the obvious person who will bear the brunt of his aggression. It won't be the Chief Constable or one of his assistants, or any decision-maker high up in the authority. It won't even be the force doctor who, without a second thought, discharged this man from the Force. It'll be the small, insignificant person, the tiny cog in the great machine, the one person whose only mistake was to be in the wrong place at the wrong time.

"A time when Alton – this great, angry predator – is searching for a target on which to prey. His message is:

"'I'm still here; don't think you can get rid of me that easily, I'll be haunting you for as long as I possibly can.'

"Again, the great blundering bureaucracy ignores the signs, thinking it will all blow over. After all, he is now concentrating all of his efforts on one individual so it's taking the focus off the organisation. The organisation knew full well that the real battle was between themselves and Alton; bearing that in mind, they sat back and did nothing.

"Alton eventually got sent to prison for his pains, an experience that gave him a taste of life behind bars; he didn't want to repeat it. A deal was done to shorten his sentence in exchange for an end to his grievances.

"He got the attention he wanted and proved his silly little point, that he didn't want to be ignored; so, at the end of the day, they'd finally got rid of him and the only one left to suffer was me.

"However, that's not the end of the story.

"Post-Traumatic Stress Disorder moves from one person to another. I develop the same anger, the same frustration, the same grievance.

"The cycle will continue from person to person until someone has the foresight to break the cycle. Again, the target of all this inherited bitterness won't be the obvious one; it won't be the Chief Constable or the force doctor or anyone else holding a duty of care.

"It will be someone whose only crime was to be in the wrong place at the wrong time, and then they will become the vehicle in which the grievance is carried on."

"When was the last time you heard from Andrew Alton?" Beth asked.

"He wrote to me from his prison cell in Liverpool, while he was held there on remand. I've no doubt that the letter, which came via his solicitors, was also for the benefit of the court for when they considered sentencing, but it built up a picture of the man and his own story and that answered a lot of questions."

"Have you kept the letter?"

"Oh yes, I'll always keep it, because it was one of the moves in the game that made sense. He was trying to explain to me the journey which took him from a detective in the Special Branch to a prisoner in a Liverpool prison cell. From time to time I read it and I reflect on my own journey, a similar one in many ways: one of a highly-commended police officer to a defendant before the Crown Court. On our journeys, we both looked to our employers for care and support before being let down and ignored, both feeling rejected, bitter, frustrated, exploited, and forgotten. I'll bring the letter with me next time and let you see it; you can read it if you like."

She scribbled away at her notes before she looked up.

"By all means, anything you want to show me is fine, that's what I'm here for."

I looked at Beth, who smiled back, and I realised that the key to this therapy was her skill at listening. Just sitting there quietly, dependable, not judgmental, allowing me time to reflect on my circumstances, giving me the space to realise my anger.

She looked down and studied her notes before speaking.

"Is it just the police that you think have let you down?"

"No, it's not just the police it's the whole God damn system. My journey through the criminal justice system has been a long and frustrating one. Sometimes, when I try and think about the journey, I try to picture myself in ways that make it easier for me to understand.

"I've often felt like I want to picture myself as a runaway train on a railroad in the old North American gold rush days: a steam train that has just been derailed by some buffalo wandering onto the line.

"I picture the scene as the wheels are lodged within the metal tracks, firing up showers of sparks high into the air, accompanied by an ear-piercing screech of steel scraping steel. I think I use the image of the train as I believe that, once you've come off the tracks, you can't find your way back until someone takes the trouble to stop the train and put you back. Not just stand there on the sidelines, judging you and complaining that you have a problem. Without proper help and care, you just continue scraping along the tracks until the inevitable happens: you crash and burn!

"Then that's the end of it. There's no going back: you've reached the end of the line and it's time to think about the times when someone could have intervened and put things right. Someone, simply by doing their job with a little more care and attention, could have prevented all that pain and suffering you've been through.

"Not to mention the incredible waste of public money that's been spent trying to get rid of you instead.

"Since becoming ill with post-traumatic stress disorder I've seen at least five consultant psychiatrists, all working for the private sector. After hours of examination, each came out with a different opinion. Two of them completely contradicted each other. It was useless; you're ill, and they just see a fast buck. For all the money they received they only produced the most basic reports with broad, non-committal conclusions. They prey on the vulnerable.

"I started to feel like I was no more than a cash cow for these individuals to milk. Meanwhile, the train just kept rolling down the tracks, sounding its steam whistle, crying out for help, warning people ahead that the train is out of control.

"I look back into the distance; galloping along through clouds of dust ride the cowboys. Faster and faster they gallop to catch up with the train and initially there's a big sigh of relief that help is coming.

"But to my surprise they're not cowboys at all: they're barristers, lawyers and doctors, all coming to help.

"They're riding up close now, close enough to help me; it won't be long before everything's back on track. One by one, their horses gallop up alongside and they make the jump across to board the moving train. I breathe a sigh of relief – I'm going to be saved.

"Suddenly, something happens that I don't understand. One of them has just taken a load of booty and has jumped back onto his horse; he's now galloping off into the distance.

"I think to myself: that can't be right. Then another jumps back onto their horse, taking with them a fistful of dollars.

"One after another, these characters take their money and go, stripping the train of everything of value, leaving the great, rusty husk rolling down the tracks. Just as I'm about to crash into a half-finished tunnel, I look back and shout:

"'Hey, what about me? Aren't you supposed to be working with me?'

"But in this scenario, they don't seem to be able to hear me; I just hear a familiar sound in the distance. Through the clouds of dust I notice that another train is approaching, running off its rails. The barristers, lawyers and doctors are now riding alongside that one, getting ready to board her.

"The train shows all the signs of hope as the professionals jump across. Then the look of hope changes to one of despair as they flee, their pockets overflowing.

"So the system continues until it's all broken. As far as I'm concerned, it's the system itself that needs one big train crash so it can start again and this time focus on the victims and not just money." I suddenly stopped talking to see Beth watching me as I spilled out all my frustrations.

A quick check revealed that my pulse was racing and my speech had been getting louder and louder. Beth was looking a little shocked. I took some deep breaths to calm myself down before a clunk from the tape deck signified that the tape had ended. We both started talking at once.

"No, Beth, you go first; I think I've said enough for one session."

"I was just going to say that our time is almost up and I think we've had a good meeting today. I think you're successfully releasing a lot of frustration and that means good progress. I think you're coming along really well, and I hope you'll soon start to see the benefits of these sessions."

She took out the tape and put it in its plastic case before handing it to me.

"There you go, that's for you. If you get a chance, please listen to it. I don't know if you've got a player in your car or at home, but when you've got half an hour, stick it on and see how it makes you feel when you play it back."

I took the tape out of her hand, already knowing that it would be in a bin somewhere between here and the coffee shop within the next ten minutes. I made a big show of putting it safely into my jacket pocket and patting it gently.

"Thanks, I look forward to hearing it; maybe it will help me put all this anger into perspective." I got up to leave, just as a slight draught blew the curtain which moved with a flutter and caught my eye. For a second, I imagined Andrew Alton himself getting up and preparing to leave. I stared at the curtain a second too long.

"Are you feeling alright Simon?"

"What? Oh, yes, thanks: fine. Thanks for all your help and I'll see you again next week. Look forward to listening to the tape!"

"Bye."

★ ★ ★

CHAPTER ELEVEN

The Plan

"So, this is the story as I see it: this guy, Alton, has been following this woman, Kate Chandler, for several days. Always the same guy, always the same vehicle: follows her around and about the place – home, work, almost everywhere."

I looked down at my papers.

"As you already know, we checked out the number plate and went to visit the registered keeper. When we got there we met this ex-Special Branch officer, Andrew Alton; he was very hostile and made a point of taking us into his garage. He refused to answer questions and eventually pushed us out onto the lawn.

"We didn't get to the bottom of what was happening; however, we did give him a warning of harassment. The warning didn't seem to cause him any concern and he actually went on to make a complaint to P.S.D.

"We then found out that he has made numerous complaints about officers and that he has some serious grudge. This grudge he has borders on some kind of obsession and it looks like he might be mentally ill.

"Following our meeting with Alton, there has been no let-up in the extent of his harassment. In fact, we have now taken a statement from Miss Chandler, who states that the harassment has got worse.

"Two days ago, when she left her place of work, he was waiting outside, and as she left he made a gesture with his fingers, like he was shooting a pistol. This has caused her and her family a great deal of distress. She has now moved out of her home to go and live with relatives. Here's the statement: I wanted you to have a read of it and see what you think."

Sergeant Moore reached out and took the papers. He then settled back in his swivel chair, resting his outstretched feet on the open desk drawer. He checked all the pages were in number order and then began to read.

Realising that this would take a while, I sat down and looked out over Shirley High Street.

It was the beginning of October, and across the road, over the park, storm clouds were gathering. A blustery wind lashed at the trees. Branches swayed and whipped each other while, beneath their great canopies, people scurried about.

Along the busy road people ran into doorways as the rain began to pour, lashing against the windows and bouncing off the pavement. A sea of coloured umbrellas appeared, bobbing about, and people dodged each other at a quickened pace.

People kept to the building line, avoiding the splashes from buses, now fully laden and lit up against the foul weather, taking tired and weary passengers home.

The eye of the storm was now over the station, black and menacing, giving a foreboding sense of things to come.

My uneasy feeling crept back, like a cold hand turning in my stomach, and every moment that passed made me feel like I was being drawn further and further into the centre of a spider's web.

I was being drawn deeper into a battle; the first moves had been played, recorded on those pages the sergeant was now holding.

After several minutes, and some re-reading, he finally spoke.

"I think it's clear now, he should be arrested and we should hear what he has to say about the allegations. We can't allow this woman to suffer any more; did you say that she had gone to stay with a relative?"

Moore looked up from the file.

"Yes. For the time being she's with her uncle and she'll stay there until she gets any news."

"Okay, then, that's settled. How do you want to play it?"

Sergeant Moore passed the papers back. I noticed he had already got his head buried in a different file.

"I was hoping to have a word with you about that one. You see, I think that someone else should take up the case."

I noticed that he didn't look up.

"What do you mean?" He turned a page.

"I've got this feeling that this Alton chap is trying to make a point, cause a fuss and stir up a load of grief. I think that if I'm exposed to every stage, from the statement taking to the investigation, the arrest and interview: he will start to focus on me. I think he's mentally ill and this is going to backfire."

Moore looked up.

"All the more reason to keep you on it. You know all about the case, you've already got a feel for what's happening, and if it is going to go to rat shit, I want as few people as possible getting tied up. Besides, everybody is snowed under; I'm not prepared to pull them off another case just to pick up this one.

"Just try and get it all sorted as soon as you can. I don't want this going bad any more than you do."

Somehow, I seriously doubted that. Anything I faced, I would face alone.

The driving rain summed up my mood as I walked out the office and joined Tracey in the kitchen area. She was spooning coffee into a cup.

"What's wrong?"

"I tried to get out of it, but it appears that I'm stuck. He won't listen."

"What did Moore say?"

She handed me a coffee.

"He basically said that I will be dealing with it and that if it was going to go pear-shaped it's better that there's limited fallout."

"Well, you did your best. No one can say you didn't express your concerns."

Tracey took a sip and looked at me over the brim. Our eyes met and, for a brief moment, time seemed to stop.

A feeling of lust washed over me, like a wave crashing, but the wave disappeared when I saw the change in her eyes. Like a mother saying goodbye to a child: a mixture of sadness and concern, with a sense of the inevitable.

Children leave home, friends split up; people go on dangerous missions and come back changed.

The mood became intense. If I were to make a move, she wouldn't resist. I could run my hands all over her and it could only make the moment more passionate.

If I wanted her, this was the time, right here, right now; I thought about the property store. We could be totally alone in there; we could lock the door, the big solid door. Just the two of us and rows and rows of cigarettes and homemade videos.

A sexy goodbye in a dark and dingy store room. A single forty-watt light bulb and nothing but a cell mattress for comfort; just the proceeds of crime bearing down on us, casting their dark shadows over our bodies.

Or, maybe the room beyond the store – the tiny cell – no one ever goes in there; you could hide there for days.

Tracy's eyes were intense, alight, her chest pounding under her crisp white shirt. I looked deeper, thinking that now was the time to follow our instincts.

When the silence was broken, her lips didn't even move.

"Simon, can you come back up to the office for a minute?"

Sergeant Moore's head disappeared behind the door.

I disengaged from the intensity of the moment and left the room, following him up the corridor, my mind full to overflowing.

"I've just had a chat with Inspector Stewart, as I think he should be kept up to date with this Alton business. What's your plan for the arrest?"

"I think that if we just go round and knock on his door, he won't answer. He'll be aware that we're after him and he'll take advantage. He'll know that we're protecting the girl and we're tying up resources. I think he will go underground and leave us chasing our tails. I think if we're going to get him, we need to do an early morning job: six a.m., hit the place. Once we've got him, then at least we can use bail conditions. I don't want to be chasing his shadow for the next few weeks."

Sergeant Moore opened another file on his desk.

"Well, we're all on nights on Friday, apart from Andy Jones who's doing a day shift. We'll go with you to lock him up. Then you can liaise with Andy who'll do the interview. Just make sure you supply Andy with a good handover package. I want this bugger sorted so we can all get back to some police work."

The sergeant resumed reading a file; I took my cue to leave.

"Early on Saturday morning then, Sarge."

I walked out, closing the door behind me. I paused to gather my thoughts and decided to check on Kate.

★ ★ ★

CHAPTER TWELVE

Anthony Hudson

It was on a crisp and foggy autumn morning that I found myself on a second visit to see Anthony at his office.

A Police Discipline Tribunal was to be held later that month, and the purpose of this meeting was to start preparing a defence. The charge was one of having a criminal conviction of common assault. The task of my legal team, headed by Anthony Hudson, was simple: try to save my career.

I took an early train from Snow Hill to Marylebone, before fighting my way through the teaming mass of people on the Underground to arrive at Chancery Lane, the nearest tube station. As I walked the short distance along High Holborn, I looked skywards and noticed that the clouds above the Thames looked turbulent, almost menacing, giving the heavens an altogether darker hue than that of the cloudless blue sky I remembered from the summer.

The north wind howled down the ancient cobbled streets. The busy Londoners scurried about, scarves tight around their faces, protecting skin from the cold air.

Above the metal railings, leaves had mottled, spattered copper and brown: some clung hopefully to their branches until torn off at the stems and blown away, tumbling down alleyways to settle in dark corners.

I turned my collar up against the wind and picked my way through the narrow archway into the gardens. Across the quadrangle, over at the South Square, I saw my solicitor, Janet, waiting for me outside the lodge and rubbing her arms across her body against the cold.

I took her gloved hand and shook it in the formal way which had become our custom.

"Anthony's going to be ten minutes late. He's just phoned me to say he's leaving the High Court and is on his way now."

"Do you think his clerk will sort us out with a nice warm cup of coffee or something? I'm frozen."

"Oh, I should think so; they're very good at that sort of thing down here. I could do with thawing out a little, too."

As we headed across the grass, Janet began with her view on how she thought we should put the case.

"I've had another chance to have a good read of the file. I think your mental state at the time of the assault is one thing that the panel should consider." We came to an abrupt halt at the doorway which lead to Anthony's rooms.

"It seems to me that although they've always had ample opportunity to take such matters into account, they seem to take a rather unsympathetic line towards you and your illness. We have to appeal to their sense of moral justice if we want you to have a chance of keeping your job. Shall we?"

"Some hope," I thought out loud, as Janet held the door open for me and I began to ascend the twisting staircase.

Waiting for us at the top, dressed impeccably in his morning suit, was Anthony's clerk. With the style and grace of an English butler, the old retainer showed us into the office and then melted quietly away, only to appear five minutes later holding a tray of freshly-brewed tea.

In answer to the cold weather, a welcoming fire had been prepared and was roaring away in the hearth. Janet quickly took advantage of the old leather chair by its side; she sat down, opened her file, and began to pore over the plethora of reports and scribbled notes.

I stood by the flames to take advantage of the glorious heat: the fire, no doubt, had been lit ready for Anthony's return to his chambers. The old clerk never missed a thing, I thought to myself.

As I warmed my legs, I noticed that the stone above the grate had been stained with years of soot from previous fires and had blackened the spot where it had been carved. I looked closer and began to see the outline of a weird and monstrous creature. I had never seen anything like it before. After peering for a while to make out the hideous details, I became aware that Janet was trying to concentrate on preparing herself for the meeting. I drifted over to the windows, drew back the velvet curtain and peered down into the old square.

Although right in the heart of the city, it was an amazing thought that I was standing inside one of the most ancient and fascinating institutions in London. For the next few minutes I did nothing but stare across the gardens, soaking up the centuries of history buried within the very fabric of the place; the rituals and customs had left their marks on every staircase and within every recess. It felt like the misty autumn weather had driven its characters into their secret rooms to keep warm and pursue their business of law with a glass of good port by the fireplace.

It was mid-morning. The London courts were in session. The gardens were quiet and peaceful, carpeted with patches of red, green and gold. Everything looked so peaceful, but the walkway below had once been the scene of a famous duel between a Captain Greenwood and a Mr Ottway, way back in 1701. It was Mr Ottway who lost his battle and didn't live to tell the tale. As a car horn sounded from beyond the trees, it was hard to imagine the clashing of swords and the bloodshed witnessed that far-off day.

For centuries, the great and the good had milled around these walkways, going about their business, but it was during the reign of Elizabeth I that this place rose in prominence: it became notable for the amazing parties and festivals it hosted. Queen Elizabeth, as patron, would be hosting, within these very walls, great banquets at special times like Candlemas and All Hallows' Eve.

It was in this very hall that Anthony had been 'called to the Bar', an ancient ceremony – a sort of graduation for barristers; it would take place once they had taken part in the requisite number of dining-in nights, a tradition dating back to the days when barristers met together and students would pick up important elements of their education whilst dining. In order for the meal to count towards the twelve required for the qualification, the student had to remain in their seats until after the coffee was served.

I remember thinking to myself as I stood at his window – it was five years, almost to the day, since Anthony had notched up his twelve dining-in nights in the Great Hall, and what a privilege that must have been.

As grand as any stately home in the land, the seventy-foot room had an exquisitely ornate wooden ceiling, like the upturned hold of a medieval warship.

At the far end was a large wooden screen masking the entrance to the vestibule; at the other, a raised dais with a grand table where notables would dine. The screen had been a gift to the Inn from Queen Elizabeth while she was patron, and legend had it that it had been carved from the timber of a captured Spanish galleon of the Armada.

Light streamed through massive, ceiling-height windows, each stained with the coat of arms of an esteemed bencher.

Centuries past, the same autumn sun had lit up the stage where the up-and-coming playwright William Shakespeare performed his new comedy to her Majesty's raucous delight.

It seemed almost insignificant that I was here now, taking advice on such a small and humble matter. The door flew open and the fire leapt higher in the grate.

I let go of the drapes as Anthony swept into the room, his gown bellowing behind him. We exchanged a firm handshake before he tossed his wig on the desk and fell back into his chair, lowering his feet with a thud onto the blotting pad. With a theatrical motion he retrieved an apple from the top drawer, and with the look of a starving man took a great bite; he then turned his attention to Janet, who remained seated with her file open.

"Did you bring all the medical reports and the Occupational Health file?"

He took another bite and examined the exposed core.

"Yes, I've got them here," Janet said as she placed her papers in order.

I must admit that, looking through them …" She was halted by a knock on the door and a shout from Anthony.

"Come!"

The well-trained clerk returned, carrying Anthony's tea and a plate of custard creams.

"Thank you, Harry!" yelled Anthony, a little too loudly, already eyeing up the plate.

"As you were saying," he continued, selecting a biscuit.

"There are lots of notes here about Simon attending appointments at Occupational Health, but there isn't a great deal of information on what they were doing for him. It appears they saw him time and time again, but it seems that it was more a case of just watching him, with no real intervention and certainly no treatment. I note from the files that they have considered the fact that he may be suffering from what they call 'Post-Traumatic Stress Disorder', but they don't take any responsibility for him and are happy to rely on Simon's GP for all the answers. On the other hand, it appears that the GP relied on the fact that Simon was under the supervision of the psychiatrist at Lloyd House and believed that they had responsibility for him. All parties have been happy to pass the buck. So, in short, when Simon became ill, he found nothing but barriers."

Anthony took time in carefully selecting another custard cream, even though they were all identical.

"What would you say about that, Simon – the fact that they weren't able to help you?" The second biscuit was dunked.

"It makes me very angry to think that I've been ignored for so long and passed from pillar to post amongst a variety of health professionals who don't know or understand much about P.T.S.D.

"When I look back, I feel that I've let myself down, you know? I should have been more demanding."

"What do you mean, demanding?" Anthony paused, his biscuit half-dunked.

"Well, I've always had a great deal of faith in people – you know, a sort of blind faith that professional people will do professional jobs and care about people. I've just been naïve. My problem seems to be, when I go to see someone, I walk in, all polite, you know, shake hands, sit down and speak to them with respect and courtesy. I believed in them; I believed that they would do their examination, speak to me, ask relevant medical questions and want to help me. But no, I've been left feeling let down and ignored, time after time.

"I feel that nobody has wanted to know about the case, and behind all that superficial gloss of a caring smile there's nothing but empty words."

Anthony stood up and paced the room, hands behind his back.

"I think we can all agree that you've been passed around and no one's taken responsibility." He paused, back to the fire.

"But that's only the first hurdle," I continued. "I've had to suffer the army of psychiatrists who follow the criminal justice system like parasites, all busily preparing reports to suit their clients' needs. They are nothing but wordsmiths, peddling their trade in spinning yarns to say whatever their paymasters want. Each report can be written to be read either way, most are non-committal; I think they call them 'medico-legal' reports.

"Churning these out in their hundreds for an insatiable criminal justice system is bread-and-butter for any unscrupulous medic. Each report comes out the same as the last: meaningless drivel about your childhood, followed by a paragraph on their own non-committal opinion. These reports are the lifeblood of a system hellbent on making the most qualified in society a lot of money."

Janet was scribbling away, Anthony toasting his backside by the fire, deep in thought. I continued.

"You know, in the field of psychology, it isn't hard for someone to engineer a report to make any point you may wish. When you consider that each report earns hundreds of pounds, and the same organisations approach the same psychiatrists, it isn't hard to work out in whose favour the conclusion will be. It took a while, but after what seemed like an eternity of suffering this kind of thing, I finally got to see the system for what it was.

"The amazing thing is that nowadays, when I complain about this practise to other doctors, they usually smile and sheepishly admit that it does happen; they just see it as an inevitable part of the system, a sort of 'Statements for Sale' psychiatry.

"But, do you know what really gets to me, what makes me so angry? It's the fact that it's always the poor, innocent, desperate patient who suffers. They suffer through lack of help, no diagnoses, and lack of treatment. The patient leaves the consultation, confused and frustrated, while the consultant packs their briefcase into their shiny new car and heads off to their large house in the country.

"While the patient is neglected, they run all the way to the bank – no doubt to use the money to send their own kids to public school, so that one day they too can exploit the vulnerable."

I paused for breath, suddenly aware that my voice was raised. I was shaking. A shocked silence had fallen over the room. Anthony and Janet exchanged glances. It was Anthony who spoke first.

"Yes, I daresay it's quite possible that it happens more than one might think. But getting back to your own case: with the somewhat inadequate medical notes that we've been provided, I have to point out that a proper assessment into your Post-Traumatic Stress Disorder is one thing we do need."

He swallowed the last of his tea and picked up his fountain pen.

I used his silence as an opportunity to continue, to vent my anger at my lack of treatment. I seemed unable to stop the flood of emotion: the urge to offload was too strong.

"I often ask myself …"

I raised my head from my hands.

"How can this be possible, how can this happen to someone? Surely in a modern, decent society we can rely on our professionals to give us the care we need? You know, I think the answer lies in how the public sees the medical profession as a whole.

"For instance, there are some professions where a mistake or lack of judgement could cost you your job; like social work, for example. The case that springs to mind is the Baby Peter case in Haringey.

"The head of Social Services, the person in charge of safeguarding children, ended up getting fired, following the death of the child.

"Why? Well, the main reason, as far as I could see, was that Baby Peter had been known to Social Services and indeed had been visited by them on many previous occasions. So it follows that the department had some responsibility towards that child and therefore a duty of care. So, following on from that logic, someone didn't do their job properly, someone should be held accountable: therefore, someone should lose their job. Now, it should be the same with mental health care, because it's exactly the same; if the standard of care falls short, someone dies.

"Even if it's just one person – one person who has sought help and then goes on to take their own life, then it's a catastrophic failure. But would the general public ever expect a psychiatrist to be held accountable? Would there be a similar witch-hunt? The answer is no.

"So what would happen if there were two tragic suicides in the one health care area, straight after each other, perhaps both children? Would that create a problem for the local doctor? What if there was a whole 'suicide cluster', a situation with teenagers hanging themselves from trees in parks, would the psychiatrist be under any pressure to account? No, not at all.

"I'm thinking, of course, about Bridgend. In that area of Wales, they witnessed the largest teenage suicide cluster of modern times. Over two years, twenty-five young people committed suicide, all by hanging. Yes, it was a huge story at the time: the area had news crews descending on it from all over the world; headlines of "internet death cult" and "cyber-suicide ring" jumped out at you from every paper. But quickly it was forgotten.

"The public and the press moved on, leaving the families grieving, hurting, needing answers. Mothers sat in chairs at the fireside, clutching urns that contained ashes, reading letters from their health authority which tried to explain the terrible errors of judgement, the lack of resources and training.

"But has anyone tried to hold their doctors to account, or even their psychiatrists? Has anyone been fired? Have their careers ended in disgrace? No. And why not? Because, once again, the Establishment doffs its cap to the bloody medical profession – and why? Because these people are held in such high esteem by the rest of us, they simply can't be at fault."

Anthony looked sideways, his pen paused over his notes.

"The fact might be that they have failed in their duty of care; however, when it comes down to it, there is little in our employment law to enforce such a duty of care. I suppose it could be summed up as the difference between a good employer and a bad employer. What amount of resources does the Chief really want to put into the welfare of the employees? Or are they happy just to pay lip-service to the problems, while at the same time ignoring them?"

Anthony returned to his pad and scribbled away furiously.

I came round to my point.

"I've been looking on all the websites that deal with P.T.S.D. and reading about the treatment that's available. There's a doctor down here in London who specialises in members of the armed forces who show symptoms of P.T.S.D.

"Like any sufferer, they find themselves isolated, lonely, misunderstood and needing help, but until recently there was little for them. They just ended up being ignored until they could no longer cope.

"Did you know that about ten percent of the prisoner population in this country are veterans of the Iraq and Afghanistan campaigns? Service personnel coming back after fighting for our security, finding no help, no support, no understanding, just a bare cell and a prison bunk.

"Considering that a prison place costs the tax-payer £44,000 a year, the obvious alternative is better understanding and some compassion.

"Just like those soldiers, I feel I haven't been supported, the force has shown no understanding of the condition. I've seen no evidence to suggest that the police force understands anything about P.T.S.D., let alone care. There's a general ignorance, from the police doctors all the way up to the top.

"But I can tell you now, I'm determined to fight this case – then I'll continue to fight for other officers who find themselves in the same position.

"I've found an organisation called 'Trauma Support Network'. They specialise in the treatment of P.T.S.D. I gave them a ring and spoke to one of the ladies that run it, a lady called …"

I reached inside my jacket pocket and pulled out a piece of paper.

"Bethany Goodchild."

I put the note back into my pocket.

"She explained the procedure over the phone, and I must say she sounds really nice. She's just spent two months lecturing at some university in Ohio, and she's about as up-to-date as they come.

"She explained to me the system that they have over there. First, you go for an assessment, about three hours in length. She takes you through the incidents that have caused the issues and you discuss the effects they have had on you. Then, once the assessment is done and her report is written up, she'll recommend the course of treatment that's most appropriate. That could be something called 'Trauma-Focused Cognitive Behavioural Therapy', which normally takes place over twenty sessions."

"And what are the costs involved?"

Anthony paused and looked up.

"The initial assessment will cost £150 and it all goes from there. But I'm more than happy to pay for the assessment myself. As it stands, the police are refusing to acknowledge any medical condition and once the diagnosis is made I think we should insist that they take responsibility for the treatment. For that, Anthony, I'd be prepared to take them to court. I refuse to let them ignore this; it was this type of ingrained ignorance that caused the problem in the first place – for Andrew Alton himself. He was ill, he needed help, but they just threw him out of the force without any thought for the consequences."

"When do you think you'll be able to get an appointment to see this, err… "

"Bethany," Janet interrupts.

"This Bethany?"

"The first appointment she's got for an assessment is next month, so the sooner I book it, the better."

"Okay then, Simon. That's agreed: give this woman a bell and book yourself in for an assessment; let's show them that we mean business. Now, with the time we've got left, I want to have a chat about your appeal. I've sent Janet my written advice about the matter and I have to say that the chances of winning are no more than fifty-fifty. Are you sure that your instructions are still to press ahead with the appeal?"

★ ★ ★

CHAPTER THIRTEEN

The Arrest

Friday night passed into Saturday morning much as it would have done in most towns and cities across the country. Like elsewhere, Solihull had witnessed a rapid expansion of licensed premises and alcohol-related disorder had risen as a consequence.

High Street venues competed with each other, using ever more aggressive marketing practices. Huge blackboards appeared on the pavement, displaying special promotions to tempt the weekend stag parties and rowdy hen nights.

No longer were binge drinkers knocking back pints of beer and sweet white wine. Now there was a whole range of colourful, eye-catching drinks in exotic bottles, lined up in front of mirrors, lit up with bright lights, tempting drinkers to new horizons. Towards the end of the evening, the customers moved on to hitting the spirits with the result that, at closing time, they all streamed out of the clubs in one heaving mass of humanity – into the cold night air to continue their revelling.

At two a.m. that night, the High Street was crowded. Some people were dancing, others were kissing; two people cuddled in a phone box. The ring road, which just a few hours earlier had resembled a graveyard, was packed with noisy cars and aggressive drivers sounding their horns.

Up the road from where I sat, a taxi driver gesticulated as another turned his vehicle in the road, impatiently honking at his horn as a party of revellers spilled out into his path. A swirling mass of teenagers made their way towards the only chip shop open at that hour. Some of them fell over; friends stopped to pick them up, all unsteady, holding beer cans aloft and singing football songs.

A teenage girl, leaning over an overflowing rubbish bin, was violently and noisily sick. A fight started in a bus shelter across from her: one man was knocked out cold; two officers ran across and found him flat out on a bed of chip papers. An ambulance siren came from the distance, becoming louder above the shouts and screams.

A drop of rain appeared on my windscreen, too light for anyone to notice or care.

I remained seated, cocooned in the warmth of the police car. I had no appetite to get out and engage the rabble. In a few hours I had a job to do. I could not afford to get tied up with all the paperwork involved in arresting a drunk.

Heavier drops of water came out of the air. They ran down the glass and distorted the colours of the street lights, creating a kaleidoscopic, fairy-grotto scene, but not a grotto from a nursery rhyme you learnt in school. This was a different kind of fairy grotto, where the elves had discovered the secret of the falling-down water and were on the loose in a frenzy of mischief-making.

All the elves would need a good eight hours sleep before they could change back into good fairies and join the human race in the morning.

"These people are drinking like this to escape from their own lives." I imagined Tracey's voice from the empty seat beside me. "Alcohol allows them to break loose from their personal and professional responsibilities – or maybe just give them a reward for simply getting through another dull and boring working week."

My hand touched the arm rest.

The rain was heavier now, thank the Lord; it washed bright colours down the windscreen. I felt all alone. Once again, a feeling like a cold hand stirred in my stomach – a feeling of being trapped and helpless washed over me, like I was about to enter into a battle I didn't want. All attempts to avoid it had failed. I was about to face someone who was lying in wait for me, like a snake curled on a branch, watching, waiting to release its venomous anger at me.

Anger ingrained into him by a system he despised, a system that abandoned him and now he wanted vengeance – and I was the prey.

I found myself wishing that Tracey was with me, she'd know what to do.

I looked at my watch. Tracey would be finishing her packing, doing those last-minute checks: passport, visa, tickets. A couple more days and she'd be gone, starting her new life in Port Phillip. Perhaps I should have gone with her and started my own new life, with all that sun, that oceanic climate. I closed my eyes and allowed myself to drift away, picturing the two of us together.

The sudden bang on the window brought me back with a start.

"Give us a kiss, sweetheart." A woman's face filled the window, lips pursed with bright pink lipstick, top pulled down, squeezing her cleavage upwards.

"Leave him alone, Sheryl, he'll put you in his handcuffs." A woman behind her was eating from a tray of chips covered in curry sauce.

Shrieks of laughter filled the air and the group skittered down the road in their high heels. I checked their progress in the mirror; the tall one hitched her skirt up above her waist flashing her pink thong. I looked back through the windscreen, up the High Street and towards the bright lights.

Light shone through the droplets and, for a split-second, I saw Tracey's image splashed across the glass. I reached forward and touched the windscreen just as the image disintegrated before my eyes, running down in streaks and draining of all colour.

I sat back, lost in thought. If she was here now I'd probably promise my life to her, promise everything to her, plead with her, even take her into that property cupboard and throw caution to the wind – go right past that point of no return and let fate take its course.

Or is it that, just at this moment in time, I felt emptier than I'd ever felt before. Just like those binge-drinkers out there, dancing and singing outside those clubs, I was looking for a chance to escape.

The alarm on my watch told me it was time for me to return to Shirley and prepare for the morning's raid. The chip shop opposite the station didn't close until four, so I stopped off for a couple of lamb samosas and some pakoras. Back in the parade room I laid these out, together with their sauces, next to my files and devoured them with gusto as I finalised the details to give to the early turn.

Within the hour, everyone involved would be meeting here and I needed to brief them to make sure that the next part went according to plan.

First to arrive was Adrian Taylor, my new working partner, now that Tracey was leaving the force. Then came the officers from the other mobile, Mike 4, and finally Inspector Stewart arrived alongside Sergeant Moore.

With everyone sat around the table with a cup of coffee, it was time for me to begin the briefing.

I looked from face to face before clearing my throat and starting to read.

"Hello, everybody, and welcome to Shirley. This morning's operation will start in approximately one hour. It is our intention to attend the Maybrook Road on the Blythe Way estate and arrest Andrew Alton for an offence of harassment.

"Some of you already know a bit about this job, but this briefing will hopefully fill in the gaps and bring everyone up to speed.

"The facts are that Shirley police station had a complaint from a lady called Kate Chandler. She reported that over the past few weeks she's been followed around by a man. This man has taken photographs and video recordings of her and, due to the vehicle he uses, we believe this man to be a certain Andrew Alton.

"We've already been to see this man and given him a first-stage harassment warning, but it appears that the harassment has continued and, in fact, got worse. The latest incident involved him making the shape of a pistol with his fingers and pretending to shoot at her, which, you can all imagine, has left her very distressed. She has moved away to stay with relatives until this man is arrested.

"Ladies and gentlemen, this Andrew Alton is an ex-West Midlands police officer who worked in the Special Branch for most of his career. He was a surveillance operative and, as we have discovered, worked on a lot of very high-profile cases throughout the Midlands.

"Following his retirement on ill-health grounds a while ago, he has become fixated with vendettas against his previous employer. He is a serial complainer against the West Midlands police force as a whole and appears to hold a serious and dangerous grudge. It's true to say that he will be looking for any reason whatsoever to catch us out and then make one god-almighty fuss about it.

"Due to his somewhat erratic mental state, we must be on our guard at all times, particularly inside the house: remember, we watch each other's backs. We know from our previous visits that he has cameras fitted around his garage, and there's no doubt that there are other cameras and recording equipment in the house. There's every chance he might try and antagonise us or provoke us into saying or doing something unprofessional, with the objective of recording it and using it as a complaint. So just be careful. None of us relish the thought of Professional Standards breathing down our necks for the next six months.

"So that's our man, Mr Andrew Alton. Are there any questions?"

"Yeah, where do you want us?" John, from Mike 4, leant back in his chair.

"You two will cover the rear of the house, just in case he tries to make a run for it. I've got plans of the road here." I passed copies round the table and waited for them to study them before I spoke.

"As you can see, the back of the house is difficult to get to. I wouldn't be surprised if he considered running for it – if anything, just to frustrate us. So your job will be to scramble over that fence and rugby tackle him in his pyjamas."

"Okay then, everybody," Inspector Stewart put his copy down and gave a gentle cough, signifying it was his turn to speak.

"You've heard what's been said. You've heard that this Alton fella can be unpredictable and dangerous. Make sure you bear that in mind when you're with him, particularly alone, and with any luck this will all be done and dusted within an hour. Good luck folks, we'll see you there."

Within five minutes, the three police cars in the rear yard had their engines running. A convoy began leaving the station in the direction of Blythe Way.

Adrian and I were in the first car, followed by the supervision and then Mike 4 bringing up the rear; it would be their job to stop short of the premises and guard the rear, just as the first two cars pulled up at the front.

Soon, we had entered the Blythe Way estate. We worked our way through the winding roads until we arrived at the entrance to Maybrook. Mike 4 took up position while we drove in to the cul-de-sac, pulling up outside number five.

The road was perfectly still. Nothing but a slight breeze in the trees stirred at that sleepy hour of the morning.

The sky above us was a deep, dark blue – almost black – and a cloud lay over one side of the moon, creating a silver smudge high above the roof. The old oak tree stood black against the sky, its branches reaching out, protecting the house from the limitless sky above.

We were now in the middle of the road and could be seen by anyone who happened to be looking out. Still nothing moved; only a cat prowled across a lawn before stopping under a porch, licking its paw.

I stepped out and approached the door, followed by Adrian. I looked back to see the supervision car, its windows open, the Inspector in the passenger seat. He nodded and gave the thumbs up. I realised they would not be joining us at the door but would watch events from the police car, a good ten meters away.

As Adrian joined me, I knocked on the front door, stood back and instinctively eyed the garage door, waiting for it to open and for Alton to appear. A bedroom light went on. There were sounds of movement. A key turned in the lock; the chain removed; a bolt undone. The door slowly opened and there, lit by a dim table light behind him, stood Andrew Alton.

I couldn't tell whether he had been expecting us or not. I just know that as I spoke he continued to look over my shoulder, observing the road and the two police cars.

"Andrew, we need to talk to you about a complaint of harassment made by a lady called Kate Chandler. She states that you've been following her. You received a warning about this behaviour, but she reports that you have continued. I am therefore arresting you on suspicion of harassment."

Alton turned his back and started up the stairs. He, like any other police officer, would know the drill. Now he was under arrest, we would follow him, stay with him while he got dressed, and not let him out of our sight.

The landing and his bedroom were dark, all decorated with dark blue wallpaper with silver dots, which gave it the appearance of the sky outside. He pulled his trousers on and grabbed a shirt.

"I need the toilet; I need to take a piss."

He brushed past me and opened the toilet door. I took the door and held it as he entered, knowing that he must be watched. He looked over my shoulder. As I turned, I saw Adrian standing across the landing, looking out of the window.

Alton took the opportunity; Adrian was out of earshot.

"You'll pay for this. If I ever see you again you're . . ."

His husky voice was a whisper; his tone signified he meant it. This was not an idle threat by a petty criminal who curses the uniform – we're all used to those.

No, this was different. This was the voice of someone who was resourceful, vengeful. Someone with a point to prove.

Adrian had broken the first rule of dealing with a prisoner. He had relaxed, taken his eye off the ball. Alton had spotted the opportunity and was going to take full advantage.

He brushed past me. A camera sound came through the dark. I knew at once that a camera was recording on the landing. He was trying to set me up, trying to provoke a reaction.

I thought of the officers outside, sat in their car, chatting about football. I looked at Adrian, still oblivious, examining an ornament on the shelf.

"Adrian, stay with him."

I stormed down the stairs and out onto the lawn, the Inspector met me halfway.

"Gaffer, Alton's playing up, trying to create problems, I think you should come inside."

As we turned, Adrian was escorting Alton, now on his best behaviour, out of the house.

"Good morning, Sir," a polite Alton addressed the Inspector.

The Inspector looked at me then at him, a look of irritation passed over his face.

"Let's all get back to the police station as quick as we can shall we?"

He got into his car and sped off around the corner leaving us standing there.

Throughout the journey to the station I sat in the back with Alton. His eyes never left me: those angry, soulless eyes. I could see in my peripheral vision those hateful eyes boring into the side of my face.

The tension was tangible: you could have cut through the atmosphere with a bread knife. There was nothing I could do but sit there.

Somewhere in his past, Alton had been left out in the cold by an organisation that simply didn't care, now someone was going to pay the price

Psychiatrists sometimes call it 'hand-me-down hurt', and I was about to inherit.

★ ★ ★

CHAPTER FOURTEEN

Off Sick

Silence fell as the tea tray was removed. Only when the panelled door was firmly shut did I continue.

"My doctor signed me off with stress after I'd explained about the problems at work. I then received a letter asking me to attend Headquarters for an appointment with the force psychiatrist, Dr Stale."

Although I'd given these details before, for the court, both Anthony and Janet were scribbling away furiously: Anthony leaning over his rosewood desk, Janet with her papers spread out on her knees.

"How did you feel about that appointment?"

"I was quite happy; it seemed the normal course of action. I had met Dr Stale before and I knew him quite well, I trusted him. I thought that we would have a chat and he would suggest some form of help – perhaps a review of medication or something. As he was aware of the case, it was reassuring to know that it would be him I was going to see."

"And what happened during that consultation?"

Anthony turned a page in his leather-bound folder.

"The first thing that unnerved me was the lack of eye contact. We'd always had good meetings in the past, but this was awkward; something was praying on his mind. But, because I knew and trusted him, I opened up, talked about my lack of sleep and my anxiety, my reliance on alcohol.

"Out of nowhere he shot me a warning glance. I went quiet, stumbling over my words. He picked up his pen and said my condition was very complicated and therefore hard to treat. He then told me he was signing me fit-for-work. I told him he was making a mistake and why didn't he help me?"

"Why do you think he acted in that way?"

"I've no doubt that he'd been told to do it, told to get people back to work."

"Told? But he's supposed to be the doctor." Janet showed her frustration.

"There had been a number of incidents where officers who were off sick were treated very badly. Pressure came from the top and people like him wanted to keep their nice, cosy jobs – so they acted like puppets, jumping because they were told to jump.

"You see, like everywhere, the police are all about targets. And when targets are set, mistakes happen. That's the unseen cost of the target culture. But the odd casualty is a price worth paying. I believe that I was one of the officers who were given the ultimatum: go back to work or leave the force."

"How did you feel after that meeting with Dr Stale?" Janet was now pursuing the line of questioning.

"Let down. Abandoned. I had opened up to the person I trusted. To me, it was an obvious case of putting targets before care. I suppose what hurt most was the fact that he never tried to hide it. No examination, no questions, no empathy, just his signature on a form. I looked directly at him, but he never met my gaze. His eyes remained fixed on the desk."

"What happened then?" Anthony cut across Janet.

"After that shock, I complained. I had a meeting and we all agreed that an independent assessment was needed. I pointed out that if Dr Stale had signed his form already, then it would be pointless going to see his colleague. As Dr Stale was the actual psychiatrist, it was almost inconceivable that a colleague would disagree with him. But even though we agreed that an independent assessment was necessary, I was sent to see his colleague."

"What happened then?"

"Well, I attended the appointment. I wanted to do my best to cooperate. I suppose I was hoping that together we could line up some help, get some breathing space – you know, get back on track.

"I hadn't slept the night before. I'd just got this feeling they wanted me out. I went into the room, but again, the atmosphere seemed wrong from the start. I felt that the outcome of the meeting had already been decided. There was no warmth. He had his statement prepared and never looked at me.

"I knew he'd been a doctor in the Army, and boy, could you tell. He treated his patients like soldiers under his command. I suppose that's why he wanted to work for the police: a love of discipline; perhaps no one else would have him.

"He wasn't used to listening and he didn't want to help. It's a good job there are still places such a doctor can find employment – thank God for the police."

"So, take us through the meeting." Anthony was a little impatient, one eye on the clock.

"Sorry, yes, well, I went into his office, he was sat firmly behind the desk and a chair was on the opposite side. He made a meal out of arranging his papers before sitting up straight and telling me that he'd read Dr Stales's report and he agreed with it. I let out a snigger, as there was a comical feel to the futility of this meeting. I went on to explain that there seemed to be a problem with the lack of understanding.

"He looked at me for the first time and calmly told me that I was the one with the problem.

"I couldn't work out if I was angry, furious, upset or having a panic attack. I felt my throat tightening and a shortness of breath. I became dizzy and started to shake. I stood up and took one step towards a cupboard; I leaned over to catch my breath. On a pile of papers stood this model – some anatomical section of the lower spine. I remember focusing on it, then it felt like I'd been hit by a steam train."

Anthony flicked through his file.

"Yes, I've got the photographs of the office here. Now, just help me out with these, if you would. I can see the cupboard in this photograph, and I can see the pile of papers with the anatomical model of the spine. Is that where the spine was when you entered the office?"

"Yes, Anthony, that's where it was when I entered the office, that's where it remained all the time. It never left that pile of papers."

"But he said in court that you'd swung it at him."

"Yes, that's right. When officers came into the room, he pointed to the spine on the side and told them that I'd tried to pick it up. Officers verified that it was on the cupboard and so did the scene-of-crime photographs. It was when the doctor gave a statement some hours later that the story had changed into something different, something that made a better case."

"How did he explain that the spine was still on the pile of papers if you'd been swinging it?"

"He said that, in the seconds before he left the room, he tidied up, put it back. Yes, I know it sounds far-fetched, but it was the only thing he could say."

"Well the scene-of-crime examination should have shown where and how you handled it."

"Yes it would. They took the spine away but they didn't examine it, you see they knew my fingerprints were never on it."

★ ★ ★

CHAPTER FIFTEEN

Nightmare

I know where I am: I'm at the bottom of the garden, looking for the gate.

It's very well hidden, years of neglect has left it overgrown and rusted up. But I know I'm close. A patch of honeysuckle has grown over it; I pull aside the great trumpeting flowers and see the notice.

'Danger' daubed in red paint.

The hinges and locks are rusted solid, they won't give way; I see a hole where a wooden knot has fallen out. Looking through, the view is obscured by more bushes but I hear someone approaching. As the noise gets louder, I can see it's the gardener walking towards me, wearing an old leather waistcoat and carrying a shotgun.

I ask him to open the gate. He stops and takes two cartridges out of his pocket. I watch as he breaks the shotgun and inserts them. As he turns, I step back in horror; I have never been more terrified.

His face has no features. Skin covers the places where his eyes and mouth should be. He raises the barrel and brings it towards the hole.

As I peer through, the barrel joins the hole. Everything goes black. I realise what's happening and prepare for the blast.

When the trigger is pulled it doesn't make the normal sound; more like a telephone. I prepare my face for another blast. My eyes screw tight. Why is the gun making that ringing sound?

I sat bolt upright and found myself in bed in a cold sweat. I heard the phone ringing again, high-pitched, shrill. I reached out to grab it. The base unit fell with a crash.

"Hello?"

"Hi, it's Tracey – remember me?"

I tried to focus on the clock, completely disorientated; I couldn't work out if it was morning, noon, or night.

"Look, sleepy-chops, I'll help you out. It's three o'clock in the afternoon and you should be up."

My eyes focused on the clock. She was right: the display told me it was just after three.

"Hi, Trace." Still a little dazed, I could feel myself waking up. I threw the duvet off, swung my legs out, and sat up, rubbing my eyes.

"Me? Well, thanks for asking, I'm fine. It's the rest of them."

I got to my feet and padded through to the bathroom, where I looked at my face in the mirror.

"What are you up to, ringing me at this ungodly hour?"

"I wanted to ask how things went last night – you know, locking up that bloke."

I closed my eyes and gave a heavy sigh. I'd been hoping that it was all a bad dream that had just ended with a telephone ringing. But Tracey had brought me back to reality.

Her voice began to have a soothing effect and I felt an overwhelming desire to see her. She was the only person who seemed to understand and could sense the effect that the case was having on me.

"Listen, Trace, are you going to be around in about one hour's time?"

"Well, I can be," she replied in a way that sounded like she felt the same.

"I've got to get some last-minute things together for my flight so I could meet you in town if you like."

"Great. I tell you what: I'll make myself look beautiful and I'll meet you in Starbucks at four."

"How will I know you?"

"I'll be the one wearing the pink carnation with a copy of the Times under my arm."

"Okay, I'll be there. Agent Tracey Collins signing off, over and out."

The phone went dead. I dabbed my face with a towel, opened the bathroom cabinet and took out my razor.

★ ★ ★

I noticed that while Beth was listening she was busy taking notes.

When I paused, she leant forward and rested her file on the coffee table between us.

"With your permission, I'd like to run these details past my colleague, Jean. She works here most days, you may have seen her: she's got the rather striking pink hair."

"Yes, now you mention the pink hair, I think I've seen her around."

"Jean's an expert in imagery rehearsal, which is the treatment we use to reduce the effects of nightmares in cases like yours."

Beth paused for my reaction. I considered her proposal for a moment.

"I've got no problem with that. Please feel free to discuss the subject with any person you feel fit, you have my complete permission."

Beth picked up her pad and resumed leaning back in her chair.

"I think it would be worthwhile seeking her input. As you may be aware, there are various interpretations of dreams, their symbolisms and meanings. In fact, I've learnt a lot from Jean over the past couple of years, in particular regarding rapid eye movement dreams or R.E.M... I don't know if you've ever come across the phrase."

"It's something I've heard about on a radio program, and I know there's some rock band with that name but I don't really know much about it as far as my dreams are concerned."

Beth could see I was struggling.

"It's activity in the brain that can bring about R.E.M sleep. Research shows that the eye movements a person makes during this sleep correspond reasonably well with the content of the dream that the person is having. Circuits in the brain which have become particularly agitated by recent use are likely to be active and run thoughts and memories, stimulating R.E.M. Therefore, dreams tend to express events that are most important in any individual's life.

"Let me give you an example: let's say, a person who might be waiting to go into hospital for an operation may experience their first dream about two or three days before they go in. The dream is unlikely to involve detailed images of scalpels or the operating theatre but more likely, vague images developed into a story by overactive brain circuits.

"There are also dreams that are common to people in general, and there are well-documented ideas that surround these. Let's say, for example, the 'tooth dream', where people literally dream about losing their teeth. Theories about this dream include occasions when no one is listening to you, or maybe you're being overlooked at work. It's also been connected to people who are getting anxious about the natural ageing process and are feeling vulnerable and insecure.

"You've clearly been let down by your colleagues and they've put you in a very vulnerable position. You put your trust in people you thought would help you and you've been let down. As a result, you've become ill, and that in turn has made you feel that you're letting everybody else down. You've started to blame yourself for everybody else's failures, thinking that somehow you should have intervened and rescued the situation.

"But the fact is, it was for others to intervene, and you couldn't do anything to help these people. Every story you tell me about your experiences in the police, you feel that you should have done more, but the reality is that you couldn't. Like the Jackie story you talk about, where she ends up seriously ill on a mental unit and the offender walks the streets at night, laughing.

"You feel guilty, thinking you should have done more to save her. But I'm telling you that, on your own, you couldn't.

"The criminal justice system is full to overflowing with individuals, all with their own opinions, prejudices, targets, vested interests – you were exposed to too many of their failures and, because you cared, your health started to break down. The very people whose job it was to support you failed and you went into a downward spiral.

"You embarked on a journey where you met barrier and barrier. No one was prepared to listen. But, as we've seen, the dreams you experience don't come with images of cases collapsing and victims being failed. Your dreams involve characters from this book that you've been telling me about, the one Ben read before killing himself.

"When you picked up the Alice book, your brain recognised the images and began to weave them into your nightmares. Everything got jumbled up and kept playing itself back, like a record with its needle stuck in the groove. Remember you told me that you went to the local library to search out that book, to read it and try and piece together Ben's last thoughts? Well, going back to the book and reading it only made the images more vivid and helped develop the scenes that are now repeating themselves in your sleep.

"It may well be that, when you see Jean, she'll ask you to bring the Looking Glass book in and discuss it with her. This should help you to understand that these characters are fictional, from a children's book, and not the monsters that you see.

"The work she will do will help you detach Alice from what has really upset you: the image you have in your head of Ben and the problems with Andrew Alton. Jean will take the images apart, piece by piece, decide which bits are real and which are fantasies, and then, together, we will work on the real bits, leaving the fantasy to fade away."

I thought for a moment.

"Okay, Beth, just let me know when. I still have a copy of the book."

Beth gave a satisfied smile and jotted down a note to remind her.

"Right, that's settled. In order to help, would you mind going over the details again of your dream, and with your permission I'd like to tape it."

"No, by all means: go ahead. I have no objections at all."

Beth unwrapped a new tape and placed it in the machine beside her. I closed my eyes and leant back, transporting myself to White Gables. After a short pause, I heard her voice.

"Okay then, Simon – what can you see?"

"I'm in the dusty loft. Ben's body hangs by a rope. There are boxes everywhere and I can't find the hatch to get down out of the attic. It's very warm. I can see that I am naked and I feel very alone and frightened. I can hear a child softly whispering something about a nearby forest, but I can't make out the words. The sound is coming from each corner – as though there's four speakers concealed in the dark, playing the voice over and over. I'm moving boxes around and getting into a panic trying to locate the loft hatch. I start to think that I'll never get out. I'm throwing boxes into the air as the child's voice gets louder, filling the loft with whispering. I'm now kicking the boxes about in a frenzy in my bid to find the hatch and escape. Then at last I see the hatch and pull it up. The ladder is missing, I have to jump down. The fall seems to last forever, as though I'm going down through the floors, landing after landing, further and further into some underground world beneath the cellars."

I paused all of a sudden, aware that the images in my head were so vivid and lifelike, I didn't want to continue. Beth leaned across.

"How long was it, after the start of your problems, that you started having the dream of falling?"

"I think that the nightmares coincided with the time when things got really bad. I remember waking up in the middle of the night in cold sweats, you know, having to go downstairs and make a cup of coffee. It was a really bad time."

"The dream of falling shows that you are very distressed. It tells me that, at this time, your whole world is going wrong: the falling is a sign that you may be just about to suffer a complete breakdown. Do you wake up at that point or do you carry on dreaming?"

"The dream normally continues. I find that I come to a stop at what looks like the long landing, where we first saw the ladder. I head off in the direction of the stairs. As I pass each one, the pictures on the stairway seem to come alive – the faces moving and their mouths talking. Each one having its own animated discussion. The noise of all these conversations is horrendous: each one talking over the other.

"Standing in its place in the hall, the grandfather clock has developed a human face. Its hands are spinning around its face, opposite directions, the keys on the piano moving up and down, playing a tune, the stool is empty. I run through the living room, past the woman curled up in an oversized rocking chair, weeping and weeping as she rocks back and forth.

"I continue through the French windows, calling out for Tracey. Last time I saw her she was sitting under the roses in the arbour. But now the bench is empty. I run around the garden screaming her name, running over flowerbeds, searching behind stone pillars and around the hedges.

"I see the archway in the hedge at the bottom of the garden – within it there's an old wooden door, the word 'danger' painted across it. I'm desperately trying to find Tracey, so I ignore the stupid sign. With a sturdy kick, I have the door off its hinges. This time the gardener is nowhere to be seen. I pull aside the honeysuckle and woodbine.

"Beyond the gateway, I see green meadows stretching off to the horizon, a forest in the foreground, and a winding stone path that leads to its edge.

"I take the path , calling out Tracey's name as I walk. Then, just like Alice saw in the book, a young fawn wanders by; it looks at me with large, gentle eyes, but then starts back a little, before standing, staring at me.

"I approach the young thing and stroke its soft neck. But, just as I'm talking to it, asking its name, a clap of thunder sounds above the forest. The fawn takes one last look before darting off. There was something familiar about it – although it had four legs and caramel fur, it had Jackie's face.

"Before I reach the forest another fawn comes wandering up, but again, starts back when I reach out. I take hold of it and stand a while, my arms wrapped around its neck. I look into its eyes: I see Ben's face staring back at me. Again, a clap of thunder, far away, and it too darts away.

"I enter the wood and find myself walking beneath the overhanging branches. I see two identical finger signs, pointing in opposite directions. As I try to make sense of them, the letters re-arrange themselves into made-up words, words that are nothing but nonsense. I watch carefully as they do it again; then again; then I finally give up any chance of sensible directions and walk on, deeper into the wood.

"In front of me, under a tree, with their arms round each other's necks, are those characters, you know, from the book: Tweedle Dee and Tweedle Dum. I recognise their faces from pictures, their fat faces and those schoolboy grins. But it's what they're wearing that's most peculiar.

"They're wearing white laboratory coats and have stethoscopes around their necks. Immediately behind them is a road sign with fingers pointing off in every direction, including where I've just come from. I decide to ask for help.

"I say, 'Excuse me, Doctor, but which is the best way out of this wood, it's getting very dark.'

"'Can't you read a finger sign?' snarls one, and the other laughs out loud before they link arms and do their merry little dance. The letters on the finger posts are changing themselves round again, spelling words that don't even exist.

"'Can you tell me which path to take before it gets too dark?' I say a little louder. This time they don't seem to hear me, so I move my face closer and repeat myself. I don't think they can see me as they continue dancing round each other; I'm starting to feel invisible.

"Then, all of a sudden, another thunder clap, and at the first drop of rain, they stop dancing and cover themselves, sharing a big umbrella.

"'I'm getting very wet with all this rain,' I say, getting soaked through.

"'It's not raining, at least not under here, anyhow,' snarls the one with a wolfish grin.

"'But it may rain outside,' squeaks Number Two.

"'It can if it chooses,' replies Number One

"Stupid, useless idiots, I say to myself, as I walk off, following the first turn. I look back to see their arms linked, dancing around one way, then the other, making the most terrible shrieks, white coats flapping in the breeze.

"I've walked for some time and come to the far edge of the forest. I look out from underneath the last of the branches.

"I can see right across this new country and there are a number of brooks running across the meadows from side to side, the grass between them divided into squares by narrow hedges that run from brook to brook. It looks like a giant chess set together with its pieces, like the one Ben had beside him when he died.

"I look down on the squares, expecting to see movement on the board, and then, one by one, the pieces walk on and take to their squares for the start of the game. First the red set, led by the King and Queen; then the bishops, knights and castles.

"The white pieces follow, lining up the other side: a great procession of pomp and royalty walking to the sound of a great fanfare of trumpets.

"But as I survey the scene from up on the hill, I see that everything is not as it seems. It's not a normal chess set by any means. The Kings and Queens are in the correct reds and whites, but they're dressed as Judges with huge horsehair wigs trailing behind them. The bishops are like barristers, carrying paper files held with lengths of pink ribbon. The knights are doctors with surgical masks and plastic face-shields, rearing up on their huge chargers. The castles are police officers with oversized police hats the size of bicycle tyres, making them look like old-style Russian border guards in a Bond film.

"All the pieces are in place except the pawns; those squares are empty, and you can't play the game of chess without pawns.

"Then, with the bellowing of orders from the guards, sixteen cowering fawns creep in and take their places on the empty squares. Some try to back off but are whipped into place until they stand perfectly still, trembling, waiting for the start of the dreaded game.

"The red King lifts his arm high into the air. Another fanfare sounds and a red handkerchief falls from the royal hand.

"The game has begun.

"Suddenly, from a rear square, a red knight gallops over a hedge; as it lands, its great hoof crushes a fawn's skull. Blood flows from its broken skull and it's carried away to the sound of raucous cheering.

149

"The white knight replies, his steed prancing high above a frightened fawn, his sword crashing down across the animal's spine. The animal seems to fold in two; cheering fills the air and the stretcher is rushed on.

"As the scene gets bloodier and bloodier, food is brought on by a column of servants; roast meats piled high onto tables that start to creek under the weight.

The characters continue their game as, one by one, the animals are slaughtered, carried off, some fighting for breath. The teams continue baying for blood, screaming like banshees, waving paper files above their heads, pink ribbons flying like standards.

"Then the trumpeters sound the fanfare and the pieces stop still. Knights reign in their horses.

"'Dinner is now served,' the red Queen bellows.

"The chess pieces run to the dinner table and pile their plates high with slices of bread soaked in gravy. Some characters carve away at meat joints, biting into chicken legs and throwing the bones over their shoulders to the hungry dogs.

"As the last of the surviving fawns pick themselves up and limp off, the party finally breaks up.

"Each character, slow and weary due to the feasting, stops and fills their pockets from a sea-chest overflowing with gold coins. One by one, they bow low to the Queen and make their way to their carriages, home for a good night's sleep, only to return to the board and begin a new and terrible game the following day."

I sat and looked at Beth, sweat pouring from my forehead, she sitting still, pen poised over her pad.

Without a word, she reached across and switched off the recorder.

★ ★ ★

CHAPTER SIXTEEN

Custody

There was a short intermission in the meeting as Anthony ordered a fresh pot of tea. We took advantage of the break.

"Janet probably told you, I've been in court all morning, couldn't get a decent cup of tea for love nor money. And to cap it all, I've got to be back in the city at three, so I'm afraid tea and biscuits is as good as it gets."

"So there's no nipping home for lunch today?" I ask, somewhat envious of his accomplished lifestyle.

"Not likely. Though it was easier when I used to live here, in this very building. I had a top-floor flat, handy for dining, but I got fed up with living amongst so many wigs and gowns. Six months ago I moved into a flat in Knightsbridge with a friend I was at St. John's with, so I'm not too far away if I want to nip back.

"Though, I must say, these days I'm lucky to get home at all, what with holding down two jobs, but I suppose it's a blessing in disguise. The new place is a lovely little garden flat, belonging to one of Toby's relatives; perhaps a little cramped for the two of us, but it's very cosy.

"Anyway, I'm here at chambers for twelve hours a day, so I tend to just use it for somewhere to lay my weary, over-worked head."

"It must be very nice, living close to all the shops: Harrods and all that. It sounds like paradise to me." Janet looked up from her file.

"Never get time to go there myself."

A light tap at the door; the clerk entered and placed the new pot on the desk, putting the old one on the tray. He placed the biscuits in front of Anthony and faded out through the door, shutting it firmly behind him. Anthony selected a pink wafer and pointed it towards me; I was miles away, staring at the fire.

"In case you're wondering, it's a Griffin."

"I beg your pardon?"

"The carving, in the stone above the fire. It's a Griffin."

I stood up and moved a little closer to the exquisite carving, reaching out and feeling the cold stone blackened into a plume of old soot. I could just make out the details of the peculiar creature. Its demonic form had the body of a lion but the head and wings of an eagle, with a fierce-looking beak and razor-sharp talons that sprung from its feet.

"An ancient crest from the old coat of arms," Anthony interrupted. "As you can see, the Griffin is a mythical creature, half-lion and half-eagle. In mythology, its usage is to protect treasure, apparently. The female of the species builds the nests and lays sapphires in them instead of eggs. The Griffin is said to protect gold: that's why so many banks in London have them carved into their stonework."

My thoughts went back to the scout camp in Kingshurst and its old pair of Griffins, but for some reason my eyes stayed fixed on the carving before me.

"Now, Simon, I hope you don't mind, but if I can just bring you back to business for a moment?"

"Yes of course, Anthony, please go on."

Anthony raised an eyebrow at me and then returned to his notes.

"When you said earlier that it felt like you'd been hit by a train, what did you mean exactly?" He devoured the wafer and began to pour his fourth cup of tea, one eye on the old clock above the door.

"He got up before I had chance to move. Hit me with a rugby tackle, knocking me back against the couch and winding me in the process. He thought I was about to hit him."

"And why would he think such a thing?"

"At first I hadn't got a clue. I thought he'd just overreacted – don't forget he was in the army: he was just trained in combat and suchlike. But a few days later, I got a chance to read his statement.

"According to his account, he was under the impression that I was a violent person who had previously attacked his colleague. This was a misunderstanding that he received from a third party. In short, he was expecting me to be violent and was prepared to deal with it himself."

"Why don't you think he wanted to have someone else in the room as a witness?"

Anthony looked up from his desk.

"As I say, I think he wanted to deal with it himself. But he'd got the facts wrong and no one had tried to put him right. He must have been expecting an angry, violent customer – a situation he was more than happy to deal with himself.

"The fact of the matter is, he was never in any danger of being attacked. He'd got the wrong idea and acted too quickly. I think his bedside manner needs a little work, but then again, that's why people like him work for the police."

Anthony took a sip of tea and continued to read.

"And then, it appears, after the struggle, he opens the door and shouts for help."

He placed his cup on the saucer.

"It was at that point that the room filled with other officers who just happened to be in the waiting room, is that correct?"

"Yes, that's correct. They all rushed in. Two of them took hold of me and one of the others, a female I think, led the doctor out."

"Did he have time to put this. . ." Anthony turned the page. "This model of a spinal column back on its stand?"

"No, he didn't have time to touch anything; everything was left in situ and remained like that until the room had been examined by S.O.C.O. As I said, he was led straight out into the corridor and away from the room. You see, as police officers, we are trained to separate parties as fast as possible and keep them separated. As I say, that spine never moved one inch throughout the whole incident."

I reached over for my cup of tea while Anthony flicked through another file of notes.

"Okay, let's go over the injuries to the doctor once again. Did you see any blood at all?"

"No, I saw no marks on him and there was no blood on him when he left the room. He was taken by colleagues to the City Hospital – a routine thing for such a case."

I took a sip of tea.

"They took him to the City hospital." Anthony turned another page.

"Yes, that's correct." I cradled my cup in my hands

"Well, I have the report here: the doctor in the casualty department examined him and recorded no marks or injuries to his face. This puts us in quite a quandary because, as you already know, in the Magistrates Court he testified to having a string of facial injuries which he claims you caused, although he has never been able to provide evidence to support this."

"That's my entire point!" I leant over and replaced my cup.

"Yes, I see," Anthony replied at length. "But we have to remember that he's a doctor, and a doctor makes a very sound witness in court. He was very convincing with the testimony he gave; he did it very eloquently and it appears that the court was quite prepared to believe everything the man said. A doctor who has served in Her Majesty's Forces and then goes on to serve in the police makes a very convincing witness, even in the absence of medical evidence."

Silence fell over the room as the realisation struck me of the mountain we would need to climb. The sound of the fire in the hearth was quietly comforting, together with the sight of Anthony, feet on his desk, munching away at a biscuit. He finally broke the silence.

"Janet, have you got the full custody record there? I only seem to have an edited version." Janet dug a copy out of her file and handed it over.

Anthony turned the page and began the process of absorbing every detail with his computer-like brain. I found my own thoughts drifting as I stared out of the window in much the same way as I did when I was at school.

My old teacher was a particularly boring man who could spend whole lessons scribbling logarithms on the blackboard, unaware of the chaos behind him. I'd often gaze out over the playing fields on those crisp autumn days, longing for the lunch bell to sound so I could spend the hour walking along the avenue of trees, chatting to Sue.

Once again, in those quiet, warm chambers, while Anthony pored over the case, I felt myself drifting into some dusty corner of my memory. As the memories came back, I focused my eyes on a leaf that floated to and fro across the window until it came to settle on the sill.

I watched as the wind tried to lift it, but the leaf held firm, flapping in the wind until it blew against the glass, its flat blade pressed against the window. It was golden brown, with traces of green in the pattern of its veins, the green merging into the gold edges daubed with patches of brown. It looked like a leaf from a horse chestnut tree, like the one in my own garden. No doubt, scattered amongst the red and gold carpet of leaves, would be the familiar horse chestnut seeds – like the ones we used to collect at school, threading them with old shoelaces to play our games with.

I looked away from the window and focused back on Anthony, who was studiously turning the pages. I was sure he'd have a few questions about my period in custody and I didn't want to be caught staring out of the window. The old voice of Mr Manders comes back; the sound of a ruler hitting the blackboard. I shook the image out of my head and ran through the details of the police station.

I remembered Steelhouse Lane and the feel of those Victorian cells, the architecture outdated and neglected – more like a museum than a police station. I remembered thinking that the place belonged to another era: the late nineteenth century, when the plot of land was set aside for the city's first Magistrates Courts.

The surrounding buildings all had the same Neo-Gothic style: the General Hospital, the Methodist Hall; all designed with Gothic arches, steep gables and towers, a fairytale town built of red terracotta.

Some forty police cells were built for Birmingham's Court. In those thick defensive walls, small grated windows allowed in light through murky glass, four inches thick.

Inside, the prison was a three-storey cathedral of steel galleries, and along each gallery a series of stone-framed cell doors were recessed into the stone walls. The prison resounded with the ceaseless banging of doors and shouts of distress echoing up to the vaulted roofs, intermingled with the jangle of keys and the sound of steel toecaps on the gangways.

Outside on the street, there was little clue to the number of unfortunates banged up in those dismal cells. It's a bleak reminder of Victorian Birmingham – a place they forgot to close down. Only years of under-funding and neglect has saved the squalor of that dimly-lit labyrinth.

If you are ever unfortunate enough to arrive at that police station, you first go before the custody officer, the person ultimately responsible for you, whose job it is to listen to the facts of the arrest and then, if appropriate, authorise your detention. With years of experience, the custody officer will have become slow and methodical, almost robot-like. A machine from a science fiction novel, programmed to take in data, refer to the rules and churn out the Act and Section in a perpetual monotone.

There is little point in arguing with the machine: it has been tried, tested; it's like a hardy perennial from an English forest – in a word, unshakeable. This officer was built like a tree, her hair scraped back into the tight bun and not a line of humour on her face.

"When was the last time you slept?"

Her stubby fingers hovered over the dirty keyboard, ready to record the reply.

"The night before last, I think. I think it was … sorry, everything's a bit of a blur."

A list of further questions flooded from the machine. Once it had enough data, it could compute its next action. Invariably, this would be the selection of a cell and instructions for you to be escorted up the metal stairs, out of harm's way.

Up we went, up the steel stairway, along the gangway to a blue cell door in a grey doorway. I sat down on the hard wooden bench. Above my head the low ceiling was domed, making the space close in around me, emphasising the feeling of solitary confinement. The stonework gave the feel of a subterranean bunker, where the lost souls of society could be kept apart from everyone else, hopeless and incommunicado.

At first, there was the feeling of loneliness, total solitude, but after a short time, my eyes grew accustomed to the light and saw it: above my head, perched up where the wall curved into ceiling, was the little black window, the all-seeing eye. Made of toughened glass, protected from attack, it showed no sign of life. But behind the eye there was life, lots of it, monitoring my every move and feeding the machine its information.

Back down in the custody area, the machine studied the prisoner, watching their every move, an incarnation of Big Brother.

The past hour had left me traumatised. Tiredness washed over me. I curled up on the bench. Comfortably numb with fatigue, my eyes followed the lines of grey bricks that lay just inches from my nose. They stared back at me; cold, silent, impregnable.

I turned over and focused on the cell door; like the gate in my memory, it showed signs of age and rust.

For a moment, I pictured the door as the gate, the bricks either side became the hedgerow, the mortar became the honeysuckle, stretching its way across the gate. The cell door and the gate had much in common. On the one side was safety and security; on the other, evil, greed, misery and hurt: the people who use, exploit, and feed off you like parasites.

I turned over to get more comfortable, adjusting my position on the solid wood.

Somewhere down the hallway, the machine turned to the monitor, detected no movement and recorded: 'Prisoner Fast Asleep'.

★ ★ ★

Starbucks was unusually busy that afternoon, probably due to the heavy rain.

In the first-floor seating area, the whole side of the room was a giant picture window looking out over Poplar Road and its high-street banks. Tracey had managed to find two large leather armchairs commanding a bird's-eye view over the town.

On the low table between us were carefully positioned large cappuccinos and two smaller cups containing very strong espresso on the side.

"Hi, sleepy head! Glad you could find the energy to crawl out of bed." She navigated round the table before throwing her arms round me and giving me a big welcoming hug.

"Well, you've certainly pushed the boat out. I'll have to be careful if you've started mixing your drinks this early in the day."

"I just thought that you could do with a nice strong shot of something to get you started, even if the rest of the world is on their way home."

We released our embrace and took our seats.

Outside, the rain lashed against the window, making me feel like I was in a ship's cabin during a storm at sea. I looked down at the colourful umbrellas darting around the busy pavements below. Further down the road, to my left, was the very spot where I'd sat in my police car the previous evening, waiting patiently for the long hours to pass before the raid.

Images flooded back from the previous evening.

Neon lights, an ambulance siren, the lady at the car window, the words "Give us a kiss, sweetheart!" all flashed up in my head.

Just as I'd felt then, the same sense of foreboding – as though a huge net had closed around me.

But, there and then, in the warmth of the coffee house and sat opposite Tracey, I was filled with a welcome sense of relief, the sort of calmness that only Tracey could bring.

I selected the strong black coffee and eased myself back into the chair.

"I'm glad you rang; I wasn't sure that I'd actually get a chance to see you before you went."

"Well, I couldn't fly off to the other side of the world without a proper goodbye. I also wanted to make sure that you would be coming to my leaving do on Thursday evening at the Coach."

"Isn't it Friday morning that you fly out?"

"Yes, so Thursday's going to be a bit of a sad day. I've got to say farewell to friends who have meant so much to me over the past years and there are some that I'm never going to forget."

She reached across and took hold of my hand. I felt a gentle squeeze; its warmth ran through my body like electricity. My eyes met hers.

"How did it go last night?" Her voice was soft and gentle. Her eyes were intense, I felt her grip tighten and the softness of her hand. I suddenly felt like I was under a spell which was slowly paralysing my muscles and turning my body to stone. I wanted to join her and curl up in her arms; to feel the heat of her body against mine. I wanted to feel the soft skin of her cheek against mine as she told me that everything was going to be all right.

"Simon, are you okay? How did it go last night?" A shadow of concern drifted across her face.

"Yeah, I'm fine, just a bit tired – you know what these bloody nights are like."

"I take it that you got him in this morning?" Tracey let go of her grip and settled back in her chair to listen.

I gulped down my espresso.

"Yeah, we got him in. Six of us ended up going; he must have thought he was Britain's Most Wanted, the way we all turned up in a posse. Sally and Mick on Mike 4, the gaffer and the sarge, then Adrian Taylor with me. Mike 4 took the rear, Adrian and I knocked on the door and the supervision stayed in their bloody car. I think he must have been expecting us because there was none of this garage nonsense, he just calmly opened the front door, we arrested him and he went upstairs to get dressed."

"How was he with you?" She sipped her espresso, her cigarettes lying in a sealed box on the table, a timely reminder of the days when you could light up just about anywhere.

"As you can imagine, he doesn't like me at all. While Adrian was wandering around upstairs in some kind of daydream, Alton started, whispering his threats in his quiet, menacing way. Adrian's such a dipstick; I remember saying that no one should be alone with this nutter, but he still walked off.

"Then we end up in the cell block just as the custody officer is changing over. There was no one else in the custody suite, but they left me alone with Alton in the holding area as they took their time with the handover. Adrian had buggered off again, giving me some crap about doing some checks, and there I am again, sat there, just me and him waiting to be called in."

"Did he say anything else to you?" Tracey picked up the box of cigarettes and started to toy with the seal.

"No he didn't. He just sat there staring at me. Burning holes into me with his eyes. He didn't take his eyes off me for a second. If I got up to stretch my legs, he just sat there perfectly still, staring. That was really menacing, as though he's right in your personal space, eating away at your confidence.

"I remember watching a documentary on Saddam Hussein, following the first Gulf War. Somebody from his Revolutionary Command Council had escaped to America and was interviewed, you know, just his profile in shadow and an actor doing the voice. He was saying that the most dangerous thing you could do was to look Saddam straight in the eye. People got used to looking at the centre of his chest when they were speaking to him; even people high up in the regime and close to him would never look him straight in the eye. Saddam believed that the eyes were the window into the soul and he could see into people's eyes and see their innermost thoughts. He could tell if someone was a traitor if they looked at him straight in the eye. That's how powerful eye contact can be, and I'm sure that I could see the innermost thoughts of Andrew Alton as he sat there staring at me."

"What did you see?" Tracey had taken a cigarette out of the packet and was toying with it.

"I saw hatred – deep personal hatred – the sort of hatred you might see in a mother's eyes when she sees her son's murderer in court. Someone who is irrational and deadly, driven along a path of revenge; someone who is brooding, able and willing to take their time until they reach the day of reckoning, when old scores will be settled and only then can they find peace."

Once again, I felt the warmth of Tracey's hand on mine. I remained trance-like, gazing out of the window through the rain. For a few moments we didn't speak. I found the peacefulness combined with the touch of her hand somehow comforting.

Neither of us was in any hurry to break the silence – perhaps that was why we were such dear friends: we didn't feel the need to keep talking and we didn't find silences uncomfortable or testing. We could sit there enjoying each other's company in silence.

The heightened craving for a smoke brought the peace to an abrupt end. She had an unlit cigarette between her two fingers and her deep-red lips had adopted a smoker's pout. I nodded to her, swallowed my coffee and followed her down the stairs. The cigarette was now firmly between her lips, the lighter flicking away in her hand. As I held the exit door open, she lit up and left wisps of smoke in her wake. The smoke mixed with her expensive French perfume and produced a smell I was now used to: a smell that would always be Tracey. The smell hung in the air and I took a moment to breathe it in.

Perhaps I'd taken her for granted for too long. Perhaps, if things had been different, she wouldn't have felt the need to travel to the other side of the world. It occurred to me that, ever since people had the means to emigrate, they'd gone to pastures new for a whole range of reasons: the urge for a fresh start, to escape the past, to make a change to the mediocrity of everyday life or to deal with a feeling of underachievement when people's expectations of you are impossibly high.

I guessed that with Tracey it was the fresh challenge that drew her to the furthest corner of the globe. I was just sad and a little bit bitter that she was leaving me here while she made this new start.

"You will be there on Thursday, won't you? You're not thinking of backing out and not saying a proper goodbye?"

"Of course I'll be there. I wouldn't miss it for the world."

She threw her arms around me and the hug lasted a fraction too long, as if she didn't want to let go. She gave me a soft kiss on the cheek.

I felt a tear rolling down my face. I tried to say something but I choked. In my mind, I'd already got my excuse.

★ ★ ★

CHAPTER SEVENTEEN

The Diamond Tribunal

"Are we ready to start, yes? Okay, for the purposes of the record, the time is now 13:33, Thursday, 8th January 2009.

"We are in the fifth-floor conference room at West Midlands Police Headquarters, Lloyd House, Birmingham. Mr Samgrass, I presume you're the presenting officer; for the purpose of the record can you please state your name?"

Superintendent Samgrass looked up, straightened his tie and shuffled the papers in front of him.

"That's correct, Ma'am; Superintendent Giles Samgrass from the Professional Standards Department."

"Could you please tell the panel the name of the officer subject to misconduct charges?"

A clearing of the throat and further nervous shuffling.

"It's Police Constable Simon Davies from Solihull, Ma'am." He returned his attention to the file in front of him with a self-satisfied smile.

"PC Davies, my name is Bernadette Diamond. I'm an Assistant Chief Constable with the West Midlands Police and I'll be presiding over the misconduct hearing today. I'll ask my colleagues to introduce themselves."

On either side of her sat a male Superintendent, dwarfing her slight frame and making her look like she had two bodyguards. The three of them sat in a row on the top table and there was the slightest suggestion that the men were slouching back to compensate for the size difference. Bernadette, however, sat bolt upright, working very hard to appear at ease.

I couldn't help noticing that her hair had been done especially for today: it was perfectly fixed in place. Her makeup was understated and her uniform had been pressed.

Her smaller body made her insignia of rank look even larger, almost comical; a lace of silver oak leaves ran down each collar and on her shoulders sat two cross-tip staves embroidered with silver wreathes. She sat, her eyes surveying the room, while her colleagues introduced themselves.

"I see that you are legally represented, PC Davies." She cast her eyes towards Anthony. "Can I ask you to introduce yourself for the purpose of the record?

Anthony was already head down, scribbling, and didn't bother looking up.

"Anthony Hudson, barrister."

He spoke as he continued to write.

"Thank you very much."

Bernadette was not accustomed to people answering her without looking at her.

"PC Davies, you know that you face a misconduct charge on assault proceedings. Are you satisfied that all the preliminaries have been dealt with and complied with and you've had all the relevant statements and documents?"

Anthony looked me in the eye and nodded.

"Yes, Ma'am," I said on cue.

"Thank you very much. PC Davies, can I ask you to stand?"

It sounded more like an instruction.

Anthony nodded his approval. I pushed my chair back and stood up straight, looking directly out the window, twelve inches above her head.

"The charge is one of Criminal Offences contrary to Police Regulations 2004; that being a member of the West Midlands Police you were convicted of a criminal offence, in that you assaulted Dr Strictly by beating him, contrary to Section 39 of the Criminal Justice Act 1988. Do you admit or deny the charges"?

I looked down at Anthony who nodded his assent.

"I admit the charge, Ma'am."

"Thank you very much, please sit down."

Bernadette turned her head to the presenting Superintendent.

"Mr Samgrass, would you kindly read out the circumstances of the case."

After adjusting his tie one final time he cleared his throat.

"Ma'am, the officer appearing before you today is PC Simon Davies. The officer appeared in court on the 6th August charged with assaulting Dr Strictly. The officer denied the offence but after a full trial he was found guilty. The circumstances of the incident are as follows:

"On 20th of July ..."

While listening to the officers' report, I poured a glass of water from the decanter in front of me.

After a little nervousness and an initial stumble he began to get into his stride. An aura of satisfaction surrounded him. He had been appointed as Discipline Superintendent of the Professional Standards Department because this was what he was best at: routing out the bad apples.

From behind his desk he had prepared files on a number of officers, all of whom had failed to live up to the high standards expected.

His outlook was simple – there was no place in this force for anything other than exemplary behaviour.

He continued to read from his thick file, punctuated everywhere with bright pink post-it notes. I studied his tie. It was a navy blue and no doubt made of silk. It had a repeating pattern of a university crest, embroidered in a contrasting shade of blue. The crest looked like a shield in two sections: the field was blue with a silver band at the top. A diagonal line of five gold diamonds joined one side to the other. On the silver band I could just make out an open book bound in red between two black hammers and a red torch held aloft.

"And those, Ma'am," he gave a wry smile, "are the facts of this case."

He paused in a way that looked as though he expected a round of applause; instead Bernadette tilted her head in Anthony's direction.

"Mr Hudson, I now formally invite you to present any evidence that you may have as to the character of PC Davies, in order that it may assist us in determining the appropriate sanction."

"Thank you, Ma'am. We have submitted to the panel two statements of character from supervising officers, who describe this officer as a hard-working and caring individual who has suffered from a truly traumatic ordeal and had been struggling to recover from it.

"Indeed, this is an officer who has suffered over the past few years and made mistakes, but it appears that those mistakes are themselves directly the result from the suffering that he has endured.

"In other words, Ma'am, my submission to you today is that, as well as punishing PC Davies, this panel may consider that it is their duty to protect him. Not only is it appropriate for this panel to give a sanction, but he also requires support, and it's for those reasons, Ma'am, that my respectful invitation to this panel would be to impose a discipline sanction that fell short of dismissal or requiring him to resign.

"I'll structure my submissions as follows. I'll take you through five discrete points. Firstly, his record as an officer; secondly, the incident of harassment that you've heard mention of; thirdly, the medical situation and the incident that caused the medical condition; fourthly, the incident of common assault, and then, finally, I'll tie the points together."

Anthony paused and I looked to Superintendent Samgrass, who was studying the backs of his fingers.

I refilled Anthony's glass with water.

"I'll make some submissions as to what my view would be as to a suitable sanction.

"Madam, you've received our written character reference from Simon's previous Detective Inspector. He describes Simon as hard-working and caring and he was a valuable member of the team. We've also heard from his Chief Superintendent who very helpfully brought to your attention the officer's considerable record of commendations and awards. These span the officer's career and include five commendations for bravery. He also received bonus awards in 2003 and 2004. So, in other words, Madam, this is someone who has consistently shown a high level of service to the West Midlands Police. He genuinely wishes to continue such a high level of service but this aim has suffered as a result of difficulties beyond his control in recent years.

"The difficulties – and now I'm turning to my second submission – were a series of incidents which occurred in the first half of this decade while Simon was at work, in his usual way providing a high level of policing, quality and commitment to members of the public. He attended a call from a lady who was being persistently harassed by an offender who, it turned out, was an ex-police officer in this force. Through his commitment to see justice done, he put himself in the line of fire and became the target of a prolonged period of harassment. It was from this incident that he became ill and turned to his force for support.

"I now come to the expert reports into his mental condition that have been prepared for this tribunal. What the experts agree on is the fact that Simon was at work when he had cause to attend the address of a Mr Andrew Alton, a former member of the police Special Branch. It is clear now that this Special Branch officer was suffering from psychiatric problems at the time he was removed from the police. It appears now that while PC Davies was doing his job, protecting a vulnerable member of the public from this officer, the tables were turned on him. What started off with simple aggression from Mr Alton led to a series of threats and criminal behaviour against Simon.

"His life was threatened on more than one occasion. One can only imagine the result of such threats and such terrifying comments, particularly to a caring officer such as PC Davies, and the tension and anxiety they must have caused.

"Mr Alton did serve a term of imprisonment but, at the same time, PC Davies began to suffer from medical problems. These have been outlined in the expert reports as Post-Traumatic Stress Disorder. During the time of the harassment, he felt quite unable to protect himself or his family. Though he looked to his force for help, his perception was that there was no protection for him from that direction.

"The anxiety caused by these experiences resulted in his complete mental collapse and brought about a series of marked changes in his personality. His social life and marriage crumbled to pieces. The report in front of you states that there is a course of treatment available through the Trauma Support Network, called 'Trauma-Focused Cognitive Behavioural Therapy' that would help Simon to deal with this condition. It would last up to six months but would help him recover from his P.T.S.D. It then follows that it is possible he would be in a position to continue acting as a police officer in the force."

"Has he had that treatment?" Bernadette Diamond interrupted.

"No Ma'am, he hasn't had any treatment yet. These reports simply outline the treatment recommended for his condition.

"Can I bring your attention to the Trauma Support report?"

Bernadette shuffled her papers impatiently, attempting to find the relevant forms.

"The counsellor reports that Simon has suffered major psychological problems as a result of attending a police incident when he had cause to fear for his life. He felt helpless and was not adequately supported by his employees. It would appear that his situation would improve sporadically with various anti-depressant medicines, but the following collapse in his marriage led to a return of the P.T.S.D. symptoms and a major depressive episode. It is clear that the incidents in question would be serious enough to bring about the onset of P.T.S.D. in a normally healthy individual.

"To summarise, Ma'am, both the reports that you have in front of you make the link between PC Davies's mental health issues and the incident with Dr Strictly. And both are clear on the treatment that is necessary for his health. In other words, there is a glimmer of hope at the end of the tunnel and that is for you to give him the opportunity to receive the protection and the support that he needs. It is clear that he would then be in a position to make a full recovery and to continue with his excellent police work. Madam, it seems to me, as I refer to the medical examination reports, that whilst he has been convicted of an offence, that offence itself was not caused by some defect in his character. It doesn't show that he would make a bad police officer. It does show that he was suffering from mental health problems which, on the day in question, caused him to act in a way that was entirely out of character.

"Madam, if I can turn now to the facts of the incident itself – this is the incident on which the panel will be deciding on a sanction, and is no doubt the incident that will be causing the panel some concern.

"By any consideration this was a serious incident: an assault upon a member of the medical service who was there to help and assist PC Davies. PC Davies accepts his guilt of that offence and he has expressed his remorse. However, Ma'am, it is entirely crucial that the incident is considered in the context in which it arose.

"As you've already heard, it arose from a meeting that took place between the officer and Dr Strictly when the subject of his return to work was being reviewed. Dr Strictly stated that it was his opinion that the officer was fit for work. PC Davies, for understandable reasons, disagreed with that prognosis.

"You have in front of you some very detailed expert medical reports which refer to serious mental health issues at the time of the incident. When we consider these reports, one can perhaps understand something of the frustration the officer felt on that day in front of the police doctor, Dr Strictly.

"It is also important to consider the exact mental health situation over that time. The panel has heard reference to the interview in the Birmingham police station. It was there that the solicitor representing the officer brought up the fact that PC Davies had not slept for the past seventy-two hours and had also taken himself off medication, against the advice of his GP. It was clearly the opinion of the solicitor and the Police Federation official representing PC Davies that, at the time, he was not fit to be interviewed.

"He had not slept during the twenty-four hours that he was held in custody. In other words, this was someone who wasn't acting in his normal fashion, who was suffering from a severe mental episode, who hadn't slept and hadn't taken his medication. Not a normal situation for this person to find themselves in.

"Now, Ma'am, if I could bring your attention to some of the comments made by the learned District Judge during the hearing. District Judge Nash stated that when the incident occurred, it was clear that PC Davies was suffering some mental health difficulties. He went on to say that the mental health problems were made worse when he stopped taking the medication. The Judge stated that the officer was unusually agitated before the incident and that was evidence of a mental health problem.

"In summing up, the Judge was eager to point out the fact that PC Davies was somebody of previous good character. The punishment of a conditional discharge was clearly the appropriate penalty, bearing in mind the state of health and mental well-being of PC Davies. In other words, Madam, it's not just the doctors and medical experts who made the link between the incident and mental health problems, but even the Judge who considered the case.

"Now, Ma'am, the panel here today is made up of three experienced senior police officers. All will be fully aware of the sentencing possibilities that were available to the court. And yet they were right to impose a sentence of a conditional discharge in this case. That must, in some way, be an indication of the mitigating factors – not least by consideration of the fact that this was entirely out-of-character for PC Davies.

"Madam, those are the main thrusts of my submissions. This is someone who's had an excellent record as a police officer and has been of previous good character. It's someone who is suffering from a serious mental health issue but with the right care and help can progress to a recovery. For all of those reasons, I would ask the panel to consider a sanction that does not involve removing PC Davies from the force. I ask the force to consider their duty of care.

"Unless I can assist you any further, those are my submissions."

"Thank you for that. Mr Hudson. I now ask my colleagues if they have any questions."

Bernadette looked to the officers on either side of her, who shook their heads.

"In that case, the panel will now adjourn to consider the sanction to be imposed. For the purpose of the tape the time now is 14.02hrs, same day and date. Thank you very much".

★ ★ ★

"Okay, for the purpose of the record the time is now 15.42, same day and date, which is Thursday, 8 January 2009, and the same persons present in the room. This is a continuation of a misconduct hearing regarding PC Simon Davies.

"PC Davies, can I ask you to stand, please.

"PC Davies, you have pleaded guilty to the charges preferred against you at this hearing today. We have listened to the circumstances of the case as outlined by Superintendent Samgrass. In considering sanction, the panel have taken into account the evidence of character presented by Superintendent Jones and the evidence of character submitted by Inspector Reid.

"The panel note the positive early career history and your receipt of a number of commendations, awards and bonus payments. We are cognisant that the mental health issues appear related to a particular investigation and the subsequent harassment that you suffered personally and on behalf of your family. Given that your mental health issues appear to be work-related, we have very carefully considered the psychiatric report compiled by Dr Hibbert and the P.T.S.D. assessment report submitted by Bethany Goodfellow. The panel accept that you have suffered and potentially are still suffering from mental health issues.

"We note that, after a course of treatment, some of the associated symptoms may dissipate. However, there are a range of symptoms described in both reports that cause the panel concern – for example, the ability to control yourself and being aggressive, to name but two. Your counsel, Mr Hudson, has outlined our duty of care to yourself when considering sanction. We note in Dr Hibbert's report that, and I quote, 'one of the perpetuating factors in his psychological difficulties is his anger towards the Police Service, and it is difficult to think that his issues towards the Police Service have completely resolved and would not resurface in the future, should there be any complications in the path he perceives should be available to him on his return to work'.

"The circumstances of the assault have been tested in Magistrates Court and in Crown Court on appeal. Both found against you.

"Whilst the panel acknowledge the punishment was a conditional discharge, the panel do find that an officer assaulting a colleague on police premises is a very serious incident.

"Behaviour reflects public confidence in the police service; therefore the conduct of all police officers should be of the highest standard. Integrity and professionalism of police officers is of paramount importance and fundamental to the trust and confidence that the public have. Police officers should not behave in a way that is likely to bring discredit on the police service.

"The sanction therefore is a requirement to resign forthwith.

"The time is now 15.45, same day and date, and that brings this misconduct hearing to a conclusion."

CHAPTER EIGHTEEN

Acacia Avenue

"Beth's just rung. I'm ever so sorry, she's going to be about ten minutes late. There's been an accident on the motorway and she's stuck in traffic. Can I get you a coffee?"

"Yes, please, that would be great."

Susan scurried back into the inner sanctum. I found myself alone, staring at the four walls peppered with information, like a plague of locusts. But there was that particular one: the one that had haunted me since my first visit.

My eyes were drawn towards it, the same way your eyes look at a bloody scene in a horror film; you try to look away but the force is too powerful.

I tried to fight the temptation, distracting myself by looking at other posters, but they seemed lame and meaningless compared with the lady in the bare room. I forced myself to back away, carelessly bumping into Susan's desk and knocking over a mug. An inch of cold coffee spilled over the desk. I grabbed a tissue to mop it up, managing to prevent it from reaching her paperwork. A bead of sweat appeared on my brow.

I scanned the floor for a bin; I didn't see one. I looked behind me; there was that collection of postcards pinned up on the window frame behind the desk. Holding the wet tissue, I checked the cards.

The Greek Island was still there, as was Edison's lighthouse. I looked down the row. There was a new addition: someone had been to China.

The postcard was dog-eared and looked old, like it had been kept in a chest for years; a closer look told me that it came from the mausoleum of the first Emperor of China.

The grainy black-and-white photograph showed an incredible scene. Row upon row of terracotta figures standing in long lines, heads poking out above the excavated pits. Among them were rows of warriors, horses and chariots, together with lines of acrobats, servants and musicians; literally, thousands of statues.

I eased the postcard from the wall and examined the writing. It was from Jean, the lady with pink hair, who had gone to Shaanxi in May; addressed to 'the office', it had a smiley face drawn in the corner.

The card had an official text on it, explaining that the Terracotta Army was built for the Emperor to lead him to victory in the afterlife, to conquer and rule the heavens.

Not only were there his great armies, but a great walled palace was also built, buried alongside him, with enormous palisades, gateway entrances and mighty fortifications. The scale of the building was awe-inspiring, indicative of the power that would accompany the Emperor on his journey.

I mopped a bead of sweat with the wet tissue and considered the photograph.

Surely, when people pass on to another world, they couldn't take with them the brutal repression from this one.

The afterlife can't be made up of the same miserable conditions, the poor and the weak exploited by the rich and powerful. All this magnificence for one person's passage to the afterlife; thousands of people living their lives in misery, just so one person can have such luxury.

The idea that the next world would be just as tedious as this one drew a dark cloud over me.

I stared out across to the castle's walls, thinking about the Emperor's armies marching above the clouds through the limitless sky. All the time fighting, slaying the innocent and building new empires. For all eternity, the souls of the dead from the battlefields reborn to the next life, finding the same pain and suffering, just fighting for another brutal dictator.

I looked over to the poster of the lady slumped in the corner. It always reminded me of Jackie. Once, Jackie was so low that she told me she would never bother the police again: she'd given up on the whole world, its injustice, its greed and inequality.

So, what could possibly be worse than to be abused and murdered, only to find yourself facing the same thing again in the afterlife?

Jackie was lucky; last time I'd heard she was still alive. Maybe she'd found some happiness after all. Maybe someone was loving her, showing her warmth and human kindness, not beating her black and blue with a cane.

At least, if you find some hope in this life, you can hold some hope for the next.

You could dream of a better place, no more pain or disease, no more hate and violence. No more angry husbands using their wives as punch bags. No more divorces ripping homes apart, daughters violated by fathers, widows struggling to raise families. No one tormented because they are too fat or too skinny or simply a different colour.

For Jackie's sake, there had to be a better place – but then again, what about people like Margaret? I wiped my brow, leaving coffee stains across my face, and heard a voice behind me.

"Hi, Simon, sorry to keep you; I got stuck in traffic. Have you had a drink?"

As if on cue, Susan came up behind her with the coffee and handed it to me. As I reached out I realised I was still holding the postcard and the wet tissue. Susan looked perplexed.

"Do you like Jean's card?" she enquired, one eyebrow raised.

"Sorry, I'm just interested in the story behind the terracotta army." One big lie.

"Don't start Jean off on the subject, she's got three photo albums full – you'd never get away."

"I must have a word with her about it sometime."

I was sounding less and less convincing and perked up when Beth changed the subject.

"Shall we go through?"

★ ★ ★

The memory of Margaret and Acacia Avenue had upset me and she could tell. Nothing got past Beth.

"How's this week been for you? Is there anything special you want to talk about?"

I wanted to tell her all about Margaret but something stopped me.

Part of me thought that I should be talking about Alton. Maybe all this would turn out to be a complete waste of time if I kept avoiding the point.

However, I had found comfort in talking to Beth, so maybe that was helping me open up and get better.

"You seemed lost in thought. You were looking at Jean's postcard and looked as if you'd seen a ghost. Is everything okay?"

I noticed her summer dress of blue gingham with a bow at the waist. Her hair bounced softly over shoulders.

"Do you ever have people coming in here, maybe they're terminally ill, asking you if you believe in an afterlife?"

"Yes, sometimes. People who have been recently bereaved often like to think of their loved ones in a peaceful place, watching over them. They sometimes ask my opinion, but I tend to let them picture where they think their loved ones are and encourage their own peaceful thoughts."

"As for you, Beth, do you believe in heaven and hell?"

"Yes I do, but I'm a Christian. Everybody has different opinions and images of heaven and hell and what they think they'll find there. But yes, I do believe that there is a heaven for people who live good lives."

"And how do you visualise heaven and hell?"

I sat up straight and leant forward, realising that I was the one asking the questions.

"Well, as a Christian, when I think of heaven I think about the Garden of Eden: a peaceful place with no hatred and no wars, no greed or hunger. A place of lush green hills covered in flowers, with all the animals of the earth roaming freely under a bright sun."

"And hell, how do you see hell?"

"Well, hell is quite the opposite: fiery and painful, a place of guilt and suffering. Although some people view hell as freezing and gloomy. If you read Dante's 'Inferno', you'll see that he portrays the innermost circle of hell, not as a fiery furnace, but as a frozen lake of blood. So you see, there are many different visions of heaven and hell. I believe that people should be allowed to believe what they like."

Beth considered me for a moment

"Is there any reason why you ask this – is there something you need to talk about?"

"I suppose I was thinking about that postcard, the Chinese one, with the terracotta army. It made me think whether or not we go to a similar world after death. A place with the same anger, violence and inequality as we find on earth. Can somebody die after years of pain and abuse and find themselves born into another world of just the same, maybe even the same people doing it?

"It makes me scared. I was thinking of some of the people I'd come across who had been killed or committed suicide – what if it never ends and they wake up with the same?"

I paused for thought, my mind travelling back, bringing up vivid images.

"I saw a vision of hell in a nightmare. I remember it clearly. Hell was the mouth of a cave, surrounded by darkness. A thick fog surrounded the cave, the rock all sharp and jagged like teeth.

"From out of the cave came people, the most desperate souls you ever did see; the air filled with the wailing and crying.

"Out came children calling for their mothers; then came mothers, screaming for their children. Then came a soldier, dressed in red, with a tall black hat, his tunic torn; his arm was missing at the elbow, face white as a ghost.

"Then out came what looked like a king from the East. He was struggling to carry bags of gold but stumbling under the weight on his back. He was trying to buy his way out. His robes were turning to rags as he crawled around in the dust, begging for mercy."

Beth put her file down and reached for my hand.

"What's on your mind, Simon? Is there something you want to tell me about?"

Her hand squeezed mine gently; I looked up and caught her stare.

"It was just another job, one from my days as a family liaison officer. Sometimes, if I think the world is unjust, I remember this job; it was a murder of an old lady.

"You may have even heard of it; it got a five-minute slot on the News at Ten. But I tell you this: there's no amount of news coverage that can portray the real suffering of a family that's lost a mother, particularly in this case where it could so easily have been avoided."

Beth released my hand and returned to her notes.

"The job of a family liaison officer can be very demanding. I have clients who have undertaken that role and they, themselves, often find they need support. But what happens when you don't have the answers? When you become angry yourself and you're trying to explain things that don't make sense to you?"

Beth placed her notepad on the coffee table and pushed herself back in her chair, signalling that she was ready to listen.

"Come on then, Simon, let's have it: what's on your mind?"

★ ★ ★

A light drizzle hung on the wind as it swept along the platform towards the old footbridge. Loose pages from a newspaper had been left on the bench; the pages had taken to the air and were now being blown across the safety line onto the tracks.

I felt moisture on my face and realised I was exposed to the weather.

When this station was built as part of the Great Western Railway, there would have been a wrought iron canopy to shelter travellers, even a roaring coal fire warming the waiting room.

Now, the waiting room was locked for repair and the rain fell on the passengers.

I sat on one of the benches and looked up and down the platforms. One person put up an umbrella; two moved back into a doorway. With the rain on my face I looked up at the clouds.

An announcement came over the loud speaker; slow and muffled, it suited my senses which were now numb and strangely detached.

I felt light-headed. My eyes filled with rainwater, making objects blur and fade in front of me. My eyes narrowed and I looked towards the railway tracks.

I saw two parallel rails, huge bolts locking them to the sleepers below. Stone ballast filled the gaps, littered with cigarette ends and plastic cups.

I thought about what society had done to this railway and, likewise, what it had done to me. How, once upon a time, this very station had been fresh and new, built for a new railway system that ran through this beautiful country landscape.

It had freshly-painted fences and stone walls and all those romantic sounds from childhood: hissing, puffing, the shrieking of brakes and the steam whistle blowing through the night air.

Now the place felt tired, unkempt and unfriendly. The fire had gone from the hearth, the shelter had gone from the canopy; there was nobody to help you if you were lost.

A shadow passes over me, bringing a feeling of darkness and despair, of being all alone, abandoned. I realised that I had no fear of dying and I wondered what sort of relief it would bring.

I wanted to escape the arrogance and bitterness of other people, the way they always let you down. The lack of thought and compassion in the way people treat each other, the absence of care.

Through blurred vision I saw a face forming on the tracks. It went in and out of focus. The words 'duty of care' whispered in my ears, getting louder all the time – so loud, I put my hands over my ears and screamed.

The words 'duty of care' acted like a trigger that started off a train of thought, a dangerous train of thought. The face swimming in a vision between the tracks became clearer. I saw her uniform, the embroidered insignia, all shiny and silver; she sat on the top table mouthing the words 'duty of care' like a taunt, taunting me to jump onto the tracks.

I sensed movement; people moving to the edge of the platform, standing in line, as though they were going to jump too.

I looked down the tracks and saw this huge engine getting larger and larger, filling my whole view. I heard the hiss of its brakes as it slowed down, the screeching of metal on metal filling the air.

The people boarded the train and sat down in the warm carriage. A buzzer sounded, the wheels turned, the engine roared, the iron horse pulled itself along the tracks and left the confines of the station.

The noise and turbulence faded with the last carriage and a page from the newspaper floated down, settling at my feet. I looked around to check that I was the only one left on the platform.

As the final sheets of newspaper fluttered down, the air was filled with a deathly silence. A silence that suggested the world as I had known it had been blown apart. I was taking the first tentative steps out of my shelter.

In this brave new world, the rules would be different. The old rules didn't work. Those rules included such notions as respect for society and respect for your elders.

When I needed help and actively sought it, I found nothing but selfishness, neglect and incompetence from people who just got richer and richer, living off the very systems they fought tooth and nail to retain.

I found hypocrisy, abuse and greed when I expected to find care, understanding and treatment. So now, on reflection, the rules had changed, and so had I.

There was no longer that fear of appearing anti-social, no longer a fear of not fitting in; in their place, the deep satisfaction of marking out my own territory.

I wouldn't consider suicide; that moment had been buried with the old rules.

The approaching train had presented an opportunity for me to end it all, but the vision of her face between the tracks had filled me with inner strength. Now I had to gather my thoughts and plan my next moves for the months ahead.

The only thing I needed to find out was, "Where the bloody hell am I?"

★ ★ ★

CHAPTER NINETEEN

The Roseby Case

Margaret Roseby was a little over sixty-two years old when she died.

Although I never had the pleasure of meeting her, in the weeks following her death I heard a lot about her and her charity work.

I knew that she had lived at Two Acacia Avenue ever since the bungalows were built in 1959. I knew that she had brought up two children, that she was fond of baking and that she loved cats. She had always owned a cat. The latest one had come from a re-homing programme after it had been abandoned with its litter by the side of the M40; the family named her 'Banbury' after the nearest junction. Her children had presented her with a rather playful Banbury after she spoke about her loneliness following the loss of her husband.

She was a longstanding member of the Methodist Church but she struggled with her faith; her attendance waned and for three months she was hardly seen in church at all.

Among her friends at St. Mary's was the minister's wife. They had known each other since Girl Guides, and it was to be Doreen's evidence that proved crucial in the subsequent trial. You see, it was Doreen who first noticed the changes in Margaret's behaviour.

It's often the friends, and not necessarily the relatives, who are the first to pick up on changes: they don't take each other for granted.

Although most ladies of her age had suffered losing someone dear in their lives, most people were shocked when they saw how deeply Arthur's death had affected her. She had always been considered a stalwart of the community, with a long list of interests and hobbies, always willing to donate her time and effort.

For her, the past had been hard, trying to bring up two children while her husband was overseas. She had learnt how to stretch a housekeeping budget, always providing good meals and making sure her children were immaculately turned out, even if it meant that she went without.

Sam had been ten when he went on a trip to France. He had pleaded with his mum to let him go and spent days throwing tantrums and locking himself in his room. At the end of the week she had told him that he could go and bought him a new pullover to take with him. At around the same time, Sam noticed that his mother wasn't wearing the gold necklace she'd been given as a child. Six months later, after his mum had worked her fingers to the bone, the necklace reappeared around her neck; the pawnbrokers on the High Street had made its profit.

Margaret had that old-fashioned quality of always being able to keep calm and carry on. Through good times and bad, she always had a smile on her face and time for her friends. But after Arthur's death, Doreen was first to notice the lonely, vulnerable side that emerged.

If you were to ask Doreen today, she would tell you that not a day goes by without her thinking that she was somehow responsible; after all, it was she who had introduced Margaret to Oswald.

Now, it just so happened that George Oswald joined the congregation of St. Mary's shortly after Arthur's death.

Margaret seemed to be coping with the steady flow of tea and sympathy, but then became distant and avoided company.

Some people even found it awkward to speak to her. They found it strange to think of her without Arthur: the two had been inseparable since he was discharged from the Air Force.

To her closest friends, it seemed something was missing. A part of her was buried alongside Arthur. In her lowest moments, she'd long for the time when she could join him again in heaven – something she believed in passionately.

Oswald was quick to notice her but didn't approach her directly. He said that people always needed their own space to grieve. But he would often listen intently to other people's conversations when the subject of the unhappy widow came up.

In one of these conversations, he learnt that Margaret had been asking the minister for advice on how she should invest her savings. Later that Sunday, Oswald suggested to Doreen that the two of them should meet; after all, he knew all too well the pain of losing a partner: his own wife had died in a tragic house fire. Maybe he could help her, comfort her and see her through these difficult times. Doreen could see no harm in this idea and believed that they might find strength in each other. So she asked Oswald along to the Friday coffee morning, where the two of them could meet.

Margaret found him totally charming and started to enjoy the stories of how he had travelled in the years following the awful accident and how one day, just as friends, he'd like to show her the place that she'd always longed to visit: Salzburg.

He talked about how he had lost contact with most of his friends and relatives since the fire.

He was kind and generous, a good listener who proved to be quite a handyman. No job would be too much trouble, and before long he'd set about painting the whole bungalow, inside and out.

She started to wonder how she'd managed without him, he seemed to be a constant source of support. She would tell Doreen that he wouldn't accept so much as a penny for his work and she so enjoyed his company. The only thing he asked was that he be allowed to keep his tools in Arthur's shed, just so he didn't have to carry them with him all the time. She readily agreed, still grateful for the help, and was even impressed when he purchased a new padlock for the shed.

"We wouldn't want the tools to get stolen before I finish!"

They both laughed.

"Such a lovely man," she told Doreen the following Sunday.

It was when she missed church for the second week that Doreen got concerned.

Her absence caused a great deal of gossip at the coffee morning and a decision was made that Doreen would pop round the following afternoon to check that she was all right.

When Doreen got round there, the first thing she noticed was the garden. Where there had been a neatly kept patch of grass, a cherry-red American Buick rested on piles of bricks. She had seen cars like this on the television and in films but had never seen one on a friend's front lawn. She then looked up at the house.

The front aspect consisted of one large gable, weather-boarded down to window height. She recalled that this had always been painted white and there had been a row of hanging baskets across the window bay. The hanging baskets were nowhere to be seen and now the weather-boards were painted black, with a satellite dish fixed in the middle.

Doreen climbed the three steps and knocked the door. She stepped back, holding the Victoria sponge like a trophy. After a couple of minutes, she put the cake down and knocked again, this time a bit harder.

She waited. She was sure she could hear a man's voice inside and a quieter feminine voice replying. Doreen banged even harder and shouted through the letter box.

"Margaret? It's Doreen – I've come to see you and brought you a cake!"

This time, the man's voice was louder, more insistent, and, after a short pause, she heard the sound of a chain being released and bolts being pulled.

The door opened, no more than ten inches, and she saw Margaret's face, tired and withdrawn. She held a handkerchief to her mouth.

"Margaret, how are you love? We haven't seen much of you these past couple of weeks. I've baked you a sponge cake," she announced, holding it up, as though Margaret had never seen a sponge before.

Margaret glanced back at the kitchen door, and then at the cake.

"It's very kind of you, but I've been feeling a little poorly lately. I think I've got one of those bugs that's going around. I don't want to give it to anyone."

"Nonsense, nonsense, Margaret, that doesn't sound like you. A bit of fresh air is what you need, maybe a ride down to the supermarket in the precinct. I think it'll do you good."

Margaret looked back down the hall once again. She looked nervous, her face forming deep furrows; she looked back at her oldest friend.

Doreen thought that her eyes held a pleading, desperate look – one that said, 'Please go away, maybe come back again at a different time when I can talk.'

Doreen craned her neck to look down the hallway. She thought she saw a shadow on the kitchen wall, a tall, ghostly shadow against the wallpaper.

"Okay then, Margaret, I'll be off now," she said, projecting her voice down the hall, her watchful eyes on the kitchen door.

Then she lowered her voice to a whisper.

"Margaret, for God's sake, ring me, do you hear me, ring me!"

But as Margaret closed the door, it didn't seem like she was listening: she made no reply. The light faded from her eyes, like someone caught in a web, knowing they were trapped.

It took a while for me to work out what had happened.

Dorridge Station was two stops further down the Chiltern Line. I couldn't remember passing through Olton or Solihull, but could only assume that I must have done to get here.

I knew I hadn't fallen asleep. I pondered the five-mile walk back home; however, sat there in the peace and quiet of the railway station, the bench seemed to provide the perfect sanctuary to gather my thoughts.

"I'm sat on a bench at Dorridge railway station," I told myself, putting the pieces of the jigsaw together.

"I've travelled by train from Birmingham."

Everything was becoming clear.

"I've just been kicked out of the Force and thrown out of the building."

An alarm bell sounded in my head as I began to recall her words.

Anthony had been scribbling away furiously, recording everything, but I had been lost in thought, not able to concentrate.

I remembered the words 'duty of care' on her lips, her eyes insincere. Then the impact. "You are now dismissed from the Force."

I remembered being helped up and led out of the room. The lift had been called and was waiting for me. Its doors were open, like some toothless mouth, ready to swallow me up and take me away. I was ushered in and the doors closed behind me, blocking out sound and leaving us cocooned in a box of mirrors. The lift must have been moving but there was no sense of motion.

Suddenly, the doors opened, revealing the lobby; beyond that, the outside world, full of buses and taxis, horns sounding, brakes screeching.

The discipline officer said something about wishing me good luck; something to that effect.

The floor of the lobby had just been polished. There were yellow A-frame signs on the ground, warning people to be careful. They each displayed a black figure, suspended in mid-fall: one arm raised, the helpless figure crashing down with an almighty thud. There were no words – the picture told the story.

It felt as though the signs had been left out especially for me: a final goodbye after twenty years.

As I looked back, I could swear I saw those little black figures raise their arms and wave.

My senses began to dull and I walked through the revolving doors, out onto the noisy street, looking back at the eleven-storey office block.

The sound of a car horn broke the silence. I had stepped out in front of a bus.

Things became a little hazy. I know that I managed to board the correct train but found myself two stops away from my station. I could see where I was and how I got there, but I had to sit and clear my mind.

Like an engine starting from cold, my mind turned over once, then again, and then finally sprung to life.

Images from my past flashed in front of my eyes, like a slideshow with pictures of people's faces. No particular order; I suppose my brain was going through its filing system, sorting things out. After twenty years of service, there was a lot to sort out.

The first image I remembered was Tracey, leaning against a cell door; short skirt, knee-length boots, her black hair styled up on top, smoking a cigarette.

Then came Ben, his lifeless body hanging from the rafters.

Then Jackie, poor old Jackie, sat on the floorboards; red dressing gown, nails digging into her face.

Then Margaret, face drooping to one side, lying naked on that trolley.

Last of all, I saw Alton, the man who had orchestrated my downfall.

I recalled the day of the arrest: the threats, the hidden cameras, the anger. He was interviewed later by officers and he produced a letter from a company of solicitors, explaining that they had engaged his surveillance services to gather evidence in a divorce case.

It was true that this person's surveillance abilities were among the best available. He had indeed worked for Special Branch. But the fact remained that he was mentally unstable.

He was out there with a point to prove but without the ability to regulate his behaviour. He would soon break down completely and take innocent people with him.

The letter from the solicitors did the trick: the hierarchy wanted out; they washed their hands. Alton was released without any further action.

As he left the station he made his way to Kate Chandler's place of work, where he sat outside in his car for the rest of the day.

He had not yet finished with her.

★ ★ ★

A train sped through the station.

It gave me a start. I sat up straight. I'd got back to thinking about Margaret.

I remembered her children were called Sam and Leslie; they were twenty-one years old at the time. Sam was a computer programmer and Leslie was at college, studying to be a hairdresser. It was after careful consideration that Doreen decided to ring Sam.

Sam had been very busy with his new job and had to admit that he hadn't been to see his mother for a while, but he agreed that he would pop round the following day, just to check that everything was okay.

He saw no reason to worry his sister. He left work an hour early, knowing how much his mum liked to talk.

When he arrived he saw the big American car with its huge tail fins.

He was slightly curious as to why she had allowed anyone to park such a thing in the front garden. He rang the doorbell.

All the curtains were closed. Doreen had told him that his mother said she had been ill. Sam assumed that she was in bed.

Having lived there himself, he knew where the backdoor key was hidden. He checked that the avenue was clear before scaling the side fence and jumping over. He was surprised how untidy it all seemed, as though the garden had been left to go to seed. He kept thinking that maybe he should have offered his mum some help and instantly decided that once he had sorted her out, he would make sure that he and Leslie got together to discuss regular visits.

Before trying the rear door, he took a good look around the garden. He expected to see Banbury appearing from one of the beds and sidling up to a tree.

There was no sign of the cat, so he walked over to his father's old shed, still calling out Banbury's name. He tried the handle. It was fastened with a brand new lock. He looked through the cobwebbed window.

Inside was a little shelf where seeds could germinate: he could see a yoghurt pot, a ball of string and his father's pruning knife. Beyond that everything was in darkness.

A sudden feeling of frustration came over him and he scanned the ground around the vegetable plot to find something with which to force the door. There in the bed, where his father had grown runner beans, was a little patch of disturbed soil, no longer than a foot in length.

A little cross made of tomato canes stood at the head.

Panic rose within him and shot around his body. He ran to the rear door and kicked over the earthenware flower pot; it smashed against the wall. Then, with a feeling of anger rising, he got down and began searching for the key. His fingers sieved through the soil. A sharp piece of crock cut deep into his finger and blood began to flow, splashing little purple patches on the slabs.

Peering through the keyhole, he could see that the key was on the inside. He took out his mobile phone and dialled the house number.

The kitchen curtain was drawn. He tried to peek through a gap. He terminated the call and dialled his sister.

"Leslie, is that you?" A heightened state of panic in his voice. "Get yourself round to mum's as quick as you can!"

She replied with a slow, puzzled response. Sam butted in.

"Leslie, I said as quickly as you can."

★ ★ ★

The tannoy announced the delay in the 15:02 train to London.

The voice reminded me of Beth. At a time like this, I could have done with Beth – I wondered what she'd say.

"Of course, it was me who had to go and see Kate Chandler and explain that he had been released from the police station with no further action. You can imagine how she took it."

"How did she take it?" Beth looked over her half-moon glasses.

"She put her head in her hands and started shaking uncontrollably. Harry, that's her uncle, tried to comfort her but she ran into her bedroom and slammed the door. I must say, I expected a mouthful of abuse, telling me I should have done better and that the police were a disgrace, but he was very understanding.

"He told me that he knew I cared deeply about his niece and had tried my best. He even said he was impressed in that I always made personal contact, even when the news was bad. I told him I was very grateful and that I would do my best to keep an eye on things for her.

"We shook hands and Harry showed me out through the hallway. I could hear crying coming from Kate's room; he went and tapped the door, announced that I was going, but there was no reply.

"It was after my rest days that I managed to raise the matter with Sergeant Moore. I found him in his office, wading through a pile of paperwork. I sat down and began to fill him in on the details of what had happened: you know, the arrest, no further action, the state of Kate and the chat I'd had with her uncle.

"There was a look of concern on his face, which I took as a good sign. I thought that he must feel the same as I did; the fact that it wasn't a fair decision and that something needed to be done.

"As I spoke, I noticed that he was looking worried and I half-joked that he looked like he could do with a holiday. He didn't reply and something made me go quiet.

"The silence seemed to last an eternity before he passed me a piece of paper. I didn't look at the paper as my eyes were still fixed on him. He pointed to the paper and suggested I read it."

★ ★ ★

Leslie arrived at her mother's house within the hour.

She found her brother leaning against the side of a large American motor car on the front lawn.

She took a slow walk around the vehicle as someone might do if a space ship had landed. She looked at Sam as if he'd left it there; Sam shrugged and nodded towards the satellite dish.

"Sam, what the hell's going on here?"

"I don't bloody know," Sam shrugged. "I had a call from Doreen saying she was concerned about mother. I came round here and saw this bloody car. There was no reply at the front door so I climbed over the back to get the key. It wasn't where it should be, you know, under that old pot. I tried the shed but that's all locked up too. On top of that, the bloody cat's nowhere to be seen. I tried ringing the house but there was no reply; that's when I called you."

"I knew I should have come round sooner." Leslie started to panic

"Well, never mind that, we can sort these things out later. Have you still got your key?"

"Yes, of course, I keep it in my bag."

Leslie opened her handbag and started sorting through all the contents. She passed Sam her lipstick and nail varnish while she placed her diary on the bonnet of the Buick. After some rummaging she brought out her mother's key, holding it aloft with relief.

"Well go on, then, open the bloody door."

Sam's manner was making Leslie flustered. She continued to fumble with the key-ring all the way to the door.

She tried the first key but that one didn't fit.

She tried the second one; that one didn't work either. The third key went into the lock but refused to turn.

"Let me have a try."

Sam took over, nudging Leslie to one side. Like Leslie, he couldn't get the key to turn. It didn't matter how much he tried to force the keys, they wouldn't turn.

"For God's sake!" Sam shouted as he kicked the door, before pressing the bell hard until his knuckle turned white.

"Sam, that's not going to help, is it?"

"I've got a good mind to just kick this bloody door in."

"Sam, mum could be out or away or something. If you're really concerned, do you think we should call the police?"

"Oh yes, and say what? I can't open my mother's front door with my old key, please come round and kick it in for us?"

"Well can you think of a better idea?" Leslie began to cry. Sam softened up.

"Look, Les, I tell you what we'll do. Scribble a note on a piece of paper, just asking mum to call us as soon as she can; say it's urgent. Then, if we don't hear from her by the end of today, I'll come round in the morning on my way to work and give it another try. If we don't get any luck by the end of tomorrow, we'll call the police."

"Okay, if you think that's best, but no longer than tomorrow, I need to know mum's all right."

Leslie went to sit in her car while she scribbled the note. When finished, she got back out of the car and approached Sam, who was still leaning against the Buick.

"Here you go, I've just written, "'Mum, give me or Sam a ring as soon as you get this. Haven't seen you for a while and we are worried. Can't wait to speak to you, lots of love, Les and Sam.'"

Sam took it and read it again, as though he was a school teacher checking her grammar.

"Right, we post this now, and if we haven't heard anything by tonight, I'll be round in the morning."

"Agreed!" announced Leslie, realising there was no option.

Sam posted the note through the letterbox and stood back, looking at the house.

On the other side of the door, a man's hand, scarred with burn marks, retrieved the note and crawled back to the kitchen.

★ ★ ★

Horton & Co.

The Officer in Charge
Solihull Police Station
Solihull

Without Prejudice

Dear Sir,

We are instructed by our client, Mr Andrew Alton, to write to you.

Our client informs us that he was arrested last Friday and held in custody for ten hours. He was later released without charge and without any further action.

Our client wishes to know why it is that PC Davies continues to harass him, even when it is obvious that our client has in fact done nothing wrong.

Our client is most upset at this unfortunate treatment and our client informs us that there are members of his family who are also very upset and cannot understand PC Davies. They are indeed very angry and our client is trying to stop them from taking this matter into their own hands and seeking out the officer.

Our client, however, does admit that he is in possession of all of PC Davies' personal details e.g. vehicle and house details. Although he states he has no wish to use them at this stage to endanger PC Davies, he cannot guarantee the same from his family.

Our client is most concerned that you put into place all the necessary protection for the officer to ensure that he remains safe while our client seeks to ease the matter.

Yours Sincerely

Horton & Co.

I held the letter while I read it again.

Sergeant Moore broke the silence.

"That letter was received here this morning; it was delivered by hand."

I looked up from the sheet of paper.

"I tell you one thing: that's the strangest solicitor's letter I've ever read; I'd go as far as saying it's not a solicitor's letter at all."

I started to read it a third time.

"Yes, I'd agree with you on that one. In fact, we've already checked the directory of solicitors and there is no company registered as Horton & Co. I also agree that is not the language any solicitor would use. I can only suggest that you are right, in that either Alton or an associate has written it. Having read it twice myself, I would suggest that it's come straight from him."

"So what happens now?" I passed the letter back.

"I have spoken to Lynn Bailey and I've read her the letter; she wants the original kept securely for her to pick up. I think I can safely say that she is doing her nut over all of this. She's demanding to know whose decision it was to arrest him and why the arrest was made so early in the morning.

"In the meantime, you are to have nothing whatever to do with Andrew Alton. I've also spoken to Inspector Stewart and we're going to stand by you one hundred per cent on this one. Inspector Stewart will provide you with any help you need. He suggests that you remain vigilant at all times. In short, watch your back."

"Can I keep a copy of this letter?"

Sergeant Moore passed back the letter to me.

"You might as well have this copy. Simon, just be careful."

As I left the office and walked down the corridor, my sense of panic switched to a feeling of fear. It was not the threats that concerned me: as a police officer you're used to dealing with threats, it's part of the job.

What concerned me was the man and his state of mind. This man was playing a game and he considered the people around him as fair game. What was even more worrying was that he had the commitment, the knowledge and the will to create anarchy.

The hierarchy, on the other hand, were happy to sit back and watch him from a distance. If this man went as far as trying to kill me, they would simply put him in prison; they were happy to wait and see.

As long as he was attacking me, they knew where he was.

I walked down to the locker room, removed my utility belt and put my coat on. Without telling anybody, I left the police station and crossed over to the park, sat down on a bench by the children's play area, put my head in my hands and started to run through my options.

★ ★ ★

Sam sat quietly in the McDonalds, moving his scrambled egg round the plate with a plastic fork. He was deeply troubled.

Following the visit to his mother's house, he had rung Doreen to get some advice. Doreen was equally concerned at seeing her old friend in such a poor state and was contemplating what to do.

What worried her was Oswald.

She hadn't seen him in church; he had simply vanished.

It turned out that no one in the congregation knew much about him, other than what he had told them.

He had spoken about travelling through Europe, in particular Germany, but never anything specific about himself. When he met someone who had visited and knew a particular country well, he would change the subject. It was only when he had mentioned sailing down the Rhine through the city of Stuttgart that the alarm bells rang. Doreen went to her local library. What she discovered there confirmed her deepest fears.

Meanwhile, Sam was waiting for the right time.

He didn't want to arrive too early; he wanted to knock at the door at exactly nine o'clock. He knew his mother's habits and they ran like clockwork: nine o'clock, a boiled egg, toast and marmalade and the breakfast show on Radio 2.

Swallowing down the last gulp of coffee, he got up from the table and made his way out to the car park. Within five minutes he was sat in his car on the corner of Acacia Avenue and Willow Drive. From this angle he had a good view of the front of the bungalow.

Another glance at his watch: eight thirty, just half an hour to go. He switched on the car radio and tuned into Radio 4.

Hilary Clinton from New York was debating health care with a senator from Chicago, both of whom were running to secure the position of Democratic candidate for the US election. Sam pictured the headlines coming hot off the presses: 'America's First Female President!'

"About time," he muttered to himself. The debate continued.

"Let me tell you something."

The female voice from New York sounded formidable.

"When it comes to finishing a fight, Rocky and I have a lot in common. I never quit, I never give up, and neither do the American people!"

Sam found himself looking at the radio dials at the very moment the man left the house. The first movement he saw was a white male, aged about fifty, opening the boot of the Buick and removing a small rucksack. The man looked up and down the street before slinging the bag over his shoulder and walking off in the direction of the station.

Sam turned off the radio, leaned forward and peered through the windscreen as the man disappeared from sight.

He gave it a couple of minutes, then jogged across to the house.

He was sure that his mother would be alone, and that was how he wanted it. As he approached the front door, he paused at the car and tried the boot. It was locked. He tried the driver's door. It opened with a firm clunk, and Sam looked inside.

It was impeccable, done out in white and shiny chrome, in contrast the cherry-red of the exterior. The front bench design was in white leather, matching the newly-fitted carpet. The steering wheel looked beautiful but deadly, with gleaming, butcher's-knife radials, chrome-plated, and a white leather rim.

He slammed the door and jogged up the steps to the front door, banging his fist against the wood, shouting, "Mum, it's Sam, open up!"

He had decided that he would keep banging on the door until he got a reply – or, if need be, kick it in. As his fist struck the old door in a drum rhythm, the first sign of blood started to appear.

"Damn." He sucked hard on his knuckle. Stepping back, preparing for a good kick, he heard the sound of a bolt. He paused and listened.

A key, a chain, a bolt; the door opened a few inches before a brass door chain halted its progress.

A familiar voice, just a little frail, answered. "Yes, who is it?"

Sam craned his neck and peered through the gap.

"Mum, it's me, Sam. We're all worried about you, can I come in?"

"I haven't called you, Sam, and besides you're very early, your dad's still in bed."

Sam felt an icy hand gripping his stomach. What made the realisation hurt more was that neither he nor Leslie had been around to see her becoming ill, and now there was some man in on the equation.

"Mum, I'm going to get you to a hospital. Come on now, open the door."

His mum's face and eyelid were drooping, as though one side of her was asleep.

"I've told your dad that he's got to get you both to school today, but I think he's still in bed."

Her face was heavily lopsided on the right. Her head did have the habit of being slightly lopsided after a tendon was damaged during surgery as a child, but this was much worse. Around the front and side of her neck was bruising of differing shades. Sam took his phone out and began to dial for an ambulance. He heard a panic in his mum's voice.

"No, not hospital, Arthur couldn't cope without me – please, no, Leslie, please no."

"Mum, it's me, Sam. I'm not leaving you like this. You're going to hospital, do you hear me?"

Sam was frantically jabbing his finger onto the phone keypad and realised that he needed to calm down. The door slammed loudly in his ear.

"Damn!"

He punched in the keypad for his phonebook and pressed the dial button with the words 'Dr Becker' next to it. After two rings a friendly voice came on the line.

"Doctor Becker's surgery, how can I help you?"

"I want to make an emergency appointment for my mother to see Dr Becker, it's urgent."

★ ★ ★

I had been very slow to realise what was happening; in fact, as the car pulled in front of me, my first thought was to walk around it.

Then I recognised the car, and everything started to happen in slow motion. I froze to the spot and stood rigid, watching the electric window lower and a familiar face stare up at me.

"Hello. I've been wanting to have a quiet word with you."

Two possible options shot through my mind.

One: walk on, ignore him; possible consequences, he would continue to follow me and simply choose another moment.

Two: stop and listen; possible consequences, he could get the point off his chest and leave me alone.

I stood and listened.

"I don't know how you think you can get away with treating people like this. I'm a law-abiding citizen, you ask any of my friends and neighbours, they'll tell you. But no, you have to get involved, don't you?

"I told you at the time you were going to pay. You must think I'm an idiot. You think you can upset me in any way you like. I was policing the streets before you were born – yes, I've done things you couldn't dream of. I could give you the names of MI5 officers who would vouch for me. Does DCI Bailey ever mention me?"

"No, I don't often get the chance to talk to her, she's normally too busy."

"Well, Simon, I want you to talk to her today. I want you to apologise for the way I was treated, she'll know that's all I want. If I get an apology then it all finishes right here, right now. Do you understand?"

"Well, I can talk to her but I don't know what she'll say. I can only do my best."

"I'm relying on you. I don't want to go into what happens if I don't hear. I know people who are very angry and want to help me; these people are very dangerous. One day, you'll just be out and about minding your own business, you'll feel a tap on your shoulder, and that will be that. I'm warning you as best I can; please, do as I say."

The electric window slowly closed. The car reversed and made off in the direction it came. I wrote the registration number on my hand and walked the last five minutes to the station.

I headed straight for Sergeant Moore's office and sat down opposite him.

"I've just had the pleasure of meeting our friend, Mr Alton. Apparently, I have to get him an apology, otherwise I will be propping up the new motorway bridge over the M40." I tried to chuckle at my own joke.

Sergeant Moore got up and closed the door before taking his seat behind his desk.

"Well, just so you know, DCI Bailey's been back on the phone." He glanced at his notes.

"Yes?" I said. "Apparently, that's who he wants this apology from: he wants me to talk to DCI Bailey, get her to say sorry for anything and everything, and then he'll leave me alone."

The first feelings of deep anxiety welled up. I started to take deep breaths.

"Simon, they've made it very clear. If you apologise in any way to Andrew Alton for anything, you'll be disciplined. There's no compromise on that. They will throw the book at you. The view of PSD is simple; it's been spelt out to me in words of one syllable by Lyn Bailey herself. If you apologise, it means you have something to apologise for and you will be up there so fast you won't know what's hit you: she's said that to me. Do you understand?"

"Yes I do, but it's my life in danger, not hers. I'm the one caught in the middle and getting fired at from both sides. I tell you something: I can't cope with this much longer."

"She's instructed Inspector Stewart to give you anything you need – personal alarm, house alarm, anything. She's made it very clear: we're here to help you."

"What's the point? This bastard wrote the book on causing mayhem. I'm sorry to say it, but if I had to put money on someone winning, I'd put money on him."

"Well, maybe so, but in the meantime we all have to take this steady. Her instructions are that you will not be allowed out of the station without somebody else with you. However, I think I now know why they're going to such lengths to protect him."

"And why's that, then?"

"It's a very long story; but first, have you ever heard of 'Cider Nightmare'?"

★ ★ ★

"Mr Roseby? Dr Becker asks if you would go through."

"Yes, of course, thank you."

Sam put the magazine down and went back to the room where he had deposited his mother just ten minutes earlier.

On entering, he found the two of them sharing a joke, although his mother looked slightly confused.

"Sam, I've just given your mother a thorough examination and I've come to the conclusion that she's suffered a stroke."

Sam took hold of his mother's hand and squeezed it gently as he leaned forward to speak. His mother's laughter had transformed into a faraway, glazed look.

"I've heard people talk about strokes. I suppose my questions are: what exactly is one and what happens now?"

"A stroke can be described as a rapidly developing loss of function due to disturbance in the blood supply to the brain. A stroke can affect a patient physically, mentally, emotionally, or a combination of all three. The results of a stroke can vary widely depending on the side and location of the lesion and the dysfunctions corresponding to the areas of the brain that have been damaged. To assess the damage, I'm sending your mother for a series of scans at the local hospital. You'll initially be referred to the rehabilitation unit, who will sort out the details by the end of the week."

"Does she not need to go to hospital right away?" Sam's attention was fixed on his mother's face – her expression had turned blank.

"No, I believe she suffered the stroke some time ago, so there is nothing I can do today to help."

Sam continued to stare at his mother, expecting her to spring to life and tell everyone to stop fussing, but there was not even recognition of her surroundings.

"Sam, I wonder if you'd take your mum and give her a seat outside and then pop back in and see me?"

Sam helped the old lady up. She just stared at the old family doctor, not even recognising him. He sat her down in the waiting area and wiped a tear from his eye before returning to the room.

"Thank you for coming back in, Sam; I just wanted a little word."

Sam sat back down in the same chair and instinctively prepared himself for more bad news.

"Sam, while I was examining your mother I found evidence of extensive bruising to the side of her neck. It's almost as though your mother has been wearing something very tight around it. I'm concerned that what ever has been the cause of this bruising could have been responsible for the subsequent systemic hypo-perfusion, or in other words, the decrease in the blood flow causing the ischemic stroke."

Sam sat in silence, wondering how much more information he was expected to take in. A tear rolled down his cheek.

"Are you suggesting she's had something put around her neck on purpose?"

"In short, Sam, I think this is a matter for the police."

★ ★ ★

"Well, Simon, I must say: things would have turned out very differently if someone hadn't vandalised the phone box on Corporation Street," Sergeant Moore began.

"I was a police cadet. My brother was an officer in Aston and was working the evening shift. We hadn't experienced anything quite like it before; the whole of Birmingham went into meltdown.

"My recollection from that evening of 21st November 1974, was helping to direct traffic along Steelhouse Lane as people blocked the road, arriving to give blood. I counted a total of forty ambulances. When one ambulance pulled up, no one got out. Both causalities were dead.

"It seemed that every alarm in the city had gone off together; it would be hours before they were silenced.

"I helped the blood donors into lifts and we took then to areas away from the injured and dying people; even the canteen became a blood bank.

"A young Asian doctor walked past me in the corridor. His white coat looked like a butcher's apron. I asked him where to take the rest of the volunteers; he walked past me in a trance.

"Back on New Street, police removed the cars that were written off when the two bombs ripped through the pubs. The scene was one of carnage."

"What was the problem with the phone box?" Sergeant Moore had my full attention.

"At that time, it was generally accepted that warnings would be phoned in to local newspapers, giving information of where the bombs were. This would give the emergency services a fighting chance to save lives.

"That evening, there were three bombs planted, the first two at city centre pubs, the Mulberry Bush and the Tavern in the Town. The third device was planted outside a branch of Barclays Bank on the Hagley Road.

"The planters had done their jobs well; it just fell upon the informer to ring the Birmingham Evening Mail.

"But when they got to the phone box, it was bust. Five minutes later, twenty one people lay dead. The Barclays Bank bomb failed to detonate."

"Okay then, Sergeant, I know a little about the Birmingham Six, but how does all this history relate to me?"

"The Birmingham Six were found guilty and sentenced to life imprisonment. Evidence obtained at Steelhouse Lane was discredited when it was suggested that these men were tortured before their confessions. In 1991, the six were released by the Court of Appeal. A huge amount of pressure was put on the then Chief Constable, Sir Ronald Hadfield, to find the real bombers; hence, 'Cider Nightmare'."

There was a sudden knock at the door.

"Come!" Sergeant Moore shouted.

"Can I get you a coffee, Sergeant?" A young probationer appeared.

"Yes, please. Can you fetch Simon one as well? Both white without sugar."

The door shut.

"Where was I?"

"Sir Ronald Hadfield."

"Of course. I was saying – the hunt for the bombers. The best men were picked. Techniques in surveillance and interception were very advanced and Alton, known in surveillance talk as 'Merlin', went to work."

"Which was?"

"His job, to nail the only suspect: the man known as 'The Cardinal'."

★ ★ ★

Sam sat in the front office and, not for the first time that day, found himself looking at his watch.

He didn't want to take his mother home and insisted on going to the police station at the first opportunity. They had been sat there for just under three hours.

"Margaret Roseby, please!" A police officer appeared in fluorescent jacket and over trousers, a utility harness strapped across his chest.

Margaret made no response to her name being called. Sam got up and approached the officer.

"Just Mrs Roseby, if you don't mind sir." The officer eyed him suspiciously.

"I just need to let you know that my ..."

"It really would be better if we could speak with her alone. Is she here?"

"That's what I'm trying to explain: that's my mother over there." Sam pointed to the lady staring at the floor. "She's very ill and we've ..."

"Has she been to hospital?" the officer interrupted, thinking that by the time they returned he'd be long gone.

"No, she doesn't need to go to hospital."

They were joined by another male officer who stood behind his colleague and eyed Sam as if he'd come to cause trouble.

"We've been to see our doctor and he has found some bruises on my mother. We think that she's being abused by a male who's moved in with her and we want to report it. Can you help us?" Sam felt his face reddening with frustration as the two officers looked at each other. They nodded.

"Just bring your mother in here, sir," instructed the first officer, ignoring Margaret.

Both took a seat in the tiny, windowless room. The officers

disappeared. They returned, half an hour later, with some statement paper and several forms.

"Right, shall we get started? This is going to take a while; then we'll see what we've got. First, we're going to need your mother's details."

Question by question, they completed the pages of who she was, who lived with her ... once they'd got all of Oswald's details, one went off to check the intelligence system. Another form was pulled out and a further list of questions appeared.

"Why do you need to ask everything again?"

Sam was getting a little tired.

"We always do risk assessments for cases like these."

"But why don't you just go and arrest this freak and make sure he keeps the hell away from my mother?"

"All in good time, sir; all in good time," the officer said with a chuckle. "The risk assessment is a valuable tool. It goes to one of our analysts who'll place it all on a computer programme. The computer is then able to tell us the likelihood of further incidents; it will also automatically generate a letter."

The officer looked at the new form longingly.

Sam gave a deep sigh.

He could see that the officer had total faith in his computer, so he answered all the questions once again.

The second officer returned to the room and everyone shuffled around to make space. Sam squeezed into the chair next to his mum.

After carefully eyeing Sam up and down, the officer whispered to his colleague, who nodded with interest and ticked a box.

The task of taking a full statement then began. Margaret turned to her son and asked, "Can we go now?"

It pained Sam to think that his mother had given up. He feared that if she went home alone, she might sink deeper and never come back. The stroke had done more than just affect her physically; it had taken away her confidence. Her trauma had drained it from her. As her confidence receded, Sam knew there would come a point when she ceased to function, and that would be fatal.

For Margaret, losing Arthur had been a deep trauma. Everything had then depended on her entering a new life and building bridges as she moved on. She had needed someone to throw her a lifeline and pull her to safety.

But a predator had found her and preyed on her. He had started off charming and caring, helpful and attentive, but then, like some dark shadow, had taken over her life. Now she could barely understand that she was in a police station, trying to make sense of things, trying to find words to explain the nightmare.

Amidst her tears and the stories of Arthur, she managed a few sorry details and a picture formed.

It always happened at night. It would be dark when he visited. First, he put on his portable tape player and started his music. She recognised the voice of Elvis; the song, always the same: 'Amazing Grace'.

It was not how she remembered the song 'Amazing Grace' from church. This was very different: a slow, southern drawl reaching through the darkness, taking a safe tune and haunting her with it.

Then the unthinkable would happen: something that only Arthur had ever done before. But just like Elvis on the tape, this was not like anything she remembered: an action that once had filled her to the brim now made her weep.

She'd feel his rough hands around her neck, squeezing. She lay there hoping that this would be the last time; but no: God was cruel. The pain continued.

She would feel herself choking. Each time, just as consciousness was ebbing away and her senses were dimming, he would finish.

She would hear him groan. He would sit up, then pad his way through to the box room. She'd be in darkness, waiting for the tape to finish. She kept some of the details to herself. She wanted some dignity and had no strength left to suffer any more violation.

They took photographs of the bruising and finished with a final tick in the last of the boxes. Then, looking tired and hungry, the officers stood up and showed them out.

"We'll be in touch, Mr Roseby". The door slammed behind them.

★ ★ ★

"The Cardinal was being watched and, by all accounts, Merlin was making progress. On the back of several miscarriages of justice involving the then 'Serious Crime Squad', a tidal wave of public support accompanied the inquiry. The inquiry had enough manpower, the budget was sufficient and the brief was simple: bring the perpetrators to justice and restore faith in the criminal justice system.

"However, in the corridors of power, things were changing and 'Operation Cider Nightmare' was about to come to an abrupt end.

"Up until 1990, the country was run by Prime Minister Margaret Thatcher, a hard-line politician who refused to negotiate with terrorists. This made her popular with the far-right but alienated the nationalists.

"Her tough line on Republican terrorism became well documented when the first major showdown occurred in 1981. The Maze hunger strikes became a defining moment in Northern Irish politics. Prisoners were protesting for a return to political status, but Thatcher branded them 'criminals' who should be treated as criminals. A man called Bobby Sands began to refuse his food and a string of others followed suit in a well coordinated campaign. The Prime Minister refused to budge and ten Republican prisoners lost their lives, but it was not without huge cost to the British Government. Her stance managed to enrage Republicans and was the single most important factor in bringing Sinn Fein into the mainstream.

"The first hunger striker, Bobby Sands, was elected to parliament as the member for Fermanagh and South Tyrone.

"An Act of Parliament was rushed through to prevent any further hunger strikers from being elected and soon after, Bobby Sands died.

"It was only after the tenth death that the strike ended, but the battle lines were drawn. A negotiated peace could not succeed while the Iron Lady was in power. What eventually toppled her was not, as many people believe, her stance on foreign policy or even her views on Europe: the Conservative Party would never oust its leader for being rude to foreigners.

"It was the Poll Tax. She had wanted to find an alternative way to raise local government finance and chose to remove the old system, based on the rentable value of your home, and change it to a tax based on people who were registered to vote. Many argued that this would shift the tax burden away from the rich and towards the poor and it was made clear to her that such a move would be extremely unpopular.

"She wouldn't have a word of it.

"Tens of thousands of people rioted through Trafalgar Square and the Party's popularity slumped to an all time low.

"And that was it: the lady had to go. She was replaced by a more centre-ground politician, John Major. With a better ability to listen to public opinion, he abolished the unpopular tax and replaced it with the Council Tax. He also worked tirelessly for peace in Northern Ireland and almost immediately authorised a series of secret negotiations with the terrorist leadership. Of course, this was strenuously denied in the House of Commons, but the parties involved were able to give the press a detailed outline of the talks.

"The work that was started in 1990 led to an IRA ceasefire in 1994 and the beginning of a very successful peace process, which has no doubt saved hundreds of lives. But for negotiations to start, key people needed to be in circulation so that contact could be made – you didn't just pick up the phone. There had to be an element of treading carefully, of developing trust and building bridges.

"I've got no reason to believe that 'The Cardinal' was high enough to alter the course of history, but taking him out could have jeopardised the whole process. There were people around who simply weren't prepared to take that risk.

"Once it was clear that there was no other way, the funding suddenly dried up. A press statement was issued to say that no one else was being sought in connection with the inquiry.

"Everybody went home happy. That is, everybody except one."

★ ★ ★

It was at eight o'clock that evening that they came and he was waiting. He'd figured it out earlier, when he arrived home to find that Margaret had gone. All he had to do was wait.

He sat peering through a gap in the curtains, the only light coming from the new television set. He was watching an American Sports Channel. Dallas were playing the New England Patriots at the Cowboys' Stadium.

Some months later, a psychiatrist concluded that George Oswald surrounded himself with American culture after developing an obsession with the assassination of President John F. Kennedy in 1963.

In 1990, at the same time as being diagnosed with an 'attention-seeking personality disorder', he changed his name by deed poll in recognition of the person said to have pulled the trigger. Like his namesake, he was practiced in exploiting the suffering of others in order to gain attention for himself.

It's typical for people with this disorder to create opportunities to be the centre of attention by intentionally harming others and then stepping in to save them.

Few people would realise that the injury caused was deliberate. When Oswald was not playing out his saviour role, he was highly resentful of the individual – his victim – and as the house fire had proven, there could be horrific consequences.

At the second knock on the door, Oswald switched over from the Dallas Cowboys to a religious program he'd previously noticed in the listings.

He then opened the front door and made sure that it was he who spoke first.

"Oh my God, no – tell me she hasn't had an accident! I was just about to phone you. Tell me it's not Margaret."

"What do you mean, you were just about to phone us?" asked the sergeant, caught off-guard.

"My partner, that's Margaret Roseby, has been very ill – she's been having terrible nightmares and is becoming depressed. I've been doing my best to care for her, but sometimes she just wanders off on her own and forgets where she is. She makes up the most incredible stories.

"I got home at five o'clock and searched the house but couldn't find her. I looked round the nearby roads, hoping she hadn't wandered off too far, but no luck. I was just going to pick up the phone when you knocked. Please, tell me she's all right."

"Well, sir, it is Margaret Roseby we've come about. But as far as I'm aware, she's perfectly safe at the moment. Margaret was brought to the police station earlier today with bruising to her neck and she complained of assault. We need to talk to you in connection with this complaint and I am therefore arresting you on suspicion of assault. Do you understand?"

"Well, as I say, I tend to care for her, and of course, officer, I'll come with you and help in any way I can. I just fear that it's her mind deteriorating so quickly. I only wish I could do more. Let me just get my things."

Oswald grabbed his coat and made sure he looked flustered as he searched for his keys. As he started to pull the door the officers heard the sound of hymns being sung on the television.

"Make sure you switch that TV off, sir!"

"Oh, silly me – I'd forget my head if it wasn't screwed on."

He switched off the set and closed the front door behind him, all the time chatting away merrily. It's true to say that they had the power in law to search the whole property. If they had, this story might have had a completely different ending. For, hidden away under a tarpaulin in the shed, they would have found the chair, the ropes, and the videos. Behind the shed, in a black bin liner, they would have found the masks and the gags.

But now, they were in their warm vehicle on their way to the station, talking to a calm, happy guy, who appeared relieved to know that his partner was being cared for.

Oswald remained the model of courtesy as they went through the station procedure. He was polite and humorous and built up a rapport with the officers who even started to enjoy his sense of humour.

"So what happens now, officer?" he enquired, after the formalities had been completed.

"We're going to interview you and luckily there's an interview room free, so we can get straight on with it. Are you sure you don't want a solicitor?"

"Oh, no, officer, there's no need for that. I just want to be as much help as I can to try to get to the bottom of this. I'm ready when you are."

"All right to go straight into Number Two, Sergeant?" the officer asked the custody sergeant, who nodded without looking up.

A joke was shared and the sound of laughter bounced around as they headed into the soundproofed room.

★ ★ ★

No one was to pick up on it, but Andrew Alton was having a nervous breakdown. The end of 'Cider Nightmare' had been somewhat premature and the levels of stress had reached a crucial level. In short, at a critical time, and at the very top of his game, the rug had been pulled from under his feet.

Months of living in the shadows and playing a deadly game had come to an abrupt end. Merlin was not going to get any explanation. He was left on a high, and the breakdown can be explained by the coming down to earth with a crash.

For three months, along with his team, he had remained undetected in his own discreet and secretive world. The levels of mental and physical stress had been increasing and there was no outlet. There would be days of fast-moving action and days when nothing happened, but the level of alertness was always high.

Add to that the fear on every watcher's mind.

The ambush.

As terrorism became more and more sophisticated with counter-surveillance techniques, his job took on new dangers.

Suspects could test the likelihood of having 'grown a tail' by the occasional running of a red light or doubling back on themselves. On several occasions, officers had to make the decision to back off through fear of being lured into a trap.

In the world of terrorism that would invariably mean one thing: being kidnapped, tortured and shot.

He had become a victim of his own shadowy world – a world where a certain level of paranoia kept you alive. But when it was all over, you needed help to slide back into normality; and that's precisely the point: there was no help.

Another knock at the door.

The young officer brought in the coffees. I took time to reflect on the news.

A sense of injustice swelled up in me as I realised that Alton and I have something in common – we were both victims. Victims of the generals who watched from a distance in the belief that life is expendable.

A tin foil parcel appeared from the sergeant's desk drawer and he removed a cheese and pickle sandwich. For him, the world moved on and now was his lunch break. My world, however, was standing still.

The game had become too dangerous for me and I wanted to find the way out.

The sergeant studied his sandwich.

"Remember, if there's anything I can do." He took a bite to signify that the meeting was over.

For me, it was about waiting for the next move, the next letter, the next phone call. Two days later, it came along with an urgent request to go and see Inspector Stewart.

"There have been more threats," he said, staring out the window.

★ ★ ★

It was Leslie's turn to check on her mother, so it was she who found the body.

Six o'clock in the evening. She was on her way back home after a busy day.

She parked her car and walked up the drive to the front door. This was the day after Oswald had been arrested and the first time she had been there since Sam had taken his mother to the police station.

The locks had been changed on all the doors and windows. She had her new key.

She said later, in her statement, that as she turned the key in the door, she immediately knew something was wrong.

There was a stillness about the place, an emptiness that was evident to someone who had grown up there. The sense of homeliness and security had gone. Coldness hung over the place like a blanket.

She pushed the door open and crept through the hall on tiptoe, calling out for her mum. There were no lights, no noise from the television; just the faint sound of a dripping tap. She opened her mother's bedroom door and looked into the room. She would never forget what she saw.

Tied to the four bed posts were lengths of rope that lay across the crumpled duvet. There was no doubt that something terrible had gone on.

She began to weep. All the clues had been there and still, somehow, they didn't manage to protect her; something, somewhere had gone wrong.

The dripping tap was still going, but she felt glued to the spot, unable or too frightened to move. In the deafening silence, the drip was talking to her, telling her something. She knew what to expect. She slowly entered the bathroom. The bath was full. Water was up to the brim and the occasional drip sent out tiny ripples across the mirror-like surface. She stepped forward to turn the tap off and saw something floating on the surface.

It looked like a wig, the same colour as her mum's hair.

Why, somebody has left a wig floating in the bath!

Then she looked down and saw the feet.

As her brain took in the full story, the whole body rippled into focus.

Below the surface, staring up at her through the water, was her mother.

Margaret Roseby was dead.

★ ★ ★

CHAPTER TWENTY

The Long Walk Home

The second train to pass me was the intercity on its way to the capital, shattering the peace and scattering litter across my feet. I must have been sat there for over an hour.

A piece of newspaper lifted slightly before settling back as the last carriage rumbled down the track. A bold headline stared up at me.

'Democrats select first black nominee in race for White House.'

I reached for the article and began to read the story.

Apparently, this man, with the unusual name of Barack Obama, had defeated Hillary Clinton in the primaries. He now faced a new campaign against a much older and more experienced Republican from Arizona. It went on to say:

'Senator John McCain, a Vietnam War hero, shot down and held as a prisoner of war!'

There were photographs of the two candidates, each wearing stars-and-stripes lapel badges and sporting the widest smiles.

I looked at my watch, wondering where the last hour had gone. It was as though my whole life had just replayed in my mind.

I noted it was medication time, so I decided to find a shop and get a bottle of water. I estimated that I must be at least five miles from home but felt that the walk would do me good. I threw the paper onto the tracks and moved off.

As I plodded along, something Sam had said kept going round in my head.

I'd spent quite a lot of time with him and his sister following the death of their mother. The last time I saw them was at the Crown Court when George Oswald was sentenced. The two of them had worked harder than anyone to bring that animal to justice; without them there might not have even been a trial. But the more I got to know Sam, the more I realised that he blamed himself for everything that happened.

Following their visit to the police station, Margaret had stayed with Sam. Maybe if Sam hadn't been involved in such a big project at work he would have taken some time off to care for her. But the deadline of that multi-million-pound contract loomed and his boss was, as the Americans might put it, kicking butts.

Sam arranged for the locks to be changed. Although he tried to persuade his mother to stay a couple more nights, Margaret did not want to be a burden. So Sam also arranged for a panic alarm to be fitted with a triggering device that was to be worn around his mother's neck.

Two days later, Oswald broke into the garden shed and hid there, surviving on a diet of dry cornflakes and cherry cola for three days.

On the Tuesday morning, Margaret went into the garden to hang out the washing. Oswald grabbed her from behind and ripped the cord from around her neck. He carried her upstairs and showed her no mercy; she had no strength to try and hide.

Sam told me that letting her go back home was the biggest mistake of his life. He felt that he could only rest again once Oswald was where he belonged – locked in a prison cell for the rest of his days.

The first of two post mortems recorded an Acute Cerebrovascular Attack or 'Stroke' as the cause of death.

I attended the examination after the family had immediately cried 'Murder' and petitioned the Chief Constable. There were indeed question marks about the death. I attended the mortuary on a very wet Monday morning.

The mortuary itself was an ultra-modern suite built underneath the Victorian sanatorium. The Gothic towers above ground were home to the administration department. An old, rattling service lift or a spiral stairway offered the only access from the house above. Cadavers were brought to a ramp behind the building where they would descend by ramp to the body reception area. A family-friendly viewing room was situated to the side of the ramp, as it had the benefit of natural light coming from a ventilation grill by the old kitchens.

Underground, the place looked like a space station, but the smell reminded me of a butcher's shop I remembered, where pigs would be hung up on giant hooks in the window. The staff would not see daylight from the start of a shift to the end: they became part of the furniture in their own subterranean world.

From the plastic-screened viewing booth, just above the dissection table, I could see the body of Margaret Roseby.

There was a whole team of technicians surrounding her body, photographing her and preparing her for the pathologist. Only when they had finished, and as if on cue, the old man entered, gloved hands in front of him, to take up position at the side of the corpse.

Before switching on the tape recorder, the assistant brought him a pink rubber block which he placed under the torso, causing arms and neck to fall back, pushing the chest up. Dr Rossenblaum surveyed the body, nodded his satisfaction and held out a hand into which a scalpel was quickly placed.

Carefully but deliberately, from the top of each shoulder, he sliced through the skin, the cuts meeting at the base of the rib cage. He then extended the cut down to the pubic bone until a red 'Y' shape appeared on the body; all the time, speaking softly into the microphone, just like he was telling his children a bedtime story.

It was a peculiar scene to behold.

Standing at just over six foot tall, he weighed no more than ten stone. His surgical gown could have wrapped around him twice; his thin, tortoise-like neck protruded from the top.

He had an emaciated, skull-like face; half-moon glasses, perched on the end of a pointed nose, missed nothing. Only one small tuft of hair grew on the left side of his head, which he combed over to the other side, curling up as it met the top of his ear.

Above the noise of the air conditioning, the only sound was his voice speaking, slow and steady, missing no detail as he peeled back the fleshy flaps, exposing the chest cavity. His assistant handed him a pair of shears and the old man went to work on the rib cage. The chest plate was then taken away, exposing the heart and lungs.

Bit by bit, the body was plundered. The lungs, the liver and the heart were pulled out and held up to the light for examination by the expert eye. He paid particular attention to the heart, turning it over and poking his fingers into its holes. It didn't look red like a heart should; it wasn't even heart-shaped: just a lump of muscle, encased in fat and stone-cold.

When he'd finished with the torso, he nodded to his assistant and the rubber block was placed under the head. It was time for him to examine the brain.

He inserted the scalpel into the soft skin behind the ear and cut over the crown of the head to the other side. The skin of the scalp was then pulled down from the top, the front flap resting under the chin; the rear flap was pulled down to the base of the neck. The assistant then handed over the electric saw. With an ear-piercing whine, the saw cut a circle in the top of the skull. He removed the cap with a twisting motion, as if he was taking the lid off a jar of pickle.

After examination, the cap was placed back and the assistant began the process of reconstructing the body. He lined the gaping cavity with a large sheet of cotton wool and placed a plastic bag, containing the organs, back into the void. The chest plate was slotted back into its former position and the skin stretched back across the rib cage and was sewn up with thick stitches.

When Margaret's body had revealed all its clues, it was wheeled back to its resting place: an air-tight fridge, two degrees centigrade.

★ ★ ★

"I'm signing you off for an initial four weeks," my doctor announced, tapping away at her keyboard. "You've been exposed to a significant amount of stress. I'm recording the condition as work-related. It's not an uncommon problem; it manifests itself when the demands of your workplace are beyond your own coping capabilities.

"On examining you, it's evident that you are suffering from fatigue, tension and a high anxiety level; some time off work is essential."

She handed me the note without even looking at me.

"Come back and see me in four weeks. Goodbye."

I thanked her and trotted out. Her time was valuable.

I phoned Inspector Stewart from my car; he listened to my story very carefully

"Sorry to hear that. I'll give welfare a call, they'll contact you in due course. All I'd say is have a good a rest and let me know if there's anything you need."

The receiver went down.

I received no such contact. The next visit to my doctor resulted in another four-week sick note.

At the time I had no idea, but what had actually begun was a saga of passing the buck. Where early intervention could have prevented a collapse in mental health, I was to receive an arm's length, 'someone else's responsibility' approach.

The first contact came after seven weeks. I was called in for a chat, but when I saw Lyn Bailey waiting for me, I became suspicious.

"We're worried about further threats made regarding your safety and we need to check that we're doing everything we can."

The fact was, there was nothing they could do, and they knew it.

The offer of support was a hollow gesture to protect themselves from the fallout that was to come. It was now a matter of damage limitation.

It was clear that Andrew Alton was mentally ill, out of touch with reality – in other words, psychotic.

He had been abandoned without the necessary care and the damage was clear. Years and years of high pressure had taken its toll and all the signs of mental trauma had been missed.

His breakdown came shortly after 'Operation Cider Nightmare.' His behaviour had been dismissed as insignificant and before long he was back out there watching from the shadows, away from reality. This was the last thing he needed.

He had no intention of causing me any physical harm; he could have done that already. No, this was a different type of revenge, harder to understand: a sort of 'dirty bomb' causing maximum disaffection, stress and panic right in the heart of the organisation.

Only when he could create his havoc could he disengage. My own personal breakdown was part of the package.

★ ★ ★

As I continued walking, rain started to fall.

Sam's voice was still bounding round my head, like a ghost in the attic.

The case went round and round in my mind. The problem was the death certificate. The cause of his mother's death was recorded as 'ischemic stroke caused by systemic hypo-perfusion' or 'a general decrease in blood supply to the brain'. Dr Rossenblaum's explanation was that brain tissue ceases to function when deprived of its supply of oxygen for more than a minute. Over a period of time, the patient suffers irreversible damage to the brain tissue which can result in death.

A list of injuries was also in the report. Among these were bruising to the side of neck and abrasions to the wrists and ankles. Dr Rossenblaum had indeed stumbled upon the correct cause of death but had failed to connect all the injuries.

Sam and Leslie refused to let it go, and it was their next course of action which made the real breakthrough.

★ ★ ★

I was still off sick when Lyn Bailey asked me to attend the station.

A flood of complaints had been received from anonymous sources and there was evidence to believe that I was being followed. The police had recovered diaries and computer records detailing all my movements for the past two months. There was a great deal of concern about his motives. He had approached someone to do his dirty work for him.

The man he approached wanted absolutely nothing to do with it. He knew that Alton spelt trouble and if his other business interests were going to flourish he had to publicly distance himself from him. The man contacted a senior police officer.

In the underworld, this is not unusual. Police informants are commonly found in the world of organised crime – a world where people are generally aware of who's responsible for what.

Quite often, informants will provide information to the police in order to obtain lenient treatment or have some of their own criminal activities 'overlooked'. Informing can be a way of getting rid of the opposition or having them shut down for a while. In this case, it was quite the opposite: the man had a friend in the police and had been helped out on a previous problem; he was now returning the favour. Alton was arrested for conspiracy to commit grievous bodily harm.

This was not going to become a botch-up like the Oswald case.

A team of experts were brought in to deal with Alton and a very thorough search was done. Along with a collection of items seized were his computer and all the software, which was sent to the high-tech crime unit. Their experts extracted every piece of information it held.

The file marked 'Cider Nightmare' was easy to find. It was set out in diary form, revealing the surveillance brief and, best of all, the identity of 'The Cardinal'.

The Alton case was now in a special category of damage limitation. It fell to a senior person to broker the deal and this person was picked for a very specific reason: they had worked with Merlin throughout the operation; since then, while Merlin had stayed in the shadows this officer had risen to the top. Most of all, he would be listened to.

Even with all that paranoia and bitterness, Merlin would listen to a colleague who had been there with him, out in the cold. Saving the life of a colleague was something that generally came with the territory, and years ago, in a back street in Belfast, he had saved Merlin's life.

After two weeks on remand in Strangeways, Andrew Alton was given a two-year suspended sentence.

For me though, the problems were just beginning. Within the next few months I was about to understand the irony of the term 'duty of care.'

I was about to meet Doctor Strictly.

★ ★ ★

A sudden torrential downpour caused me to look for shelter under a tree.

I sat down on the wall of someone's front garden and waited for the rainclouds to pass over. Unsure what to do, I closed my eyes and turned my face to the heavens. Water gathered on my eyelids. I let the rainwater trickle down my cheeks.

In my mind I saw Margaret, laid out on that trolley, the doctor holding her heart in his hands, turning it from side to side. I thought back to Sam.

The problem with the Roseby case was connecting the injuries to the cause of death. The report compiled by Dr Rossenblaum was adamant that the cause of death was a stroke. Therefore, the murder case was blown out of the water: if the doctor said death was caused by a stroke then death was caused by a stroke, and that was the end of it.

However, Sam and Leslie knew their mother better than anyone. They'd seen a side of her they hadn't seen before. They saw a lady who had become distant, someone who seemed frightened and beaten into submission. For them, that could only mean one thing: their mother was being abused.

They read the post mortem report about the injuries to her body and could only conclude that the injuries were linked to her death. Their first job was to find out exactly what had happened in the police station when George Oswald was taken in.

After careful consideration, a formal complaint was submitted.

It turned out that George Oswald had spent less than two hours in custody – about half the time that Margaret had spent waiting to report the matter.

He had been interviewed about the injuries to Margaret's neck and gave an account that the officers believed was entirely full and frank, if not a little bizarre.

Oswald had done well to appear awkward and embarrassed when he said that Margaret had introduced him to a thing called 'rope play'. He explained that he was shocked and sceptical at first but, after consideration that whatever took place would do so in private between consenting adults, he agreed. He stated that Margaret had become reclusive following the loss of her husband and that these episodes of increased sexual activity were part of what he thought was a mental breakdown.

His view was simple. He cared very much for her and was in the habit of praying for her every night. He took part in these activities in the hope that it would provide some relief and escapism from her mental anguish, while in his prayers he prayed for her soul. He was sure that God would forgive him, as he gained no satisfaction from the activity itself.

The officers were convinced that Oswald was an honest man. The interview was terminated and the CPS was consulted.

The Crown Prosecution Service in England is responsible for criminal cases beyond the stage of the police investigation. Once the evidence has been gathered, it is they who must decide whether the case should be pursued in the courts. They will only consider prosecuting a case when there is enough evidence to provide a realistic prospect of conviction. Each case has to be shown to be in the public interest.

A realistic prospect of prosecution is an objective test. It means that a jury or bench of magistrates hearing a case, and being properly directed in accordance with the law, is more likely than not to convict. They have to consider that a court will only convict if the case is proven beyond all reasonable doubt.

The CPS have to consider a number of things, including the explanation of the defendant: is it credible; could it be true?

Then they have to consider the credibility of the witness and whether there are any concerns over the accuracy of their account. As for that point, the police reported that Margaret was vulnerable and confused and there was evidence of short-term memory loss as the result of her first stroke. The young CPS lawyer, recently qualified, wanted to follow the guidelines to the letter.

The phone call to the CPS was therefore a short one. There was not enough evidence to pursue a prosecution and the prisoner should be released forthwith.

That evening, the young duty lawyer sat back in his chair in the dimly lit office with the satisfaction that he had saved the tax-payer money by not authorising further action on such weak evidence.

During the investigation of the complaint, it was conceded that failure to complete a legal search of Oswald's premises had meant that vital evidence had been lost. It was also conceded that the taped interview had not been of a thorough enough standard to allow Oswald to account properly for the list of injuries highlighted by Dr Rossenblaum.

In the light of this, the family pushed for, and were allowed, a second post mortem. This was carried out a month later by a senior Home Office Pathologist by the name of Dr Gilbert Howser. He was experienced in the examination of bodies that were believed to have died as a result of either rope-play or erotic asphyxiation.

Dr Howser's report opened up further questions that led to a case review and finally the arrest of Oswald on suspicion of murder. In short, Howser was convinced that Margaret had suffered a series of minor strokes caused by periods of reduced blood supply to the brain.

He believed that he could prove this by measuring the levels of carbon dioxide in the blood, which were high compared with the levels of oxygen. He was convinced that the deceased had gone through a regular practice of having her blood restricted on its path to the brain, and, in turn, he was convinced he could prove that this practice of restricting blood supply, simply by applying pressure to the artery in the neck, had resulted in a cumulative process of damage to the brain.

He was able to testify that, in his opinion, Margaret Roseby was killed by a form of strangulation – a method by which twenty or so people in the UK are killed each year.

His evidence was dynamite. George Oswald was remanded in custody and a trial date was set.

In this case, the CPS had authorised a murder charge on receipt of new medical evidence, but their senior advocate still had concerns. This was because the prosecution was now relying solely on the medical evidence from one doctor.

As with all murder trials, there was no victim to testify. Oswald had been ultra-careful in his planning.

The trial itself was going to be hard enough, but then something quite earth-shattering happened that no one could have foreseen.

★ ★ ★

CHAPTER TWENTY-ONE

The Ripple Effect

The shockwaves from a legal bombshell were reverberating across lawyers' desks as the Oswald trial neared.

Professor Sir Roy Meadow was an eminent paediatrician, who rose to fame in the late 1970's for his work in the area of child protection; his work in this area earned him a knighthood from the Queen.

During his distinguished career, he had appeared for the prosecution in several trials in matters of suspected child abuse. His evidence was crucial in the Sally Clark case: the trial of the lawyer wrongly convicted in 1999 of the murder of her two sons. After three years in jail her conviction was quashed. This case led to a root-and-branch shakeup for the world of expert medical evidence.

The opinion of one expert could be enough evidence to convict a person, even if other experts have differing views. The view of the Courts had been that if a doctor appeared as a witness for the prosecution and made a statement, then that statement might as well have been written by Moses himself.

One might have expected that this increased use of doctors in courts of law, would have resulted in some input from universities regarding legal and ethical practice; after all, this is common in other countries. But our universities saw no reason to fund forensic medicine departments simply to provide a free service to the courts. The focus was on individuals giving their opinions based on their own personal work.

In some cases, two experts working at the same clinic could be called as witnesses for the prosecution and defence. Counsel would instruct them that on no account should they discuss the matter with each other. Foreign lawyers found this system incomprehensible and questioned whether the purpose of our courts was to find the truth or to allow experts to see who could score the most points. The lives of real people were involved, these people often being the most vulnerable in society and deserving more than to be used as pawns in a game.

The upshot of the Professor Meadow inquiry was a look into trials where the main body of evidence came from one medical expert, as juries would be more careful to convict in future. As far as the death of Margaret Roseby was concerned, it was this dilemma which led to the offer to plead guilty for manslaughter.

Oswald was advised that if he pleaded guilty to that offence, then he would be accepting responsibility for Margaret's death but not with malice aforethought. Instead of being found guilty for murder, where the only sentence available was life, he could avoid trial and receive a lighter sentence.

He took the deal. In October that year, he appeared in Crown Court and admitted the manslaughter of Mrs Margaret Elizabeth Roseby.

Evidence as to the cause of death was given by Doctor Gilbert Howser. In the witness box he testified that Margaret died of a series of incidents where blood supply was interrupted to the brain by some physical manipulation of the neck. The periods of reduced oxygen had the cumulative effect of brain damage and death was caused by a massive stroke.

Oswald's lawyers admitted that this behaviour formed part of a sex game, common in their relationship, where a practice known as 'erotic asphyxiation' was consensually undertaken by both adults.

He was sentenced to eight years' imprisonment, with three months taken off for remand; this meant that George Oswald would spend less than four years in prison.

I happened to be sitting next to Sam as Oswald was taken down from the dock.

For a few minutes he didn't speak, he never even had a tear in his eye. After a short pause he said, "If I could have seen what was going on, and if I'd known that I would only do four years in some easy open prison, I would have gladly murdered the monster myself."

The more I thought about it, the more I felt I'd have done exactly the same.

★ ★ ★

"For I, the Lord your God am a jealous God, visiting the iniquity of the

fathers upon the children to the third and forth generations of those who hate Me."

Exodus

Iniquity means fault or perversity. Even today, in some religions, there is a belief that all of the world's problems and troubles can be blamed on old, unresolved issues, passed down from generation to generation.

As far as people's mental health and welfare is concerned, studies that have taken place in every corner of the world demonstrate that, in much the same way, trauma and suffering from unresolved issues can be passed down through generations from the old to the young, and so on.

Psychiatrists call it the 'intergenerational transmission of trauma'. Sufferers of this particular phenomenon are often overlooked by professionals because their cases can be more complex than those of patients whose problems are occurring in 'real time.'

After extensive studies, it has been well documented that the offspring of Holocaust survivors have a much higher risk of developing Post-Traumatic Stress Disorder, and are more likely to suffer after traumatic events. It has also been discovered that children whose mothers were sexually abused are more likely to display the behaviour of an abuse-survivor themselves, even if they have not been abused themselves.

The result of all of this is what's known as the 'ripple effect'. As the disorder is passed through to the next generation it spreads like an infection which, if untreated, can continue down the line.

What can make matters even more complicated in the diagnoses and treatment of sufferers is the tendency to identify with their abusers, instead of blaming the abuses on faults within society or an institution. Thus, a hatred and disregard of officialdom can develop at the same time as a sympathetic view of the perpetrator.

In my case, I blamed the organisation more than I blamed Alton for the nightmares, the mood swings and the work problems.

I was indeed becoming the classic P.T.S.D. case, with a complete checklist of symptoms; however, the organisation I worked for would go to extraordinary lengths to avoid a diagnosis. To diagnose would be to accept responsibility, an acceptance that the failure to treat an officer had directly affected an officer of the next generation.

Failure to accept responsibility was now ingrained in the very fabric of the organisation and all the time, albeit unwittingly, I was taking on the persona of Andrew Alton. I was developing problems relating to authority and becoming prone to sudden, irrational rages. I could be shaving and, whilst looking in the mirror, Alton would be staring back at me from my own face; if I peered deeper into the glass, my own face would come back into focus and any suggestion of his face would fade away.

Inevitably, there was a rising tension between myself and the Occupational Health Department. I was complaining of irrational mood swings and violent outbursts and they were telling me that there was nothing wrong and that I had a problem with respect. When I found that I couldn't cope anymore, I was given the ultimatum: back to duty or leave the police.

There was about to be a showdown and Dr Strictly was busy preparing for it, but it wasn't going to be the real me that he would confront. It would be the irrational victim of handed-down trauma, angry at being ignored, vulnerable through lack of support, who turned up that day. And there would be no gentle talk-therapy from this police doctor. The matter would get out of hand as the whole system of care failed.

In court, I was to appear before a specially-appointed Judge by the name of Graham Nash. The day itself remains very clear in my head, for it was there and then that this book began its journey.

The warm and stuffy atmosphere of Court Number Three had sprouted the seed in my mind and from there, the first notes were made.

As I wrote down the names of the characters, I focused on the length of pink ribbon that Anthony had left strewn across the desk in front of me. Slowly, the characters took shape and I wrote down the title before underlining it with a marker pen.

The District Judge droned on, his words melting into each other like water colours on a canvas, mixing into one great puddle of noise. As his words blurred, I noticed the Royal Coat of Arms fixed to the panelling above his head.

I was mesmerised; so delicate in detail, the beautifully coloured patches of blue and red. In the centre was a great shield, quartered: the first and fourth quarters displayed the Plantagenet lions of England in shiny gold with red tongues.

The second quarter displayed the rampant lion of Scotland in a deep maroon; in the third stood the golden harp on a bright azure background, depicting Ireland.

To the left, supporting the crest, was an English Lion, wearing the coronation crown encrusted with jewels; to the right, a Scottish unicorn, chained to the royal crest, a dangerous and unpredictable beast.

To the right of the coat of arms was a single door; no sign or lock, just a small handle. Beside the exquisite artwork of the crest, the door was plain and ordinary, like a thousand others, but it was what was behind this door that caught my imagination.

The heat became overbearing. I loosened my tie and undid my collar. I couldn't make out how, but the door was moving around the wall like a shadow. An invisible hand with an invisible brush began to paint across the door. Slowly, the word 'Private' appeared in red paint that dripped down the wood like blood.

My head began to swim; I made a grab for the water jug.

Before my very eyes, the jug slid out of reach, or was it my chair being pulled back? Either way, I felt something lift me into the air. Up I went, six foot above the carpet, my feet narrowly avoiding Anthony. The exhilaration was breathtaking as I rose higher, even performing a somersault over people's heads.

Up there, on my own with nothing to pin me down, I was able to do as I wished, so I made a circle of the room, looking down at the faces in the seats below.

As the Judge continued, the private door creaked open a few inches; I wanted to see behind it, to discover the secrets it held. So, with a breaststroke motion, using the air around me like water, I swam across and hovered by the crest to get a view inside.

At first, the unicorn was defensive and raised a cloven hoof. The unicorn was the gate-keeper: I needed permission, but it soon settled back in place, supporting the crest. I took my opportunity and looked inside.

I'd heard of this place before, for this was the Star Chamber, the place where only the very highest in the land could be tried.

I cut through the air and took my place among the rafters, like a barn owl watching the floor below. This was no ordinary room; this was the great hall where Anthony used to dine, two hundred foot long and one hundred foot high. The chandeliers lit up the roof with a sea of crystals, and between the sparkles I could make out the people below.

They all sat feasting along wooden tables that groaned with food; this was a very special night and the guests included the Queen herself.

Her dress was magnificent, encrusted with jewels, a high collar and ruffle about her neck, sleeves puffed and slashed with the finest silk. She applauded the young Shakespeare, performing his Comedy of Errors alongside the Chamberlain's Men.

Down each side of the hall sat the barristers; between them, police officers; then a group of surgeons dressed in theatre gowns, with knives and scalpels spread out in front of them. Lawyers in evening dress smoked cigars and drank claret, engaging in raucous banter.

In the void, between the second chandelier and the flying buttress, appeared the faintest wisp of a ghost. Pale and drawn, the figure of Ben came into view. This was followed by the ghosts of Jackie, then Tracey, then Margaret, all appearing as an illusion.

From the midst of the group, a fifth figure grew. The apparition had the face of Alton, tired, worn and pitiful; hands begging for forgiveness.

They all looked toward me with sorrowful faces, wanting to hear the truth. This was far and away the best opportunity to speak and the figures gathered around me to listen.

"You see." I cleared my throat. "You all believed in a perfect world, a place where humans care for each other and do their best. But the greatest in society, all here gathered today, have formed into groups and professions that will always look after their own interests first.

"The people down there below are so wrapped up in themselves, the procedures and mechanics of the roles they play, that they have lost sight of their original purposes. Instead of serving you, the public, they have chosen to ask what's best for them and their organisations. Because of their selfishness and arrogance, we have all lost something dear.

"Go now; go from here, lower your expectations and you will not be hurt the same way again."

I felt a tug on my sleeve. Anthony's face came into focus.

On the paper in front of me were my notes, the outline of my story. All I needed was the title. I looked up at the Judge who was still speaking.

"I have to say that I have not a shadow of doubt that you committed the offence and therefore I find you guilty."

★ ★ ★

CHAPTER TWENTY-TWO

The Appeal

The last stage of appeal was the Police Authority Tribunal. Eight months after the dismissal, I was about to face them

Sir Richard Fox was a senior barrister from prestigious London Chambers; he had been chairing such appeals for ten years. He sat in the same chair that had been occupied by Assistant Chief Constable Bernadette Diamond. His role was to hear the appeal against the level of sanction imposed.

Sir Richard had three people with him on the panel, all experts in their own fields. There was Sir Oliver Beacham, a former Chief Constable, recently retired from a position at the Home Office. Next was Counsellor Vanessa Craig, and the fourth member of the panel was John Barryman, an officer representing the Police Federation.

I sat down. Janet Ross and Anthony Hudson did likewise. Once all the people in the room had been introduced, Sir Marcus invited Anthony to make his submissions.

Anthony took his time arranging his papers, took a sip of water, looked up at Sir Richard and started to speak.

"Sir, PC Davies respectfully appeals against the decision of the Disciplinary Panel chaired by Assistant Chief Constable, Bernadette Diamond.

"Before I set out the grounds on which this application for appeal is brought, I'd like to provide the panel with some background.

"PC Davies has served in this force for over twenty years and up until the tribunal he had a flawless disciplinary record and had never received any reprimand, fine or warning. During his service he received a variety of commendations, two special bonus payment awards and two 'Quality Achiever' awards for outstanding police work. His file has many comments regarding the level of commitment he has to police work.

"It was during a routine operation that he became a victim of threats made against his life by a former Special Branch officer. There was a long delay in the investigation before this man was finally brought to court and pleaded guilty to conspiracy to commit grievous bodily harm. It was as a direct result of these life-threatening experiences that PC Davies suffered a breakdown in his mental health. The expert assessment from Beth Goodchild, the counsellor at the Trauma Support Network, states the following:

"Mr Davies was subjected to an extremely unpleasant and life threatening experience that continued for several years. The stress caused by this experience, directly resulted in his complete mental collapse and brought about a marked change in his personality. The ongoing health problems have had a serious effect on his personal life and have led to difficulties at work that were completely unheard of before these incidents…"

"One of these difficulties involved an incident with Dr Strictly after which PC Davies was convicted of common assault and given a conditional discharge.

"At the disciplinary panel he admitted the charge made against him. In mitigation, the disciplinary panel's attention was brought to the diagnosis of Post-Traumatic Stress Disorder, the considerable record of outstanding work, and his desire to continue to contribute towards the police service.

"Although no longer a member of the force, Mr Davies, with considerable support from his GP, applied to have treatment funded by the police to help him recover. After his GP's intervention, Mr Davies finally got the treatment he needed. The head of personnel wrote to him saying,

"I am able to confirm that the Force is prepared to fund a course of treatment to be provided by Beth Goodchild at the Trauma Support Network. I understand that the medical advice provided to us indicates that you will benefit from this course of treatment."

"Amongst the papers earlier submitted to the panel are a list of awards and commendations, the excellent record of service, and medical reports outlining the cause of the mental health issues. I invite the panel to inspect these as formal submissions and I would like to move on to the subject of Disability Discrimination.

"The Disability Discrimination Act applies to police officers and I respectfully submit that the diagnosis of Post-Traumatic Stress Disorder amounts to a disability for the purpose of the Act.

"By breaching the requirements of the Disability Discrimination Act 1995, the Chief Constable has discriminated against PC Davies in the following ways:

"Firstly, by failing to make reasonable adjustments in the workplace: in particular, refusal to provide the correct therapy which would have enabled him to continue his employment.

"Secondly, by dismissing him by reason of his disability, as in the first tribunal, the actions amount to direct disability discrimination.

"It is noted that the tribunal specifically justified their decision to dismiss PC Davies by referring to his disability,

'There are a range of symptoms that cause the panel concern, e.g. aggression and self control.'

"As the panel's decision was directly motivated by symptoms of his disability, I submit that he has been dealt with less favourably than a person with no such disability; which is quite clearly a breach of the Act.

"As a result of discrimination, I respectfully invite the Police Authority to overturn the earlier decision that dismissed PC Davies.

"Finally, sir, I ask that you make an order for his costs to be paid by the Authority, as I submit that this appeal is not frivolous, vexatious or without merit."

Anthony completed his statement and closed the folder to indicate that he had finished his submissions. Sir Marcus was busy making notes and there was a moment of quiet before he spoke.

"Thank you, Mr Hudson. I now turn to counsel representing the police to make their submissions." As Sir Marcus peered over his spectacles, Miss Hartford-Jones prepared her papers.

"Thank you, Sir Richard. Our case is that this hearing is unnecessary as the sanction imposed was neither wrong in principle nor manifestly excessive."

Her eyes did not look up from her file and her face started to blush as she became aware that all eyes were on her. There was a pause as she shuffled her papers, looking for a particular page. Sir Marcus leaned forward and stared at the young barrister as though he wished to give her a tutorial on being prepared for hearings, but the frantic shuffling indicated that she only picked up the file that morning and had not had time for preparation. On the other hand, Anthony had spent the previous evening poring over stated cases and had a mountain of references to use should they be required.

"Oh gosh, here it is." Miss Hartford-Jones found her paper and breathed an all too conspicuous sigh of relief. Sir Marcus stared with growing impatience at someone so young in their profession.

"Sir Richard, as for the ground of appeal concerning the unlawful disability discrimination, can I respectfully submit that the panel does not entertain this ground of appeal."

"Go on." Sir Richard was expecting an explanation.

"It is not a function of this tribunal to determine issues of disability discrimination, nor does it have jurisdiction to do so. It is for this tribunal to determine whether the actions of PC Davies, fell below the required standards and whether the sanction was appropriate. May I point out that we deny any unlawful discrimination and can I point out that any redress is a matter for the appellant to bring before an employment tribunal."

Something about the words 'employment tribunal' triggered a reaction with Anthony and he frantically scribbled a note, ending with a large question mark, which he passed to Janet. She read the note and in turn scribbled away on her pad.

Miss Hartford-Jones caught the movement out of the corner of her eye and blushed as she stumbled on.

"To conclude, the panel's decision should be considered as a whole, and when it is so considered it is apparent that the panel was explaining that, in reaching its decision as to sanction, it was taking into account all matters put before it, and in particular, the medical evidence put forward by the appellant. He was not discriminated against; he was required to resign as he was no longer suitable to continue."

Miss Hartford-Jones closed her file and took a moment to compose herself. I took a moment to reflect on how such a young person, so badly prepared, could command such an extortionate fee for a five-minute submission

Sir Marcus finished his notes and looked up to scan the room..

"The panel has heard the submissions from both sides and will now adjourn to make a decision. As our deliberations could take a matter of hours I will offer you a choice. You may remain here until the decision is made, which could be anytime this afternoon, or you may leave and the decision will be communicated to you by post."

Anthony turned to look at me and I mouthed the word 'stay', leaving him in no doubt as to my choice.

"We would prefer to stay, Sir Richard."

"Very well, we'll let you know when we're ready."

With that, we all stood up and Anthony led me out of the room, but held back to talk to Janet. He gave her his instructions and she went off to make the necessary enquiries.

"Anthony, I hope you don't mind but I'm going to take a little walk to stretch my legs. I need some fresh air; I'll be back well within the hour."

"Okay, then; we've got a little work to do here. Just don't be late."

I took the lift down to the foyer and walked out onto the street before heading in the direction of Colmore Row. It was a relief to have a moment to myself and I was glad to see some spare tables in Starbucks. I walked in and ordered coffee.

I gazed out of the window at the passers by while I considered the meeting. Something was giving me a feeling of confidence and as I sipped my drink, I tried to put the pieces of the jigsaw together to work out what it was.

I started with the obvious and that was the enormous difference in the quality of the barristers. Anthony had put forward a superb case, well-researched and put together: a highly convincing submission. On the other hand, theirs was ill-prepared, slow and stumbling, not fluent with the facts.

Then there was the fact that the panel was independent of the force itself. There was no sense of the collusion that had blighted the previous panels.

Lastly, the mood of my team was upbeat in comparison to what I had seen before. I could only hope that Janet's disappearance signalled some little trick up their sleeves.

I downed my coffee and began walking back along Colmore Row towards headquarters. I knew that I was about to face the most important meeting of my life, a decision that would shape my entire future.

The right decision would mean a new start, a chance to put 'Merlin' and 'Cider Nightmare' to sleep and turn my life around.

The wrong decision would mean a new emptiness, I wondered if Sir Richard was a kind man.

While wandering back, a commotion drew my attention to a row of bus stops opposite the Grand Hotel. A group of youths, wearing hoodies and baseball caps, had just tipped over a litter bin and were kicking the rubbish into the road.

An old lady stopped and waved her walking stick at them. While most of the group dissolved into complete hysterics, one of the yobs kicked a bottle at her. The old lady had no intention of backing down and shouted to the group to clear the mess up.

Members of the public visibly attempted to avoid the scene by skirting round the pavement. No one wanted to know; no one would support her or help her. If the youth decided to become nasty, she'd be standing there on her own.

The hoodie moved towards her, two fingers in the air, shouting and screaming. The old lady stood her ground. Two businessmen, deep in conversation stepped back to the railings, avoiding the ensuing trouble.

The boy spat on the ground by her shoe, shouted abuse and ran back to his mates, kicking rubbish as he went.

When the danger had passed, a middle-aged man walked over to her to check she was not hurt; he had been there all the time, watching from the sidelines, commenting to a street cleaner that the world had become a dreadful place and there was no respect.

The old lady thanked him, brushed herself down and continued towards the Grand. The middle-aged man watched with some curiosity as the tough old girl marched straight in through the revolving doors as though she owned the place. The smartly dressed bellboy tipped his hat.

"Afternoon, Miss Gracie." He gave a slight bow.

Scenes like this would be played out in hotels in countries all over the world; but this was Birmingham, my home town. The city and its people were changing beyond all recognition and the episode I'd witnessed had reflected my recent mood.

Many decades past, when Gracie's hotel was built, Birmingham was producing half of the world's manufactured goods; now it produced hardly anything. The city's future was in the hands of a younger generation and it was not looking good.

I reached into my pocket and took out my notebook. I'd thought of a way to conclude my book: I wanted to mention Gracie and the incident with the youths. I sat down in the bus shelter and sketched a picture of her as I stared at the hotel. Suddenly my thoughts became clear.

That was it!

The garden was the place that they wanted you to see: the rose bushes in bloom and the lawns neatly cut. But in life there's always a gate, somewhere, hidden away down the bottom of the garden ... always a gate.

Beyond the gate is the truth and today the truth is despair. I wish the earth would split into two, letting that half spin off into the void leaving us with things just the way we want them, damn the reality.

I felt hopeless – the same hopelessness I had felt at the railway station, as if society's breakdown was a mere reflection of my own: all the good disappearing, trampled into the dirt leaving only darkness.

A sudden gust blew the litter around my feet, I got up with a start remembering I had to be somewhere. I put my book back in my inside pocket, checked my watch and marched off with a quickened pace.

Back in the building, everything was as I'd left it, Anthony in his chair, feet on the table, dictating to Janet. I took a seat in the furthest corner from them and thumbed through a Police Review.

A local Police Surgeon had been sent to prison following a string of sexual offences. Dr Porlock, the article said, was starting a five year stretch at Her Majesty's pleasure, the very thought made me feel sick so I tossed it into the bin where it belonged

Three long hours were to pass before we were called back into the room, a long, lonely time; they seemed used to it and didn't fuss.

★ ★ ★

While they were working, I took out my notes and continued my sketch of Gracie. Although I didn't know my fate, there was still a story.

As for me, well, together with Beth I'd made advances and was taking the right steps to move on with my life.

For me, writing had made the big difference: it's been my own personal therapy. A chance to file my thoughts, keep a box of feelings locked away: I could still take them out from time to time, examine them, and shuffle them back in order.

I'll always feel let down and angry though.

All I know is that the day I joined up was the proudest day of my life: an achievement, a personal goal fulfilled. Even now I don't feel like a failure; I feel that they're the failures.

I've always loved the force and the people I've worked with. It was a privilege to meet them and learn about their characters – they all had a story to tell. First, Jackie; then Ben, and of course the Roseby family. I just feel sorry that their lives were blighted by failures in the system, a system that let them down, extracting the ultimate price. I can't help feeling that we could have done better, prevented the misery.

But life is a series of ordeals and maybe we should just get used to it.

Beth once told me that I shouldn't treat my life the same way that I treat my motor car. She reminded me that once a year we get our cars serviced, the brakes changed and the windscreen wipers renewed, then we cross our fingers and hope that they will stay fixed forever. We feel devastated when the thing breaks down or won't start in the morning. We set our lives upon the same principle: a notion that things will remain static and everything will stay fixed forever. We set ourselves up for intense periods of frustration and stress. Eventually, our attempts to control everything around us take their toll.

I recalled her last words: "Don't dwell on the past, it detracts from the now."

I put my pen away and closed the book.

There was a knock at the door.

A slight panic arose. I looked towards Anthony, he gave me the nod.

We all shuffled into the corridor and back into the conference room, single-file and deadly silent.

Sir Richard began to speak. I looked at the floor.

"The appellant appeared before a misconduct panel after it was submitted that he had been given a conditional discharge for an offence of common assault against Dr Strictly from the Occupational Health Department.

"It has been heard that PC Davies attended that consultation seeking help for the stress he was experiencing following a series of incidents in which he was the victim. We heard that he was initially calm but started to express anger at what he saw to be failings amongst senior officers in the force and the criminal justice system. When he was told he was fit for work the incident took place. He was charged with the assault and put before the court. We are aware that the judge issued a relatively lenient punishment of a conditional discharge and he had fully considered the fact that the officer was mentally ill at the time and was seeking help. The mental health issues were clearly a mitigating factor.

"Although the police panel made reference to the sentencing, it is clear that they did so having not heard the facts of the case. For this reason, we found that it was the court's view of culpability that was significant.

"We have seen medical evidence submitted by Beth Goodchild from the Trauma Support Network, who is working with the appellant. She states that the officer is working hard to process his symptoms and has engaged with the course of therapy very well.

"This panel believes that he is now getting the treatment he needs, indeed the treatment he was seeking at the time of the assault; he has put forward the suggestion that no one was listening to him and offering him help.

"This tribunal recognises that reinstatement of the appellant, may give rise to problems for the police in deciding his duties. We recognise that if health prevents him being posted then a medical pension should be considered.

"In the light of our decision we did not consider it necessary to determine if the officer was discriminated against because of a disability. He will no doubt be advised as whether he should take up this matter elsewhere.

"We have considered his excellent career as a police officer, the fact that the mental injury took place whilst serving as a police officer, and this contributed significantly to his actions.

"In conclusion, the appeal is allowed to the extent that the sanction is withdrawn.

"Thank you; that concludes the proceedings."

★ ★ ★

Anthony's face was a picture, Janet was in shock, I tried to take in the enormity of the news.

I took Anthony's hand and shook it vigorously, we grinned at each other, an enormous flood of relief washed over me.

"Well done, Simon, you did it; after all you've been through, you finally did it."

"Most of it has to be down to you, you wiped the floor with the opposition. I have to say, you did a brilliant job!"

"Well, Simon, I'm over the moon for you, but back to business for a moment. If you've got an hour or so, as we've got Janet's here with us, I wonder if we shouldn't have a little debrief now. I know you probably want to get on with celebrating, but it would save you a further trip to London and there's no time like the present, as they say. I can always get a later train."

I looked at Janet, who nodded her assent.

"That's fine by me, if I can just make a phone call first," I say, desperate to shout about my news.

"Anywhere you can suggest for a celebratory cup of tea, Janet?" Anthony enquired as he packed his case.

"Why not the Grand?" I suggested, butting in; there was something I wanted to check. It's only a short walk and it's just the place for a quiet chat," I added, looking hopefully from one to the other.

"That's settled, then; you lead on. Janet, I trust your expenses can cope with this?"

Anthony turned on his heels and strode out through the door, wheeling a monogrammed, Louis Vuitton case behind him.

Within five minutes we had entered the cavernous lobby of the fine Victorian hotel. Dating back to 1850, it had been built to provide travellers on the new railway system with dining rooms and accommodation. It was a truly sumptuous building. The tea rooms were decorated in a Louis XIV theme, with a scattering of large rubber plants between the tables and chairs.

We took a table below the French pavilion roof, between two Corinthian pillars. A waitress glided past.

"Could we possibly have a pot of tea for three and some biscuits, my dear?"

He always got good service when his public school tones were exaggerated. The waitress made a note then faded away amongst the plants.

"First of all, Simon, congratulations. I'm sure there'll be one or two people up there having a very bad day now, well done!"

"I'm just over the moon, thanks again for all your hard work. Is there anything else I need to do or do I just sit tight and wait for them to contact me?"

Anthony leaned forward.

"Just sit tight, old boy, they'll be contacting you. But now I need to explain some of Sir Richard's comments, particularly about the matter of disability discrimination."

The tea arrived, a china teapot, three cups and saucers, a two-tiered cake stand piled high with biscuits.

Janet took the pot and began to pour.

I got up and grabbed the waitress as she retreated to the bar.

"Sorry to bother you, I saw a lady earlier who seemed upset. I think her name is Gracie, do you happen to know if she works here?"

The waitress laughed; I thought I saw gum in her mouth.

"No, that's Gracie Chamberlain, she stays here all the time. Her great uncle was the Prime Minister, you know, in the Gulf War or something!"

I thanked her as she stepped behind the bar. I watched while she undid the ribbon on her pony tail and gathered her hair together before tying it back behind her head, all the time chewing her gum.

"So she is important," I thought out loud.

A relative of Neville Chamberlain, Lord Mayor of Birmingham and War time Prime Minister and today, she's having to walk the same streets surrounded by all that scum.

So what's gone so badly wrong? Why have things changed so much and what was it that Gracie's generation did so different?

Maybe they possessed the ability to see what was wrong and what was right; maybe they understood the rewards of endeavour, the fruits of labour and creativity.

Maybe they learnt the intoxicating nature of hard work and didn't spend their days chasing fantasy targets, moving paper around from desk to desk.

But somehow, they must have neglected this younger generation, alienated their children and made them rebel; they failed to pass on their wisdom. Their offspring grew up bitter and resentful, so youth acts like there's nothing left: no use in anything. All they see is 'Big Brother syndrome' everywhere – the desire for fame and fortune without any notable achievement, there can only be failure and the lowering of self esteem.

I felt sorry for her, but had this amazing urge to speak to her and ask her about her life.

The waitress was applying lipstick so I backed away from the bar and returned to my seat.

Anthony had just found his custard cream; he held it up to the light before biting it in half. I picked up my cup and took a sip.

"Well, now. I noted that Sir Richard specifically refused to make comment on our point that the police have discriminated against you by way of disability. However, he did comment that you may feel the need to seek advice on the subject."

Anthony jabbed the half-eaten custard cream at me as he spoke; the second half then disappeared into his mouth.

"Point is," he chewed, "Janet's already had a quick look into this one. I believe we might be on a sticky wicket."

He selected another biscuit.

"You see, the organisation has certainly spent a lot of money on the case against you and they seem to have found a way around that point. Janet's been making a couple of calls and has got her friend, an employment lawyer, to do some digging. The thing is, old boy, it appears the original panel are immune from disability discrimination. You see, their lawyers have dug out a case known as ..."

He referred to his notes.

"Metropolitan Police verses Heath. That is a little known but ground breaking case, which ruled that an internal Police Disciplinary Panel was a judicial body the same as a criminal court and so covered by the same judicial immunity from discrimination claims.

"I know this may seem hard to believe, but the police panel could do exactly as they wished, they knew they were protected in law from any claim you might have against them."

He continued to eye the biscuits as he picked up the teapot; I sat back in my chair, a little dazed.

"That's just awful, how come nobody knows about these things?"

"I suppose, you know, society works best when everything is kept quiet, hushed up and covered, old boy."

"Are you telling me that the police can discriminate on grounds of disability and there is nothing we can do about it?"

I finished my tea and put the cup down.

"Well, in their world I'm afraid you can, dark forces, eh Simon? Now old boy, allow me to pour you another cup."

★ ★ ★

THE AUTHOR

Simon Davies joined the police service straight from school and served for twenty-two years before retiring on ill health grounds.

He now lives a more tranquil life in a rural Somerset village. He enjoys cricket, writing crime fiction and is currently studying criminology.